Praise for

'We're very fond of Chris Manby. We've grown up with her frustrated females, toxic friends and unsuitable men. Chris's easy-to-read style and hilarious insights into the world of Z-list celebrity will suck you in. Lots and lots of uncomplicated fun.'
Heat on *Spa Wars*

'Smartly written, extremely readable, and gives us a fascinating and funny glimpse into the dark side of love'
Heat on *The Matchbreaker*

'Funny and inventive – prepare to be won over by an unlikely heroine'
Company on *The Matchbreaker*

'Devour it in one go'
Company on *Ready or Not?*

Also by Chris Manby

Flatmates

Second Prize

Deep Heat

Lizzie Jordan's Secret Life

Running Away from Richard

Getting Personal

Seven Sunny Days

Girl Meets Ape

Ready or Not?

The Matchbreaker

Marrying for Money

About the author

Chris Manby is editor/contributor to the *Girls' Night In*
anthologies, which have so far raised more than £1,000,000
for humanitarian organisations War Child and No Strings,
and topped book charts all over the world. Raised in
Gloucester, Chris now lives in London.

CHRIS MANBY

HODDER

First published in Great Britain in 2008 by Hodder & Stoughton
An Hachette Livre UK company

First published in paperback in 2008

1

A CIP catalogue record for this title is available from the British Library

B format ISBN 978 0 340 93701 3
A format ISBN 978 0 340 95190 3

Typeset in Sabon by Palimpsest Book Production Limited,
Grangemouth, Stirlingshire

Printed and bound by Clays Ltd, St Ives plc

Hodder & Stoughton policy is to use papers that are natural, renewable
and recyclable products and made from wood grown in sustainable
forests. The logging and manufacturing processes are expected to
conform to the environmental regulations of the country of origin.

Hodder & Stoughton Ltd
338 Euston Road
London NW1 3BH

www.hodder.co.uk

For my dear friend, Serena Mackesy.

Acknowledgements

With thanks as ever to the wonderful team at Hodder, especially Carolyn Mays and Kate Howard, for their continued support. Thanks also to my agents, Antony Harwood & James Macdonald Lockhart. And anyone who has ever turned up at my house expecting a dinner party only to find my laptop and a takeaway menu where the 'coq au vin' should be.

I don't understand how a woman can leave the house without fixing herself up a little – if only out of politeness. And then, you never know, maybe that's the day she has a date with destiny. And it's best to be as pretty as possible for destiny.

Coco Chanel

PROLOGUE

'Keep it *reeeeaaal*!' yelled the tiny blonde girl standing at the top of the steps.

'Carina! Carina! Carina!' The crowd below was going crazy, whooping, shouting, chanting her name.

The tiny blonde began an unsteady descent on very high heels to wild applause.

'Carina! Carina!'

Carina Lees was the penultimate person to be evicted from the *Living Hell* house at the end of that summer's reality TV series. First runner-up. She left behind her in the house the winning housemate: a character called 'Monkey', whose brave struggle with catatonic schizophrenia had much endeared him to the Great British Public, even though he spent most of his second month on the show having an episode that rendered him as silent and immobile as a hat stand. In fact, while Carina was making her grand exit, the surprise of winning TV's most coveted reality prize was sending Monkey into another period of paralysis that would last for the next six months.

'Carina! Carina!'

Frenzied with excitement, the capacity crowd strained against the safety barriers. Some thrust flowers, fluffy heart-shaped cushions or teddy bears in Carina's direction. Others reached out for her, like visitors to the grotto at Lourdes hoping for a miracle in her touch. They waved homemade banners professing their love for her.

'I love you too! I love you all,' she told them, arms wide like Evita.

1

The response was deafening.

All this for her? thought Carina. Just an ordinary girl from Essex? For a moment she was rooted to the spot with something approaching shock.

Jordi Flame, the eviction show's obligatory über-camp presenter, quickly whisked Carina past the fans and the tabloid photographers into the studio. Once she was safely in the famous golden chair that had cradled so many reality bottoms, he congratulated her on her 'great achievement', then, together with the studio audience and half the nation, they watched her 'best bits' – a montage of different angles on her twenty-first-birthday boob job, interspersed with spectacular crying jags and more exhortations to 'keep it real'.

'You got more votes than the entire Conservative Party had in the last election,' Jordi told her.

'Wow,' said Carina. 'Wow!' At twenty-six years old, she'd never voted in anything other than the finals of *The X Factor*. She whooped. The crowd whooped back at her.

'As runner-up in this year's *Living Hell*, you've won five hundred thousand pounds,' Jordi continued. 'What are you going to do with it?'

'I'm going to buy my mum a new handbag from Prada and get my stepdad a watch from Gucci and get my nan some shoes from Ferragamo and get myself something from Dolce and Gabbana . . .'

The studio audience applauded as though Carina had just revealed the secret of the universe.

'That's fabulous,' said Jordi. 'We all like D and G. And I'm sure your nan will love her new shoes.'

Close-up on Carina's nan in the front row of the audience. Sobbing with pride.

'I love you, Nan,' said Carina. 'I love everybody!' She stood up and blew more kisses to the crowd. She waved her hands over her head as if to better reach the people in the cheap seats. 'This is my dream come true!'

The camera turned back to Jordi Flame's six-figure-deal smile. 'Well, that's all from Carina Lees for now. After the break we'll be back with the official winner of this year's *Living Hell* . . . Monkey Gordon.'

The crowd roared their approval once more.

The commercials started rolling.

Inside the *Living Hell* house, twenty-three-year-old Monkey Gordon adopted the cactus pose in which he would remain frozen until Christmas.

Twenty miles away, in the little town of Blountford, another Essex girl's grandmother was sobbing her heart out with pride.

'Give over, Gran,' said Emily Brown. 'This is meant to be a happy occasion.'

'I know, my darling,' said Grandma Brown. 'It must be the alcopops. Always make me maudlin.'

She accepted another Bacardi Breezer all the same.

'Speech! Speech!' called Eric Brown, Emily's father.

'Dad . . .' Emily began.

'You've got to have a speech,' he said.

As Eric tapped a fork against his beer bottle in a bid to establish silence, Emily reluctantly climbed up onto a chair. She smiled down at her guests: family, friends and neighbours, all of them beaming right back at her.

'I'm so pleased you could all make it here tonight,' she began. 'To the opening of The Beauty Spot.' She flung wide her arms to take in the tiny pink-painted beauty salon that would be opening its doors to the public for the first time the following morning. 'You've all been so supportive. I don't know how I would have done it without you. I hope you're going to come to me next time you need a manicure.'

'I'll come in for a manicure!' shouted Emily's grandfather.

'Going to take more than a manicure to fix him,' heckled Grandma Brown.

'Ladies and gentlemen, let's raise a glass to . . . The Beauty Spot,' said Emily's father.

The guests obliged.

'The Beauty Spot!' they cheered as they tipped their glasses and bottles towards a blushing Emily.

'And to our lovely daughter Emily,' said Barbara, Emily's mum. 'I always knew you had it in you. She'll be a million-airess within a year,' she added. 'Mark my words.'

'May your salon be a huge success, dear,' said Grandma Brown, enfolding her granddaughter into a hug. 'You deserve it, sweetheart.'

Now Emily was crying with happiness too. 'I love you, Gran. I love everybody. This is my dream come true.'

I

While Monkey Gordon was wheeled to hospital, still standing upright and stiff as a board, Carina Lees plunged headlong into her new life as a reality star. She had wisely retained a PR agent called Mickey Shore before entering the *Living Hell* house and she exited to find that he had set up a punishing publicity round. Every tabloid and entertainment magazine published in the United Kingdom had bid for the first exclusive. By the time she left the television studio after her triumphant exit interview with Jordi Flame, Carina Lees was already a millionaire.

She gave her first exclusive to the *News of the World*. In six pages punctuated with lots of colour photographs of Carina and her brand-new hair extensions, she revealed the 'truth' about her relationship with the other *Living Hell* housemates, though she remained tight-lipped about an alleged sexual liaison with Monkey during a period of unconsciousness (his, not hers). That was worth another hundred grand, Mickey explained to his fast-learning client.

Advertising campaigns followed. Carina's obsession with keeping the kitchen clean while in the *Living Hell* house translated into a high six-figure contract to be the face of Whoosh Multi-Surface Cleaner. There were more interviews for the tabloids. More photo-shoots. More carefully timed appearances outside old restaurants and new nightclubs. Within the space of a week, Carina was linked with all four former members of a recently defunct boy-band. There were rumours that she was planning to record a single of her own, despite

5

the ample evidence (provided by the 24/7 live feed from *Living Hell*) that she could not sing a note. She got more new hair extensions. Longer. Blonder. Better. She considered a bigger boob job.

Six months out of the house, several of the original fifty *Living Hell* housemates had disappeared back into obscurity, the only column inches they garnered now in the magistrates' court sections of their local newspapers. A handful of the others were doing reasonably well. Monkey Gordon was in the news-papers almost daily, though it wasn't clear whether he knew about it. He was still in the celebrities' favourite residential mental health facility – The Bakery – standing for hours on end in a cactus pose. It was front-page news when he adopted the 'eagle pose' for twenty minutes one afternoon. Carina nodded approvingly when she read that. She'd been doing some yoga with her personal trainer. It was hard to hold the eagle pose for thirty seconds, let alone twenty minutes.

Apart from Monkey, those *Living Hell* alumni that hadn't returned to a life of shoplifting had largely moved on to yet more reality TV. Three of them were taking part in a series called *Celebrity Service Station*, in which they did the night shift at a branch of Road Chef on the M25. Tanya, Carina's rival Essex girl in *Living Hell*, was appearing alongside a former Conservative MP and a duchess on the third series of *Trust Me, I'm a Celebrity Checkout Girl*. Tanya had taken to the business of being a celebrity checkout girl very well. Perhaps that was because she had been a real checkout girl for several years before she went into the *Living Hell* house. Clare – *Living Hell*'s token 'posh bird' – was a guest star in the Danish version of the same show. She was voted out after a week, which was a good job since no one in the house could understand a word she said and she was starting to display symptoms of isolation-induced depression.

It wasn't that the reality show offers hadn't poured in for Carina as well. On the contrary, Carina was the first person every TV producer thought of when trying to cast *Celebrity Allotments* or *Roller-blading with the Stars*. But Carina didn't even get to consider the increasingly valuable reality packages the TV companies sent in her direction. Mickey Shore had bigger ideas.

Mickey's plans for Carina included a *proper* television presenting job. On the television food chain, presenting was definitely a tier above endless reality. After keeping Carina out of the reality show ghetto for six months, Mickey's foresight was rewarded when he got her a fortnightly gig on *Wakey-Wakey* – Britain's favourite breakfast show (according to a survey commissioned by their own production company).

Carina's brief on the *Wakey-Wakey* show was extremely flexible. One week she might be reporting on the plight of abandoned pets at Battersea Dogs' Home. The next she would be trying out new face creams with a bunch of middle-aged women who bore a remarkable resemblance to the Shar-Pei puppies she'd been interviewing the week before. She was even regressed to a past life by a psychic called Liyo Aslan (formerly a John Lewis carpet salesman called Terry Bostock), who told her she had been an Ancient Egyptian slave-girl. That prompted Carina to read a Dorling Kindersley book on the pyramids that inspired her to consider having her hair dyed black and cut into a bob.

'Black sucks with your present life skin tone,' Mickey warned.

So Carina kept her hair blonde. And, before long, she was appearing on *Wakey-Wakey* once a week instead of once a fortnight. The viewers loved her glamorous blonde looks. *Guardian* readers (who only watched *Wakey-Wakey* 'ironically') liked to sneer at her faux pas.

Next Mickey ensured Carina had a column. Every serious

reality star turned proper celeb had to have a column in which to slag off other reality stars who hadn't quite made the transition. All the gossip mags were keen to have Carina on board. Mickey settled on a new magazine called *Get This!*, which was already rivalling *Heat* in circulation figures, and closed a deal for a thousand words a week at ten thousand pounds a time. Even Mickey shook his head with amusement as he worked out that Carina would be paid ten pounds a word! Not that she would be writing any of them. That job fell to a hapless *Get This!* staff-writer. But the column was important, allowing Carina a regular platform for unadulterated self-promotion as it did.

Meanwhile, Mickey continued to ensure that Carina was seen at all the right parties with all the right people. Those 'right people' included another of his clients: Danny Rhodes. Danny was a former singer with a boy-band, currently trying to kick-start a solo career with a stint as the lead in a sell-out West End revival of *The Music Man*. Carina looked just perfect on his arm.

When Mickey's office received a gold-embossed invitation asking Carina to attend the country-house wedding of a Premiership footballer to a member of the nation's hottest girl-band, neither of whom she had ever met, Mickey knew that Carina had made it. She was a bona fide celebrity. The Great British Public had taken Carina Lees to their hearts.

Since the eighth series of *Living Hell* had finished and The Beauty Spot had begun, Emily Brown had also had a very busy six months.

Beauty had always been Emily's passion. She'd been obsessed by make-up since childhood and her friends were well used to her instinct to tweak and polish anyone she could get her hands on. She couldn't sit opposite someone with chipped nail polish or streaky foundation without feeling the urge to act. Many times Emily had marched mere acquaintances into the corner of a restaurant or nightclub and set about their shiny faces with pressed powder. She once set up an impromptu eyebrow-tidying clinic in the ladies' room of The Hippodrome in Leicester Square.

It was inevitable that Emily would go to beauty school when she finished her GCSEs. She graduated at the top of her class and found her first job on a cruise ship. Within three years she had been promoted from lowliest therapist to the ship's beauty salon manager. It was the perfect start to her career. With no real expenses to speak of while she was living onboard, she was able to salt away plenty of savings before she came back to dry land. On her twenty-third birthday, Emily's father matched what she had saved, thinking she might like to buy herself a car. But Emily had far bigger ambitions than ownership of a nearly new Volkswagen Golf. A year later, her savings were boosted once more by a bequest from an elderly aunt. Emily took all her money to a bank and they matched it with a business loan. She signed a long lease on an empty barber's shop a few streets from where she had grown up – and The Beauty Spot was born.

Emily had very worked hard to achieve her ambition. First to save the money, then to transform the barber's shop into something a great deal more girly. Lack of spare funds meant that she had to decorate The Beauty Spot herself, ruining her own carefully manicured nails when she sanded down the woodwork. But that wasn't to be the end of it. Six months after the opening, she was working even harder. Apart from Chloe Jones, the junior therapist who had been with her from the start, Emily Brown was the entire staff of her little salon. She was full-time therapist, office manager, accountant *and* cleaner. It didn't leave much time for a personal life. As for romance? Forget about it.

* * *

When they had a moment to talk about it, Emily and Chloe often bemoaned the fact that they'd chosen a career where it was very unlikely they would meet a future husband on the job. Emily's year group at beauty school had been exclusively female. On board ship, she was discouraged from fraternizing with other staff members, and most of the male holiday-makers under fifty were on honeymoon. The only men who visited a day spa like The Beauty Spot were married (from time to time, Emily had to deal with the hairy backs of men whose wives couldn't stand the idea of sitting next to a gorilla on the beach). Or gay.

You could tell the straight married men right away. They always looked terrified. And the bigger they were, the louder they cried when Emily got out the wax strips and went to work.

The gay guys were better clients. They spent a great deal more money. They knew that just because they were men, looking good wasn't a simple matter of a short back and sides at the barber's by the train station. These guys were as high maintenance as any of Emily's female clients. They wanted the lot. Waxing (Emily had all the right certificates, though she had yet to item 'back, crack and sack' on her service list), facials, pedicures, manicures, eyebrow-shaping, fake tan. And the gossip they shared over the manicure table made a change from the usual gripes about unreliable nannies and workaholic husbands she got from the local yummy mummies. Still, there was something strangely depressing about massaging a beautiful male body, knowing that your gorgeous client was probably thinking about another beautiful male body while you did it.

Emily could hardly remember the last time she'd touched a man during a moment of passion. Her most recent boyfriend had given up on her because she was spending too much time setting up the salon. She'd realized quickly that Mr Right was unlikely to walk in off the street and ask for an impromptu eyebrow-tweeze. And so it was that Emily felt more than a little tweak of envy as she read Carina Lees's first column in *Get This!* magazine.

Wow! What an amazing week I've had! Carina wrote. *I was so excited to get an invitation to* Get This! *magazine's annual Valentine's singles party. All the best single men in England were there, including Danny Rhodes . . .*

Emily glanced at the picture of the handsome former boy-band star, *currently appearing in the West End revival of* The Music Man. He was ridiculously good-looking. Like a Ken doll come to life. Chloe peered over Emily's shoulder.

'Isn't he . . . ?' Chloe began.

Gay is the only word for the whole evening, Carina's column continued. *In keeping with the Valentine's theme, the entire top floor of the exclusive Café de France had been turned into a tart's boudoir. Everything was pink. Pink drinks, pink cakes. Even the dress code was 'in the pink'. Lucky it's my favourite colour!*

We danced the night away to a live set (by a tribute band playing covers of Pink songs of course). And when the clock struck midnight, Danny Rhodes asked if I would be his Valentine! What did I say? You'll have to watch this space!

Emily closed the magazine with a sigh. She hadn't received a single Valentine's card. The postcard from the video shop suggesting romantic rentals for a Valentine's night spent at home definitely didn't count. But Emily had no time to dwell on her lack of love action right then. She had a customer to see.

2

'Hey, Matt.' Emily barely glanced up from the appointments book when Matt Charlton walked into the salon.

Matt was a regular client. He'd been coming in to get his back and shoulders waxed every six weeks or so since The Beauty Spot opened. He was very good looking, in a preppy sort of way. His dark brown hair was always neatly cut and parted to the left (lots of it, too, which was why he was such a regular waxer, Emily observed). He wore glasses but had chosen his designer frames perfectly so that they echoed the shape of his eyebrows and balanced the squareness of his jaw, enhancing his features rather than hiding them. When he dropped into the salon on a weekday, he would be dressed in an immaculate suit that he accessorized with adventurous shirts, like the candy-pink number he was wearing that morning. In his breast pocket, he carried a precisely folded handkerchief that matched the shirt or coordinated with his tie. To preserve the beautiful cut of his expensive Italian jackets and trousers, he carried his wallet and pens in a stylish leather 'man-bag'. Matt Charlton clearly read *GQ* very closely.

Still, Emily didn't let herself get excited about Matt's general loveliness, since she knew only too well that that level of general loveliness in a man who didn't have a wife or girl-friend (she'd ascertained as much on his first visit) suggested Matt wouldn't get excited about any girl. Emily did, however, allow her heart a little flip of happiness whenever she saw Matt's companion, Cesar.

'Cesar! You gorgeous thing!' she gushed at him.

Cesar was a white and tan Jack Russell/Corgi cross.

When the little dog rushed around the reception desk to greet her, Emily was ready with a couple of green dog-chews from the packet she kept in the drawer beneath the till. Cesar wagged his tail ecstatically and Emily was momentarily his best friend in the world.

'Do you love me?' Emily asked him. 'Do you love me more than anyone?'

Cesar loved her until he got the chews. After that he was straight back by his master's side and on duty once more.

Ordinarily, dogs weren't allowed in The Beauty Spot. Cesar was an exception.

Matt had explained the situation the very first time he visited the salon.

He suffered from epilepsy. He'd been epileptic for as long as he could remember, he told Emily. He had his first fit when he was a tiny baby. These days, advances in medication meant that Matt didn't experience anywhere near the number of fits he used to, but there was always a chance he'd be caught off-guard. Cesar was a seizure-alert dog, trained to pick up on the minute changes in Matt's physiology that heralded a grand mal episode. The second he noticed something amiss, Cesar would let Matt know by pawing at him. If Matt didn't respond to a gentle pawing, Cesar would jump up at him and, in a last resort, bark until Matt took notice.

That was Matt's signal to get himself to a place of safety as quickly as possible. Then he would loosen his clothing, lie down in the recovery position and wait.

'You know the recovery position, don't you?'

Emily nodded. She'd done a first-aid course. 'Turn the patient onto his side, lift his chin to open his airway and make sure he can't roll,' she recited. Cesar wagged his tail. 'Then what? Do I need to put something in your mouth?'

'No,' Matt shook his head. 'Might swallow it. Or bite it in half. Just stay with me. And don't tell me if I do anything particularly embarrassing while I'm out.'

Emily laughed. Nervously.

'So, you see,' said Matt, 'there's no need for you to worry at all. If I'm going to have a fit then, nine times out of ten, Cesar will let me know well in advance.'

Emily smiled brightly but, for her first three meetings with Matt, she had watched Cesar like a hawk, responding to every move the little dog made with barely concealed panic.

'He's just scratching his ear,' Matt sighed. 'And you really should ignore him when he's licking his balls.'

Several months on, Emily no longer panicked every time Cesar responded to his natural doggy urges to itch or yawn. Instead she actually looked forward to seeing him, as he looked forward to seeing her. Or rather to seeing the packet of doggy-chews. Cupboard love.

'Are you ready for me?' Matt asked.

'Come on through,' said Emily.

Cesar led the way into the treatment room.

'How have you been?' Emily asked as Matt took off his shirt and settled himself on the couch. 'Good month?'

'Not too bad,' he replied. 'I took some time off. Had a holiday.'

'Go anywhere nice?'

'San Francisco.'

Emily nodded as she checked the temperature of the wax in the melting pot. 'I've heard it's great there,' she said. Lots of her male clients went to San Francisco on holiday. In fact, just the previous week, Marco, a flight attendant with British Airways, had been telling her about a trip he was planning. He and eight of his cabin-crew friends had arranged to work on the same flight, timing it so that they would be in San Fran for the whole of that year's Gay Pride weekend.

'It's going to be mayhem,' Marco had sighed with delight.

'Got any more holidays planned this year?' Emily asked as she applied the first spatula of wax to Matt's back.

'I thought I'd go somewhere a bit closer to home for a week towards the end of the summer,' he told her. 'I was thinking Greece. Not sure which island would be best, though.'

'Oh, you should go to Mykonos,' said Emily. Marco the flight attendant was always talking about Mykonos. 'I've heard it's great. I think you'd love it there.'

'Thanks. I'll take a look at it on Google when I get back to the office. How about you?' Matt asked.

'Huh?' Emily was momentarily surprised. Her clients didn't often ask her questions during their 'me-time'.

'Are you going on holiday this year?'

Emily applied a muslin strip to the honey-coloured wax and smoothed it down with the heel of her hand.

'Holiday?' she half-laughed. 'Not this summer.'

She took the free edge of the muslin strip and yanked it in the direction of the hair growth. Matt gave a little yelp. Emily tutted. She slapped her hand down on the bare skin where the wax strip had been. Somehow doing that could short-circuit the tearing pain of having your hair ripped out by the roots. Emily didn't understand the science but it worked.

'That didn't hurt,' she said before Matt had time to complain.

Cesar, who was sitting in the corner of the room, rolled his deep brown doggy eyes in sympathy.

'Are you too busy to get away?' Matt asked, bringing the subject back to holidays in an attempt to distract himself from the pain.

'Can't afford it,' said Emily. 'Not busy enough.'

'But this place always looks busy,' Matt commented.

'I suppose it is. There are certainly plenty of "ladies who lunch" here in Essex. But . . .' Emily stopped to rip another pathway through the forest of Matt's back hair. Slap went her hand on the sore patch. She waited for him to finish groaning before she continued. 'Somehow there's still more money going out than coming in.'

'I see.'

'I had hoped to be in profit by now but I'm still running at a loss.'

'Would you like me to have a look at your accounts?' asked Matt.

'What was that?'

The end of the sentence had been lost as Matt tried to keep breathing through the removal of another strip.

'I could have a look at your books for you. It's what I do for a living,' he explained. 'I'm a small-business advisor. I work at the bank on the corner.'

'Oh.'

Emily paused in applying more wax as Matt elaborated on his job description. She couldn't wait to tell Chloe. They had speculated about Matt's job before and had him pegged as an estate agent, thanks to the smart suits.

'I could help you see a way forward,' Matt continued. 'Ow!'

A blob of wax fell from the spatula onto the small of Matt's back, taking both him and Emily by surprise.

'Sorry.' Emily rushed to deal with it. 'Perhaps we should talk about this when I'm done.'

That seemed like the best idea.

Safely back in the lobby, Matt reiterated his willingness to help Emily sort out The Beauty Spot's finances.

'I'd love to take you up on it,' said Emily. 'But I don't think I can afford your fees.'

'Then we'll barter,' said Matt.

'What seems a fair swap?' Emily asked.

'My expertise for a manicure.'
Emily stuck out her hand to shake his. 'You're on.'

From the front window of the salon, Chloe and Emily watched Matt and Cesar head off back down the street towards Matt's office.

'He always looks so smart,' said Emily. 'I love his suits. Handmade shoes, you know.'

'Fantastic backside as well,' said Chloe.

The girls looked at one another and burst into giggles.

'Shame he's so *todally* gay,' Chloe sighed.

Halfway down the street, Matt was still shaking his head at the thought of the bargain he had just struck. His business expertise for a manicure. *A manicure*! For heaven's sake.

3

Carina was very pleased with her first column for *Get This!* magazine. Who would have thought she would turn out to be such a talented writer? Her nan telephoned to say that she had read the column while sitting under the drier in the hair-dresser and she had never been so proud. Well, thought Carina, with a bit of luck she would make her nan even prouder that night.

Carina was one of the nominees for *Get This!* magazine's Reality Celebrity of the Year. The lavish awards ceremony would be taking place that evening at The Dorchester Hotel on Park Lane and broadcast live to the nation on the new digital station EvenMore4. Carina's rivals for the prize were someone called Marlon who had appeared in a programme about service stations (not *Celebrity Service Station* but an actual documentary about service stations, called simply *Service Station*) and Monkey Gordon, the nation's favourite inpatient.

It was the most important awards ceremony of the year for a fledgling celeb like Carina, and Mickey had cannily arranged it so that she would have at least two chances of getting up on the podium to receive the coveted trophy from Patrick and Trudy Blezard, presenters of *Wakey-Wakey* and heirs to Richard and Judy's daytime crown. It didn't matter whether Carina won or not, because Marlon was a no-hoper and, if Monkey won, then Carina was going to accept his award and make a speech on his behalf. It was very unlikely that Monkey would be there himself, still

standing as he was in the corner of a bare-walled room at
The Bakery (itself now the subject of a documentary called
Half-Baked).

With so much time in front of the cameras guaranteed,
Carina knew she had to look good. Lucy, Mickey's right-hand
girl at Shore Thing Talent, was on the case as soon as they
heard about the nomination, calling in dresses from Carina's
favourite designers. The public relations team at Karen Millen
sent something over within hours. As did the crew at Jane
Norman. The PR at Dior somehow 'forgot' to return Lucy's
call.

Carina was upset that the Dior dress she had picked from
the pages of *Vogue* didn't materialize, but Lucy worked her
magic, saying, 'I don't think Dior is right for this evening
anyway. This is an award voted for by the *people*. You need
to look like a woman of the people to win it.' There was still
a chance, she explained, that Carina's appearance at the ceremony could clinch it. Readers had been voting for best reality
celeb for weeks, but that night they would get one more chance
to vote by premium-rate text while the awards show was aired
live on TV.

Carina said she understood. She forgot about the Dior and
plumped for a number by Karen Millen instead. It was a
pseudo-Chinese cheongsam in pale green silk with a mandarin
collar that unbuttoned to show a satisfying amount of
cleavage. On her feet, she would sport a pair of gold sandals
from Kurt Geiger that showed off her French pedicure to
perfection. Carina had asked for a pair of Jimmy Choos, but
Lucy had to let her know that, alas, one Elizabeth Hurley
had borrowed every spare pair they had in a size six and a
half (Carina didn't need to know that the PR at Jimmy Choo
had actually snorted at the idea of sending a pair of free
sandals to Britain's 'favourite chav').

* * *

The entire week before the awards ceremony was a flurry of image-perfecting activity. It wasn't just about getting the right outfit. Carina had to be properly prepared beneath it. That meant three emergency sessions at the gym with her personal trainer Zsolt (and a crash diet of cabbage soup, which she absolutely would not mention to any interviewers). It meant half a day at Toni Tone's getting new hair extensions put in and another half-day at Malibu Tan getting a top-to-toe St Tropez. Then to a little salon round the back of Harvey Nicks to see Marguerite, the world's number one eyebrow-threader. ('Eyebrows are the windowsills of the soul,' Marguerite had solemnly declared in that month's *Vogue*.) After that, to New You Nails of Mayfair for the French pedicure (the sight of which made Mickey feel sick, though he'd never say it – toenails just shouldn't be that long, right?) and a full set of acrylics on her fingers.

And because it was a special occasion . . .

'Real Swarovski crystals,' said Elena the manicurist, bringing out a little plastic box from the drawer in her manicure table.

'Classy,' said Carina.

'I could spell out your name on your fingertips with them, if you like.'

'That'd be fantastic,' said Carina. 'Go ahead.'

The C and the S of Carina Lees were a little cramped, situated as they were on Carina's pinkie fingers, but the overall result was quite spectacular. When Elena had finished, Carina held out her hands and admired her new inch-long iridescent pink fingernails with their crystal embellishments as though she were admiring a ten-carat diamond ring.

'They're amazing,' Carina breathed.

She imagined the glitter of her new bejewelled nails wrapped around the *Get This!* magazine Reality Celebrity of the Year trophy and knew in that moment that victory would be hers. No question.

'Just don't go picking your nose!' Elena warned.

Elena need not have worried. There would be no nose-picking. In fact, Carina could do very little at all with her new acrylic talons in place. Arriving back by chauffeur-driven car at her newly built executive home (with American kitchen and Mediterranean-style conservatory), Carina suddenly realized that she couldn't even undo her jeans to pee. She got her driver to call Mickey and persuaded him to send Lucy over to Essex to help her get into her dress. Lucy was furious but Mickey calmly reminded her that celebrities were not like other people. Such little foibles were the flip side of fabulousness . . .

OK. So in the end what Mickey actually did was offer Lucy a hundred pounds in cash if she would just get down there and do whatever Carina needed.

'Because she's doing my head in,' he added.

By the time Lucy arrived, Carina very much needed to pee. Lucy patiently unzipped Carina's skintight Sass and Bide jeans (every WAG's favourite that week) and helped her wiggle them down over her hips. She was obviously too desperate to wee to remember to say 'thanks'.

'How will I, you know, wipe myself afterwards?' Carina yelled from the bathroom.

'I need two hundred pounds,' Lucy texted to Mickey while Carina finished answering nature's call.

Meanwhile, in Blountford, Emily had shut up the salon to customers and was waiting for Matt Charlton and Cesar to arrive to look over the books as promised. Emily had spread out her company accounts over the table in the staff kitchen. She'd bought cakes and sandwiches for her human guest and a dried-out cow's hoof for Cesar. The man in the pet shop had assured her that all dogs loved them. Emily hoped he was right. She certainly didn't love it. The thing smelt absolutely disgusting and reminded her of some of the worst feet she'd ever had the pleasure to pedicure.

Matt arrived exactly on time. That day he was wearing a dark grey suit with a very fine white stripe. The suit was lined with peacock blue silk that was picked up by Matt's spotted tie and matching handkerchief. He'd had his hair trimmed since Emily had last seen him and he was wearing new glasses. The German bendy-framed kind.

'You look nice,' said Emily.

'Oh.' Matt touched the fat knot of his tie, as if to say, 'In this old thing?' But he didn't say anything. Instead he blushed, and when he eventually tried to say thank you, it came out as a cough.

'We're in here.'

Matt followed Emily through into the staff room-stroke-kitchen. Like the rest of the salon, it was painted pink. Unable to afford to replace the old kitchen, Emily had sanded down the unit doors and painted them in a very slightly darker gloss pink. The room had a 1950s Americana feel to it. Kitsch. Camp.

'I like what you've done in here,' said Matt.

He sat down on one of the chairs Emily had re-upholstered in pink gingham. Cesar took up his position beneath the table with the stinky old hoof. The pet-shop owner had been right. He seemed to love it.

They made a little small talk while Emily served the sandwiches and made a pot of tea. Matt told her about his day at work – how satisfying it was to see the small businesses he advised expand and grow. Just that day he'd had a meeting with one of his very first clients – a landscape gardener – who had gone from being a sole trader with an old Ford Fiesta and a wheelbarrow to a limited company employing fifteen under-gardeners who drove around in liveried vans.

'You could do the same thing,' said Matt encouragingly.

'Get some vans?'

'Expand,' he corrected her. 'I can see it happening.'

But that was before he looked at the figures.

Matt didn't have to say anything. Emily could read what he was thinking in the lines on his forehead. With each page of the accounts book that Matt turned, the lines grew a little deeper. It wasn't good. Emily was too distressed to touch the cakes.

'It's very simple,' he said eventually. 'There's more going out than there is coming in.'

Emily knew that much already.

'What can I do?'

'You need more money coming in or less going out.'

'Well, duh,' said Emily.

'Get more clients. Or cut your costs.'

'How can I cut my costs?'

'How about here?' Matt pointed out a line on Emily's spreadsheets. 'Your beauty supplies seem very expensive from what I know about your market. I had a client setting up a salon last year. I'm sure her outgoings on product were half the amount of yours.'

Emily knew that was possible. When setting up the salon she had researched a great many different brands of beauty products, but she had fallen in love with an organic aromatherapy brand. And of course it was the most expensive range, available in tiny quantities that, because they contained so many natural ingredients, didn't last long once they were opened.

'But I can't cut corners on my beauty products,' she explained to Matt. 'This stuff is the very best on the market. I don't believe anything else works so well.'

'Your clients won't notice the difference,' said Matt.

'I would!' Emily protested. 'And I think you would too.'

'Me? I've got skin like a rhino's.'

'No, you haven't,' said Emily. 'Your skin is very soft.'

Matt looked down at his notepad and coughed. Emily realized she had embarrassed him.

'I mean sensitive,' Emily corrected herself. 'Which is why it hurts so much to wax.'

Matt said nothing. Emily decided to stop digging herself into a hole.

'Is there anywhere else I could cut corners?' Emily asked to change the subject.

'Your stationery?' Matt suggested. 'These prices are extortionate,' he added, picking up an invoice from the office supplies company. 'What are you using? Paper made from papyrus leaves handpicked from the banks of the Nile?'

'It is handmade,' explained Emily. 'I think it gives a better impression.'

Matt shook his head. 'I appreciate your love of quality,' he said.

'I can tell that from your suits,' Emily complimented him.

'But you can't buy stock for a business like you're buying for your own home. We need to create a proper budget and you need to stick within it.' He reached into his man-bag for a Mont Blanc pen. 'A piece of paper, please.'

Emily passed him one of the handmade sheets. Matt divided the sheet into two columns and began to write out Emily's business prescription.

'Item one: nail-care products. Find a cheaper brand . . .'

Emily put her head in her hands. This was going to be depressing.

Fifty minutes later, Matt was still trimming the fat from Emily's budget, but the alarm on his mobile phone chirped to let him know that an hour had passed since he had arrived at The Beauty Spot.

'Got to go,' he said. He stood up quite abruptly. 'I can't believe it's been an hour already.'

'Well, you did only promise me an hour,' said Emily. 'But can I offer you something else to finish this?'

The budget was not yet complete.

'A back wax?' she suggested desperately.

'No need,' said Matt. 'Really there isn't. I'd stay here for longer but I've got to . . .' He stopped himself.

Emily waited for him to finish his sentence.

'I've got to go to a concert,' he said.

Emily brightened. 'Then I won't keep you. Seeing anything good? Rock? Classical?'

'It's a Liza Minnelli tribute concert,' Matt muttered.

'Oh.'

Dashing to the station from where he would catch a train into Central London, Matt berated himself for telling Emily the truth about that evening's plans. *A Liza Minnelli tribute concert!* He didn't know which was worse. That he was going to a Liza Minnelli concert or that he would be accompanying his godmother. He could only hope that Cesar wouldn't howl along to 'Cabaret' like he did the last time.

But Emily wasn't thinking about Matt's cheesy taste in music. She was too busy worrying about the steps she would have to take to keep her little business afloat.

Would The Beauty Spot even survive its first year? When the salon opened, there had been a flurry of activity as the locals came to see what was new, but that had definitely died down. If it was to survive, then Emily knew that Matt was right. She had to cut corners where she could. She had no spare money to advertise for new clients right now. If she gave up on being one hundred per cent organic, she could release some money for an ad in the local paper. But Emily couldn't help worrying that, if she gave up on the organic products, she might lose some of her loyal customers . . .

It was late and she was tired and all she wanted to do was go home and eat a packet of biscuits, but alas there was still work to be done. As Matt had clearly pointed out, the salon wasn't making enough money to cover the cost of a cleaner. Changing into her tatty old jeans and donning a pair of rubber gloves, Emily prepared to do battle with the customer cloak-room.

What she needed was a miracle . . .

4

It took almost three hours for Carina Lees to be ready to leave the house for the *Get This!* readers' awards ceremony at the Dorchester. Lucy the PR assistant had, of course, booked a limousine for her company's most important client. When the car arrived, Lucy gazed at it longingly. She had hoped to be able to hitch a lift home, but because Carina took so long to prepare for the awards ceremony there would be no time to detour via Lucy's grotty flat-share. In any case, Lucy had to stay behind at Carina's house and pay the hair-dresser and make-up artist (in cash. Danger money). Then she would walk to the train station and take a filthy train back to filthy Clapham Junction.

Carina didn't even thank her for her trouble as Lucy helped her into the car like a lady-in-waiting helping Elizabeth the First into her coach.

Carina's mind was elsewhere. In the back of the limousine, she sat back against the white leather seats and imagined the glamorous evening ahead. Of the three possible outcomes of that evening's fight to be Reality Celebrity of the Year, two required that she make a speech. Mickey had couriered the speeches (written by the *Get This!* magazine journalist who also wrote Carina's column) over to Carina's house by bike so that she could learn them in the car en route. There was the speech Carina would deliver if Monkey won: *'I'd just like to say how much it means to me to be able to stand here and accept this valuable reward on behalf of my dear, dear, friend*' (whom she hadn't seen during the six months since she left the house and he went into hospital). '*I know that he's going to be very excited.*' (Not if he was still on those drugs.) And then there was her own speech, '*I'd just like to say how much it means to me to be able to stand here and accept this award. The support of the wonderful readers of* Get This! *magazine has put me where I am today! I love you all very, very much.*' Lucy had added that it might be nice if she waved her trophy in the air and said, 'Thank you, Nan,' too.

Mickey had promised Carina that he would be at the Dorchester when she arrived, waiting to give her a final briefing. He would be sitting at the same table. There was nothing to worry about.

Still, Carina couldn't help but be a bit nervous. It was the first time in her life she had been nominated for an award. That was why she felt the need to call Mickey and make sure that he was already on his way to the hotel with Danny Rhodes, who was taking a rare night off from the West End revival of *The Music Man* to be Carina's official date for the evening.

'Hey, sweetheart,' said Mickey when he picked up. 'You all set? Lucy tells me you're looking beautiful!'

Actually, Lucy had said nothing of the sort during her ten-minute/four-letter-word rant to her boss as she walked from Carina's house to the train station. But Mickey subscribed to the notion that if you didn't have anything nice to pass on to a client, you should make something up.

'I've got Danny right here in the taxi. He can't wait to see you. I just know he's going to be so proud to have you on his arm tonight.'

Danny couldn't give a stuff what was on his arm that night if it wasn't the Brazilian lad he had met backstage at Heaven the night before.

'You're going to be there when I get there, right? I don't want to be walking in on my own.'

'I'll be there,' Mickey promised her. 'Don't tell me you're nervous, sweetheart. You can take this in your stride.'

'I know,' said Carina, absently twiddling one of her hair extensions. 'I just want to make sure it all goes well, that's all. This is really important to me. My nan is going to be watching.'

'And you're going to make your nan very proud.'

Carina twisted her hair extension around her forefinger.

'Do you think so?'

'I know it.'

'Who else is going to be on our table?' Carina asked. 'It's not going to be all reality people, is it?'

'Darling,' said Mickey smoothly. 'You'll be with your own kind. Proper celebrities. People who have done something real . . .'

Carina seemed satisfied with that. She muttered on for a bit longer about how unhelpful Lucy had been when she couldn't get the ankle strap fastened on one of her shoes. Mickey zoned out of the conversation and turned his attention to Danny, who was sulking, having received a text from the Brazilian saying that if Danny really had to go to a stupid awards ceremony, he was going to meet his ex-boyfriend for dinner. As he looked at Danny's miserable face and listened to his other young charge nattering on in his ear about how great her nails looked, Mickey remembered why he'd never bothered to have kids of his own.

Danny was texting a furious riposte to the boy from Brazil.

'If she really were that important, she would have been nominated, right?' Carina was saying. 'I mean, I've actually been nominated . . .'

'Mmm-hmm,' said Mickey. He had perfected the psychiatrist's art of appearing to be giving his full attention to a conversation while in fact contributing absolutely nothing.

'And anyway . . .' Carina continued. Mickey was zoning out when . . . 'Aaaaaaaaagggggghhhhh!'

Carina screamed so loudly that Mickey dropped the phone, fearing for his eardrum. Even as his mobile lay in the footwell of the car, he could still hear Carina screaming and the brakes of the limousine she was being driven in screeching as the driver brought the car to an emergency stop. Mickey had his own driver stop as he scrambled on the floor to find his mobile phone. Danny was momentarily jerked out of his own self-pity to find out what on earth was going on.

Mickey found his phone. He pressed it to his ear. It had gone silent.

'Carina! Carina! Can you speak to me? Are you OK? Are you hurt?'

Mickey, Danny and the taxi driver all held their breath as they waited for her to reply.

All three were imagining a worst-case scenario. Danny's was worst than most. He imagined an accident between limousine and juggernaut. Carina decapitated. Bright red arterial blood making a beautifully shocking contrast to the green party dress he'd been told she'd be wearing and the soft white leather seats of the limo. He would have to go to the *Get This!* magazine awards all the same, of course. The show must go on, etcetera. And when Carina's name was called, he would accept the award of Reality Celebrity of the Year on her behalf. His face would be the picture of tragic serenity. Calm, still, perfect. Right up until the last moment when he would thank Carina's nan for raising such a beautiful grand-daughter. Then he would burst into carefully timed tears. His despair would be all over the papers . . .

'Carina? Carina?' Mickey was still trying to raise her. 'I think I can hear her breathing,' Mickey announced to his fellow passengers. 'Look, darling, I need to know where you are,' he talked into the phone again. 'I can have an ambulance with you in seconds. But I need you to tell me what's happened.'

Finally, through desperate sobs, Carina spoke to him.

'I broke my nail!!!!!!'

5

Mickey was too relieved to be as furious as he knew he should be. In Mickey's worst-case scenario, a dead Carina wasn't half so appealing as it was to Danny Rhodes. Sure, her picture would have been all over the papers for a few days, but then . . . nothing. She hadn't been around long enough to warrant more than a one-volume biography. All those advertising deals he was in the middle of brokering would be worthless. His golden goose cooked. So, Mickey was glad that she wasn't dead. But all that screaming for a broken nail? He shook his head.

'Calm down.'

'What can I do?' Carina sobbed.

'I don't know,' said Mickey. 'Haven't you got a nailfile in your handbag? Smooth it off?'

'What? You expect me to go into the *Get This!* magazine awards with one fingernail shorter than all the others?'

Mickey wasn't sure what he had expected. 'Er, yes?' he said cautiously.

Carina sent up a wail of distress.

'It doesn't matter,' Mickey tried to reassure her.

'Doesn't matter?' Carina spat back at him. 'You are joking. *Get This!* magazine's celebrity columnist turns up looking a mess? The girls from *Heat* will have a field day. Haven't you seen all the pictures they ran of Kate Beckinsale and her weird toes?'

Mickey had indeed seen the pictures of Kate Beckinsale with her preternaturally long toes poking over the edges of her Jimmy Choos. But Kate Beckinsale's weird feet were an altogether different category of interest than a broken fingernail, surely?

Not to Carina they weren't.

'Call Lucy,' Carina demanded. 'She'll know what to do.'

Poor Lucy had almost made it back to her flat when her mobile phone rang. She was looking forward to a nice quiet evening at home, deliberately *not* watching the live coverage of the *Get This!* magazine awards on EvenMore4. Instead, she was going to eat a Marks and Spencer's ready meal in front of a new episode of *Midsomer Murders*. Then she was going to take a nice long bath with some of the fancy bath oil her sister had given her for Christmas and then . . .

'I need you to find a manicurist in Essex,' said Mickey.

'I'm off duty.'

'A celebrity PR is never off duty,' Mickey reminded her. 'Unless she's been sacked.'

Thank goodness for Google and MapQuest. Like Mission Control guiding the space shuttle home, Lucy talked Carina's limo driver through the back streets of a little town called Blountford until he found himself outside a place called The Beauty Spot.

'Please tell me it's open,' said Lucy, fingers crossed. She'd tried to call but found the line engaged.

'There are lights on but it doesn't look as though anybody's there,' said the driver.

'Could you bear to go and check?' Lucy asked.

'There's nowhere to stop. I'm in a bus lane.'

'I'll sort it out,' Lucy promised. Shore Thing had a special budget for celebrity-emergency-related driving fines.

Leaving Carina sniffing away her tears in the back of the limo, the driver trotted across the road to The Beauty Spot.

He pressed hard on the doorbell and heard it ring out inside. He waited thirty seconds. No response. He pressed again. Still nothing.

Emily heard the sound of the doorbell ringing for the third time just as she turned off the vacuum cleaner. She leaned out of an upstairs window, disinclined to open the door to a complete stranger. Though it was only quarter to seven in the evening, it was completely dark outside. She wasn't expecting a customer. More likely a bunch of hoodies intent on robbing her empty till.

'Who is it?' she called down.

The limousine driver stepped back from the door and positioned himself under a streetlamp so that she could see him. Emily wasn't exactly comforted by the sight of the enormous bloke with a shaved head on the pavement outside her salon, even if he was wearing a suit. His broken nose gave the impression of someone who had spent many years working a nightclub door way too enthusiastically.

'What do you want?' Emily asked. Was this the start of the protection racket she had heard so many small businesses succumbed to?

'You open?' he shouted up.

'No,' she shouted back. 'We closed at five o'clock today. You'll have to come back.'

She started to close the window. If she just acted as though he was a customer then maybe he'd go away.

'Hey! Don't go. Girl in the back of my car is having an emergency,' the driver said, jerking his head towards the limo on the opposite side of the road.

'An emergency? Why didn't you say? There's an A and E department at the hospital in Greenford,' said Emily. 'Just follow this road . . .'

'Not that kind of emergency,' the driver interrupted.

'Well, what kind of emergency is it?'

'She's broken a nail.'

'What?' Emily's reaction was not dissimilar to Mickey's, though, in theory, as a beautician, she should have been more sympathetic.

'I dunno how it happened. It came off in her hair or something. She needs to have it fixed back on.'

'You want me to open my salon to fix a broken nail?'

The driver nodded.

'Look, I'd love to help you, but the salon is closed. I've finished cleaning up downstairs and all of the equipment has been put away.'

'Please. Pretty please,' the driver tried.

'No,' Emily imagined his passenger. Some spoilt brat on her way to a 'sweet sixteen' party. She'd seen plenty of them – children who had everything except parental discipline – vomiting out of limo windows on their way home from a bout of underage drinking.

'You don't seem to understand . . .'

'You're right,' Emily said. 'I don't.'

There was no way she was going to put herself out for some silly little girl who couldn't even be bothered to ask for a favour in person. Emily and the driver argued the toss a little longer until eventually, as though she understood how rude she was being, the passenger door at the back of the car clicked open and the passenger emerged, feet first.

Emily's eye was instantly drawn to the glittery gold sandals on the young woman's feet. They were fabulous. And when she realized that the passenger was Carina Lees, Emily immediately amended The Beauty Spot's opening hours.

6

In the time it took for Emily to run downstairs and open the salon door to her surprise celebrity customer, she knew she had to come up with a strategy. She would treat Carina with the utmost professionalism. That meant looking the part (she pulled on her overall as she raced to the door) and being incredibly discreet. And calm. She had to be calm, she told herself as she flapped her hands at her face in an attempt to cool down. She would act as though Carina were any other client. There would be no gawping.

Emily opened the door. And gawped.

Carina Lees took a step backwards as though the face that greeted her had surprised her too. She opened her mouth as if to say something to that effect but didn't. Instead, she managed a wan sort of smile.

'Hello,' she said.

'Welcome to The Beauty Spot,' said Emily, ushering her inside.

'Thank you,' said Carina. 'This is an absolute fucking disaster. Can you fix it?'

If Emily didn't already know that she was going to be dealing with a broken fingernail, she might have been offended by the way Carina extended her middle digit towards her.

'I think I can help you,' said Emily. 'You just need a new acrylic, right?'

'Not any old acrylic. It has to match these. Exactly.' Carina extended the rest of her fingers. The rhinestones dazzled Emily. And immediately worried her too. She didn't carry a lot of 'bling' at The Beauty Spot. Her customers were the kind of women who always said 'natural' when Emily asked them how they wanted their *fake* fingernails to look. 'Do you think you can do it?' Carina asked.

Emily said she would do her best.

'Well, I guess I don't have any choice but to let you,' said Carina. 'I was meant to be at the *Get This!* magazine awards ten minutes ago.'

'I'll go as quickly as I can.'

Emily had Carina sit down at the manicure table and set out by soaking off the remains of the glue that had been holding the false nail in place. As she swiped away at Carina's real nail with the special acrylic remover, Emily noticed that her own hand was looking somewhat shaky. She tried resting her elbow on the table to stop it. It didn't stop the shaking. It just made the position she was working in more awkward. When Emily glanced up, she caught Carina frowning, so she went back to her usual manicure position.

'I think I might have cramp,' Emily lied.

Carina didn't look as though she cared.

And, eventually, Emily's shaking subsided. Before she had to pick up the polish brush, thank goodness. It took fifteen minutes to replace Carina's nail with a new one. That was the time Emily usually allocated for a whole mini-manicure. Towards the end of the process, Carina shifted in her seat and looked at her watch every thirty seconds, but she agreed with Emily that it was important to get the nail absolutely right.

'The gossip magazines pick up on this kind of thing,' she said. 'You saw all the fuss they made about Kate Beckinsale's weird toes.'

'I know,' said Emily. 'You'd think her stylist would say "no sandals".'

'They pick up on the tiniest flaw and magnify it out of all

proportion,' Carina continued. 'Split ends or a sweat patch can finish a career.'

Emily nodded. 'I can imagine.'

'I think that's why so many celebs wear sleeveless outfits, even in the dead of winter. Or get Botox in their pits, of course.'

'People really do that?'

'I haven't,' said Carina quickly. 'Is that done?' she asked, nodding towards her nail to change the subject.

'It's done,' said Emily.

'It looks OK,' said Carina. 'You've matched the diamante E on the finger next to it pretty well.'

Emily took that to mean 'thank you'.

Carina was already standing up.

'How much do I owe you?' she asked.

Emily thought quickly. Should she double her usual price? Treble it? Carina Lees could afford it. Emily had read an article in the paper that said the reality star had earned three million pounds in less than a year. It was after hours. Any other industry would charge extra for out-of-hours' services. But then Emily had a stroke of genius.

'You don't owe me anything,' she said. 'Except a promise that you'll drop in again someday. In daylight. When everyone can see you!'

Carina hesitated. Then she smiled and nodded.

'If that's all it takes,' she said. 'Now I've got to go.'

Emily opened the door.

Outside, it was starting to rain. When he saw that his passenger was about to step out into the downpour, the driver jumped out of the limo and quickly came to her aid with an enormous black umbrella.

Emily remained at the open door and watched Carina hurrying over to the car. With the driver towering over her, she looked even more petite than she had done inside the salon. She was so tiny. So lovely. Emily was even more in awe of the little celebrity now than she had been when she read about her millions that morning. That was quite something, wasn't it, to be more in awe of a celebrity having met them in the flesh? Ordinarily, it happened the other way round. People usually said that meeting one's idols was a disappointment. Not so for Emily. She closed the door of The Beauty Spot and finished closing up as though she were being borne around the salon on a fluffy pink cloud. Just an hour earlier she had been thinking about quitting. Carina Lees's visit was a sign that she should carry on.

In the back of the limousine, Carina admired her *new* new nail. That Emily Brown girl had done pretty well, she had to admit. The colour match was perfect. The crystals were almost the same size as those on the other nails. You'd have to be a jeweller to guess they weren't Swarovski. It was a good job. And all for free.

Carina remembered the gleeful smile on Emily's face when she had agreed to visit the salon again some other time. In daylight. So people could see her. Well that, thought Carina, as the limo sped on towards London, is one promise I just might have to keep.

7

Mickey was waiting anxiously by the revolving doorway of The Dorchester when Carina's limousine cruised under the awning. The hotel doorman leapt into action, opening the passenger door of the limo and offering Carina his arm. Mickey took over as soon as he could, cursing Carina's slowness in those stupid French-pedicure-revealing shoes. (Yuk, he thought. Must not look down. Must not look down!) Inside the hotel's grand ballroom, the *Get This!* magazine awards were about to begin and he needed to get Carina to her table.

Danny Rhodes was also in the lobby, looking disconsolate as he punched another text message into his phone.

'Your lovely date for the evening is here,' Mickey prompted him. Danny was miles away.

'Danny?' Carina's high, thin voice cut through the other sounds in the lobby.

Danny put his phone away with a sigh.

Carina gave Danny the once-over then she turned back to Mickey with a frown.

'Didn't you tell him I was going to wear green? We won't look right together.'

'You'll look fine.' Mickey felt like a parent again. Trying to get two children to play nice. 'Let's go,' he said, pushing them towards the ballroom doors. 'Your public awaits.'

It was a triumphant evening for Carina Lees. Not only did she win the *Get This!* magazine readers' choice award for Reality Celebrity of the Year, she got to climb the stairs a second time to collect an award for Monkey Gordon as well. The staff of *Get This!* magazine had given Monkey a special prize for overcoming great personal difficulties to succeed in reality TV. The fact that he was still in hospital, and still very much under his personal difficulties, seemed to have escaped everybody present.

'This will have pride of place in his hospital room!' Carina informed the whooping crowd as she lifted the trophy over-head.

'And you'll deliver it to him, right?' asked Patrick Blezard of *Wakey-Wakey*, who was co-hosting the evening with his older wife Trudy.

'Of course,' Carina assured him. 'I see Monkey all the time.'

The crowd applauded uproariously.

Carina assured Trudy that Monkey was her very dear friend.

Back at the table, Mickey was making a note on a napkin.

'What are you writing?' Carina asked.

'Brilliant idea, that. You deliver the trophy to Monkey in hospital. Fantastic photo opportunity. We'll sort it out later this week.'

Carina blanched.

'You can't make me go there,' she whispered with horror. 'It's full of nut jobs. And Monkey freaks me out.'

'Ah ha, very funny,' said Mickey, pinching Carina on the arm to stop her from saying anything more ungenerous. They were sharing their table with one of the 3AM Girls. Those gossip journos had better hearing than the average bat and they were more eager for celebrity blood than a vampire.

From dinner at The Dorchester to the award ceremony after-party at Pink Cube, London's hottest new club. Housed in a

former car salesroom in Mayfair, it was owned by the youngest
scion of a very wealthy family; his first attempt at earning a
living after fifteen years spent getting wasted in Ibiza.

Carina clung to Danny's arm as they passed the paparazzi.
They looked very much a couple, despite their clashing outfits.
Once inside, however, they went their separate ways. Carina
to the VIP room (which was far busier than the rest of the
club), Danny to find a corner quiet enough for a phone conversation with the Brazilian boy, who was in another VIP room
on the other side of town.

Mickey was at the club too. Ostensibly to schmooze new
clients but more realistically to make sure that the clients he
already had didn't disgrace themselves. He reminded Danny
that a visit to an S & M bar would not sit well with the kids-
TV-friendly image they were trying to create for him, even if
the Brazilian boy was flying back to Rio tomorrow and he
might never see him again. Mickey also swapped every other
flute of Cristal that floated Carina's way for a glass of alcohol-
free Amé. She didn't notice the difference in taste, but Mickey
had previously noticed a difference in Carina's behaviour
whenever her drinking wasn't controlled. He didn't want the
evening to end with a fight.

At half past two, Mickey persuaded both his clients to go
home. He tucked them up in the back of two separate limou-
sines and took a taxi back to his own house in St John's
Wood. Inside he was greeted by the answer-machine, angrily
flashing 24 messages. One of his clients, a model who had
previously been engaged to the posh boy who opened Pink
Cube, was freaking out because the NYC hotel Mickey had
booked her into didn't have enough *special* pillows. Mickey
spent a half-hour talking her down. For just one night a month,
he thought, he would like to be able to stay home, eat a ready
meal and watch *Midsomer Murders*.

* * *

Emily also had a late night. Ordinarily, when she got home from a day at the salon – especially after something as stressful as Matt's pessimistic review of her accounts – she would just about make it through *EastEnders* before falling asleep on the sofa. That night, however, she was watching the *Get This!* magazine awards. More specifically, she was glued to the footage from the after-show party at Pink Cube, where Claire Paul, who had been a contestant in the first-ever series of *Living Hell*, interviewed that night's award winners.

Claire made a beeline for Carina, who was holding her award and the one she had solemnly promised to deliver to Monkey like a pair of dumbbells.

'You must be so excited,' said Claire to Carina. 'You're *Get This!* magazine's Reality Celeb of the Year.'

'I can't believe it,' Carina told her. 'I really can't believe it. Apart from anything else, I didn't think I was going to get here tonight. I had a complete disaster in the limo on my way into London.'

'Not a car crash?' asked Claire, her facial expression switching quickly to 'concern'.

'Oh no!' Carina laughed. 'I broke a nail!'

'Oh my god,' said Claire. 'I feel your pain.'

'Luckily I was able to get a new one. At this little place in Blountford. The Beauty Space, I think it was called. No, hang on. That's not right. It was called The Beauty Spot. That's it, The Beauty *Spot*. I'd just like to say thank you to Emily the owner if she's watching . . .' Carina transferred both trophies into one hand and blew a kiss at the camera.

Thank goodness for PVRs. Emily played that tiny section of footage again and again and again. Two minutes after it aired for the first time, she already had three text messages to tell her about her celebrity namecheck.

Emily was over the moon.

8

'Was she talking about us?' was the first thing Chloe asked when she arrived at the salon the following morning.

There was no need to ask whom Chloe meant by the word 'she'.

Emily nodded proudly. 'That's right.'

'You mean she was in our salon? Here in The Beauty Spot. Oh my god.'

'She sat right there,' said Emily, pointing to the pink leather chair on the client side of the manicure table.

Chloe stared at the chair she had seen so many times before like a devout religious disciple beholding a sacred relic. Recovering herself slightly, she sprang across the room to sit on the holy seat. She wriggled about on it, as though some tiny bit of stardust might be transferred from the chair to her bottom and bless her life. There was, as it happened, a little bit of glitter on the seat, but that wasn't anything to do with Carina Lees. It was from the sparkly party dress of a seven-year-old girl whose mother had brought her and two of her friends in for manicures as a birthday treat over the weekend.

'How did she sit? Like this?' Chloe stretched her hands out across the table.

'She leaned forward a bit more than that.'

'Which fingernail had she broken?'

Emily recounted the tale in forensic detail, repeating their brief conversation about Kate Beckinsale's toes and the miraculous sweat-stopping properties of Botox word for word. Chloe listened in open-mouthed admiration. Emily was to

44

repeat the conversation several times that day, for the benefit of every client who walked through the door . . . and the postman . . . and the guy who came in to read the electricity meter.

Emily's miracle had occurred.

One of her clients the day after Carina's emergency visit was a journalist from the local paper. Emily told her the story of the celebrity acrylic. The journalist wrote the story up for the next day's paper. Her editor was delighted. Any excuse to run a photograph of a reality TV star in a bikini rather than the usual shots of local pensioners looking disgruntled about spotted dick being taken off the menu at Meals On Wheels for sinister Health and Safety reasons.

The namecheck on late-night TV had definitely caused a small increase in the number of calls The Beauty Spot received, but the story in the local newspaper set off a positive frenzy of interest. Since Emily and Chloe were the only two members of staff at the salon and were often both delivering treatments at the same time, appointment enquiries were generally handled by letting people go through to the answer-machine and asking them to leave their name and number for a call-back. It quickly became clear that this strategy was no longer going to work. The answer-machine reached capacity after twenty calls and suddenly more than twenty calls were coming through every hour. Emily's grandmother took an afternoon off from the charity shop to man The Beauty Spot's phone lines.

Meanwhile, Emily's father cut out the newspaper article and had it mounted and framed. Emily put the frame in her window and the rush for appointments continued. By the time Matt was able to help Emily finish her six-month business strategy two days later, the projected figures he had to work with were very different indeed. The Beauty Spot didn't have an empty appointment slot for the next fortnight. Not even for Matt's first manicure.

'I don't understand it,' said Matt. 'You think all these customers are coming to you because of a reality star?'

'*Get This!* magazine's Reality Celebrity of the Year,' Emily reminded him.

The Carina Lees effect lasted well beyond those initial two weeks at The Beauty Spot. Emily knew that it was the celebrity namecheck that brought the new customers in, but she liked to think it was the superior quality of her salon and the services she offered that brought them back a second and a third time. There were no more quiet periods. She and Chloe were working flat out to accommodate all the new business, especially since the Carina connection seemed to be attracting quite a different type of customer. Now the salon was buzzing with wannabe WAGs as well as the usual yummy mummies. And the wannabe WAGs required a great deal more maintenance. Emily had to find a new supplier to fulfil the sudden demand for acrylics.

A month after Carina's visit, Emily was very happy with the growth in her business but she was exhausted. She hardly had enough time to do her own nails any more. Her highlights were long overdue a retouch. Fortunately, it wasn't obvious, since she wore her hair scraped back for work and covered the worst of her colour crimes with a thick Alice band.

But as the weeks continued to go by with hardly a moment to herself, Emily began to wonder if this crazy new popularity was such a good thing. She wanted some time off but she couldn't take it because if she took time off she would have to turn customers away and if she turned customers away she was afraid that they wouldn't come back. She'd lose their custom to some other salon that could accommodate their needs more quickly.

It was a dilemma that Matt understood very well. Emily outlined the problem to him as he lay on her couch having the hair on his biceps waxed off. In between yelping with pain, he offered her his take on the new situation.

'It's a classic problem for small businesses,' he told her. 'You've hit a crucial moment. Think of this salon as a seedling in a small pot. You've grown your business to the point where it needs to be repotted or it will start to die.'

Emily gasped.

'Maybe that wasn't such a good analogy,' said Matt. 'I suppose what I'm trying to say is, while you've got all this extra business, you need to take a risk on expansion. You need to take on another beautician.'

'But I can't afford to do that!'

'You can't afford not to,' said Matt. 'What's your alternative, Emily? You and Chloe are both booked out all day long. Your grandmother has her commitments at the charity shop. She can't give you any extra hours. You can't take any more clients. There aren't enough hours in the day. If you don't take on another beautician, this is as big as The Beauty Spot will ever get.'

Emily chewed her lip. She saw Matt's point but she wasn't convinced that expansion was the answer.

She needed another sign. Another push.

9

Unfortunately for Carina, her throwaway comment that she would deliver Monkey's trophy to him personally had come back to haunt her. Each time she appeared on *Wakey-Wakey*, Trudy Blezard would finish their little chat on the sofa with an enquiry after Monkey's health.

'You've been to visit him this week, of course?'

Mickey knew that Trudy wasn't really interested. She was just trying to stir up trouble. But the fact was that a large segment of *Get This!* magazine's readership were very interested in Monkey Gordon's progress. Carina seemed to have forgotten that seventy-eight per cent of the votes in that year's *Living Hell* final had been for Monkey to win.

'You've got to go and visit him,' said Mickey.

Carina tried to wriggle out of it. She claimed that she had hospital phobia but Mickey wasn't having it. He arranged for Carina to make a 'secret' visit to Monkey's bedside. There was a fine line to tread. He wanted it to be known that Carina cared for her former reality show colleague, but he didn't want anyone to think that she was so ambitious she would try to make publicity out of visiting a sick friend. Hence the 'secret' nature of the visit. Only *Get This!* magazine's personal paparazzo would be there as witness when Carina arrived, carrying an enormous box of Whittaker's Salt & Vinegar crisps. Monkey's favourite. (Mickey had high hopes he'd be able to get Monkey an advertising deal with Whittaker's, if Monkey ever got round to speaking again.)

Carina grudgingly accepted the need for the visit, but she

very much hoped that her obligations would be over when
the pap got his perfect impromptu snap of her emerging from
her new Range Rover, negating the need for her to set foot
inside the place. But it wasn't going to be as easy as that.
Monkey's doctor was waiting for her on the steps outside The
Bakery's main entrance.

The Bakery. The name of the place made it sound quite
friendly. It was built on the site of a former bakery, of course.
The offices were housed in a grand Victorian mansion that
had been built for the master baker. The accommodation was
housed in the former bakery itself. A gloomy brick building
with small, high windows.

Dr Forrest led Carina into the reception area, which had
recently been redesigned by a famous designer of boutique
hotels in boutique hotel style to give the celebrity clients ('Not
inmates,' Dr Forrest laughed) a sense of home away from
home away from home.

'We're very glad that you care enough about your friend
Monkey to come all the way here with his trophy,' said Dr
Forrest. 'I'm sure he'll be pleased to see you.'

'But . . .' Carina protested hopefully. 'Surely he isn't well
enough?'

'You'll brighten up his day.'

The girl on the reception desk smirked.

Carina followed Dr Forrest out of the reception into the
covered walkway that joined offices to the actual hospital.
Away from the plush reception, The Bakery was a very
different kind of place. The walls of the corridor were painted
in a horrible pale green gloss. Easy to wipe clean. There were
no pictures on the walls. Carina glanced in through an open
door and saw a very bleak room on the other side. A single
bed. A plastic chair. Seventies-style curtains at the window.

And then there were the noises. Dr Forrest was completely unfazed by the things that they heard as they passed. Shrieking, crying, sobbing. He didn't seem to notice at all. Meanwhile, Carina held that box of crisps like a shield.

'Here's Monkey's room,' Dr Forrest announced.

The card on the door announced 'J. Gordon'. Carina realized she had no idea what first name the letter 'J' stood for.

'I can't do it!' she said suddenly. 'I can't.'

She dropped the box of crisps and the trophy to the floor outside Monkey's room and fled back along the corridor. She didn't stop running until she was back in the Range Rover.

Dr Forrest and one of his nurses watched Carina all but doing a wheelie in her hurry to get out of the car park.

'Do you think that was a good idea?' asked the nurse.

'I don't see what harm it could do,' Dr Forrest shrugged. 'Only a matter of time before the board has us offer guided tours of this place anyway.'

When the girl from *Get This!* called to get Carina's observations of her visit to The Bakery for the column, Carina refused to speak to her.

'I'll call you when I feel like it,' Carina informed her brusquely, and put down the phone.

Carina's visit to The Bakery had left her more than a little overwrought. She was still feeling shaken when she opened the bakery section of a new out-of-town superstore in the late afternoon. Thank goodness she didn't have to drive herself back home.

Carina slumped down into the back seat of the Mercedes account car and, most uncharacteristically, turned off her mobile phone. She was starting to relax when the car took an unexpected turn.

'This isn't the way to my place,' said Carina nervously. Just the previous day on the *Wakey-Wakey* sofa, Trudy and Patrick had been discussing the rise in celebrity kidnappings.

'Why are we turning off here?'

'Crash on the ring road,' the driver explained.

He pointed to the radio. Carina listened for a moment and heard that the driver was right. A pensioner had lost control of a VW Camper van and gone careering into the back of a lorry. No one had been hurt but the road was covered with fresh-chilled fish that were making driving conditions hazardous.

To avoid the traffic, Carina's driver took the car through the centre of Blountford. It wasn't much of a place. Exactly the kind of town you'd want to bypass if you were able. However, after a few moments Carina realized they were going to drive right past The Beauty Spot. It was half past five. The salon might already be closed. But Carina could do with something to cheer her up. Her acrylics were looking a little shabby. There was a growing gap between the falsies and her nail bed. She hadn't had time to go and see Elena at New You Nails, her usual place.

'Stop over there,' said Carina, directing the driver to stop in the bus lane right opposite the little pink beauty shop. 'Run in and see if they've got time to do my nails.'

'What? I can't.' The driver protested that he was parked in a bus lane, but Carina assured him she'd pick up the fine if he got one. While a bus blared its horn, Carina sat calmly in the back of the limo and waited. When the driver reappeared with a nod, Carina had him drive around the block and drop her off right outside The Beauty Spot's front door, obstructing a bus heading in the opposite direction this time. Carina gave the passengers a little wave as she disappeared into the salon. The thrill of that would make up for any delay to their journey, she was sure.

* * *

Inside The Beauty Spot, the last two customers of the day were getting ready to leave. They lingered for a moment, pretending to be considering the possibility of future appointments. In reality, they were star-struck and wanted to hear the famous face talk. One of them sneaked a photo on her mobile phone. Hearing the tell-tale click, Carina turned and gave the offender a rather cool look.

'If you wanted a photo, you only had to ask,' she said.

The girl was too shy to ask now. Instead she scuttled out onto the street. The other customer quickly followed.

'I'm sorry,' said Emily. 'That must get really frustrating.'

'Too right. Everybody wants a piece of me,' Carina sighed. 'It's like I live my entire life on film these days, you know?'

Emily nodded. She hoped Carina hadn't noticed the framed article in the window and made a mental note to move it as soon as she had a chance.

'What can I do for you?'

Carina extended her hands.

'The usual,' she said. 'I've had a terrible day.'

Though she wasn't as nervous as she had been the very first time Carina Lees walked into her salon unannounced, Emily still wasn't quite sure how to act in front of her famous client. Prior to meeting Carina, Emily would have said that she was very good at meeting new people and putting them at their ease. A career in the beauty industry had made her an expert at chat. Meeting strangers at a party wasn't a situation that bothered her in the slightest these days. She could make small talk for England on any number of subjects: holidays, house prices, the horrendous difficulties involved in finding a reliable nanny. But somehow, Carina Lees left her dumbstruck.

She was surprisingly beautiful close-up. Emily knew that the photos of celebrities she saw in magazines were often far from representative of the truth, but Carina seemed to be an exception. Her make-up was relatively light. Emily could tell that the subtle layer of foundation rested on good skin. Very fine. Practically pore-less. No lines around her eyes or mouth. She wasn't a smoker for sure.

She had enormous eyes of a very particular blue – clear and light, like the colour of a blackbird's egg. They would have looked beautiful even without the false eyelashes that surrounded them. Unusual. Emily thought they reminded her of someone, but decided their familiarity was only due to the fact that she knew Carina's face so well from the tabloids.

Anyway, Emily was so much in awe that she decided her best tactic was to remain silent. She'd let Carina initiate the conversation. If she wanted to. Much as Emily wanted to know more about her celebrity life, this seemed the right way forward. After all, if any other client had come into the salon and decided they didn't want to chat but just relax and enjoy whatever treatment they were having, Emily would have respected that wish.

For a while, they were silent, but finally Carina spoke.

'How long have you had this place?' she asked, glancing up and around the little pink room.

'Hardly any time at all,' Emily admitted. 'About eight months.'

'Did it take you long to set it up?'

'Not too long. I'd been dreaming about having my own salon for years. I wouldn't have done it so quickly but Dad helped me out and I inherited some money from my great-auntie. Which was lucky. I mean,' Emily corrected, 'it wasn't lucky that she died, but I think she would have been happy to know that I spent my inheritance on this place.'

'All of it?' Carina asked.

'Every last penny. The Beauty Spot is everything I have in the world.'

'That must be quite nerve-wracking.'

'It is. I've got to make it work.'

'You seem to be doing a pretty good job.'

'That's thanks to you!' Emily exclaimed. 'Ever since you mentioned us on TV, the phone has been red hot.'

'Has it really?'

'Oh yes . . . I can't tell you how grateful I am.'

'It was nothing,' said Carina. 'I just mentioned the place on TV.'

'It was everything. You did me an enormous favour.'

'So did you. Fixing my nail.'

'You looked so fabulous that night. You were easily the best-dressed celebrity there.'

Carina accepted the compliment graciously. 'I was named best-dressed celeb of the ceremony by the *Get This!* post-award readers' poll . . . So, you're doing well here?'

'Almost too well. I haven't got any time for myself any more.'

Emily put her hand to her hair, subconsciously hiding her roots.

'Maybe you should take on another therapist,' said Carina.

'You know,' said Emily, sitting back as though she was hearing it for the first time, 'I've never thought of that.'

Matt tried not to roll his eyes when he dropped by the salon the following day and Emily told him that Carina Lees had suggested she get a new therapist and she was going to take her advice.

IO

A week after Carina's distressing visit to The Bakery, Mickey Shore had lunch with a producer he had known for many years. They spent a jolly couple of hours moaning about the decline of British television. When they first met, Mickey was an actor's agent and Helena was a bright young star in the realm of television drama. She'd won awards for her first drama-doc about a young girl bringing up two children all alone in a very depressing council block. Mickey had helped her to find the right actress for the part and they had remained friends ever since.

These days they still worked together from time to time but the conditions were very different. There were no actors any more. No professional scripts. Just 'real people' talking rubbish until Helena was able to edit their ramblings down to something resembling an old-fashioned television programme with a plot. They both found it rather depressing. Helena in particular. Her ex-husband was a script-writer and the rise of reality television had severely impacted his ability to pay child support.

'So,' she said after they had finished their main courses and put the world to rights. 'Here's what I'm after. The programme is called *The Way It Was*. It's all about celebrity childhoods. The grittier the better. You must have a few celebs who've had a real rags-to-riches story. Or overcome some hideous deformity to become a supermodel,' she laughed. 'You know the sort of thing.'

'Oh definitely,' said Mickey. 'Nearly all my reality stars were raised in trailer parks. In fact, one of them still lives in a trailer park,' he added, thinking of a client who had spent half a million pounds on importing a ridiculously overspecced Airstream caravan from the States.

'Can you think of anyone off the top of your head? Only I've got a meeting this afternoon and it would be nice to have something tangible to dangle before them.'

'Carina Lees,' suggested Mickey.

'Terribly difficult childhood?'

'The way she's turned out? I expect so.'

Carina was in the hairdresser's when she got the call. One of her hair extensions had come adrift leaving her with a bald patch at the back of her head. She'd been wearing a baseball cap all week.

Mickey was sure that she would be delighted with the news that he had near as damn it secured her a new television show. A whole hour-long programme dedicated entirely to her. She wouldn't have to share the spotlight with anybody. There was nothing Carina liked more than the spotlight, which was why Mickey was shocked that her first reaction was to say 'no'.

'No? What do you mean no?' Mickey asked.

'I mean I don't want to do a show about my childhood.'

'Why not? Was it very unhappy?' he probed hopefully. 'You could find the experience cathartic. I'm sure Channel Five would pay for a psychiatrist to be on set at all times.'

'My childhood was very happy,' said Carina defensively.

'Then that's great too. We need more feel-good TV. Makes a change from the whole sparking clogs and eating gravel business.'

'Eating gravel?'

Mickey forgot that Carina was much too young to remember Michael Palin as anything other than a cuddly avuncular sort who toured the world for the BBC.

'I don't want to do it,' Carina insisted again.

'Come on. Just dig out a few videos from your childhood. Everyone can have a laugh at your funny haircut and dodgy outfits.'

'I don't have any old videos,' said Carina.

'You must do.'

'I don't. And, before you ask, I don't have any old photos either.'

'What? None? Not even a school photo?'

'None at all. If you must know, our house caught fire when I was sixteen years old. We lost everything. All our family memories.'

'Well, that's a story in itself,' said Mickey hopefully.

'No,' said Carina. 'It was a traumatic time and I don't want to relive it.'

'But—'

'No.'

'You could—'

'I won't.'

'I understand,' said Mickey eventually. If there was one thing he was good at, it was reading people, and right then he understood that if he pressed Carina further, her position would become more, not less, entrenched. Mickey knew from years of experience that what he had to do now was step back and wait. It might take an afternoon. It might take a fortnight. But eventually Carina would think his proposal over and see it in a more positive light.

No pictures, though. That would be a problem if it were true.

'There will be something somewhere,' said Lucy positively. 'Her mum and stepdad may not have anything but her grandmother definitely will.'

Carina felt oddly unsettled after Mickey's phone call. She supposed it was inevitable that someone wanted to see her childhood pictures. But why? Why were people so keen to see the 'before' of the 'before and after'. Couldn't they just revel in the magnificent creature she was now?

'Nose job,' said Lucy. 'She's worried we'll find out.'

'Boob job,' said Kenny, who headed up the celebrity animals department at Shore Thing.

'Goes without saying,' Lucy laughed.

'I tell you,' said Kenny. 'I would pay a million pounds to see a photo from that girl's childhood. I don't suppose there's a single original piece of her body left.'

Emily was visiting her parents.

'You've got a letter,' her mother told her.

Emily took the white envelope eagerly, wondering who would be writing to her care of her parents. She hadn't lived with her family in years. But when she saw the headed notepaper, Emily's excitement immediately turned sour. 'The High School for Girls, Blountford', said the name beneath the crest.

'You are invited to a ten-year reunion for the class of 1997', the letter began.

Emily tucked the letter back into its envelope. She threw it into a wastepaper bin on the way back to her flat.

11

Another namecheck in Carina's column in *Get This!* magazine had The Beauty Spot booked up three weeks in advance. It was time, Emily decided, to put her fears to one side and go for it. Matt, who was finally in the salon for that manicure he'd been promised, agreed wholeheartedly.

'You'll be so glad you took the chance,' he assured her. 'I can see it. This time next year there will be a whole chain of Beauty Spots.'

Emily beamed.

'Do you think so?'

'I know it. Make sure you come to me for your business advice, won't you? Though I don't think you're going to be a "small business" for very much longer.'

'Thanks, Matt. I really appreciate your support. Now tell me about your plans for Mykynos. You'll want a back wax before you go, I'm sure.'

Matt was Emily's last client of the day. As soon as he left, Emily sat down at her PC and began to draft the ad for a new beauty therapist. She had decided to look for someone with roughly the same qualifications as Chloe. An all-rounder. Someone with all the right waxing and massage certificates. Someone with a little bit of experience but not too much. She had an idealistic notion that she wasn't just offering a job, but a chance to learn and grow alongside her beloved business.

It took her an hour to get the tone she wanted in her

advertisement, then she emailed it straight in to one of the big trade magazines and prayed that it would find its way to the right person.

Two weeks later, the right person still hadn't read and responded to Emily's ad.

Emily was aware that it was becoming more and more important that she expand her staff and quickly. Whenever Chloe complained of being tired, Emily panicked. If either one of them had to take a sick day then there would be chaos. The person left in charge of the salon wouldn't even have time to cancel the other's appointments.

At first, Emily had been greatly encouraged by the response to her ad in the *Beauty Therapist*. When twenty-five applications arrived in the first week, Emily felt sure that she would find the right girl in a matter of days. Having examined the résumés, though, she felt a little less confident. Very few had the qualifications she wanted. Very few could even *spell* the qualifications she wanted. Emily arranged interviews with the best of them, but somehow none of the girls who arrived seemed to fit.

It was so important to get the right person. With such a small staff, introducing even one person to the team would represent an enormous change. Chloe didn't feel like an employee any more. She felt like a true friend. She'd been there from the very beginning and sometimes Emily felt as though the future of The Beauty Spot was as important to Chloe as it was to her. Emily wanted the third person in the team to feel the same way. And so it was like interviewing for a sister rather than a member of staff.

Chloe sat in on all the interviews, dismissing the hopefuls for all manner of reasons.

'Her eyes looked mean. And I'll go insane if I have to listen to that voice for more than three minutes at a time.'

Emily had almost given up hope when the postman delivered a pink envelope that had a little flower drawn over the seal in green felt-tip.

She opened it during her tea break. It was a curriculum vitae. Also on pink paper, edged with a floral motif. And also written in green pen. It wasn't exactly the most professional CV she had ever seen, but Emily was desperate and that led her to suspend her judgment and read on.

The CV belonged to one Natalie Hill. It explained that she was twenty-two years old. She had qualified from the Welsh National School of Beauty and subsequently worked for two years in a salon in an unpronounceable (to Emily and Chloe at least) town near the Brecon Beacons. Her covering letter said she was about to move to Essex and was keen to start work as soon as possible. The other sheet of paper in the envelope was a reference from Natalie's previous employer: a glowing report on 'Pamper Palace' headed notepaper. All the right words were there. 'Conscientious, dedicated, good with people, punctual and a very sweet person to boot. I'm sorry to let her go.'

Emily felt increasingly excited as she neared the end of the letter. This girl sounded like a definite possibility. Emily called and left a message on Natalie's mobile, inviting her in for an interview the very next afternoon.

The following afternoon, Carina Lees was also expecting an interview of sorts. Mickey had managed to persuade the producers of *Wakey-Wakey* to consider Carina for a more significant slot on the breakfast show. She and Mickey had subsequently been invited to join the producer and the show's incumbent presenters for lunch at the Ivy.

Carina dressed up for the occasion. Head-to-toe Dolce & Gabbana, including a monogrammed baseball cap to help her hide from the paps. Or rather to signify to the paparazzi who habitually hung around outside the Ivy that here was someone worth snapping. No one but a celebrity would wear a baseball cap and sunglasses on a day so grey and misty you could hardly see your own hand in front of your face.

The *Wakey-Wakey* show's presenters, Patrick and Trudy, were already at the table. Trudy greeted Carina with a close-lipped smile that was a fraction as warm as the one she used on the TV set. In fact, you might have thought the two women had never met before.

'A makeover segment is the perfect vehicle for Carina's talents,' suggested Mickey. 'She's a style icon for the kind of young women who aspire to be WAGs.' Mickey managed to keep a straight face, though he wondered how it was possible to 'aspire' to be that kind of dingbat.

Jenny the producer nodded, as did Patrick. Trudy pursed her lips.

'We already have a makeover segment in the show,' she pointed out.

Mickey knew that. Trudy presented it.

'And very successful it is too,' he said smoothly. 'But Carina's strength is that she will appeal to a younger demographic.'

'I agree,' said Jenny.

'I'd like to think about it,' said Trudy.

'I've already thought about it,' said Patrick, reaching across the table to squeeze Carina's hand.

It was in the bag.

12

Emily was manning the front desk when the scruffy young girl walked in. She was wearing an enormous green parka, made for someone at least twice her size, and a black knitted beanie hat pulled down to her eyebrows. Emily tried not to let her irritation show on her face as the girl tripped over her own enormous feet and knocked into the coat stand sending coats and jackets and umbrellas flying. Instead she stepped out from behind the desk with her most welcoming smile and helped the girl set the hat stand and herself upright again.

'I've got an appointment,' the girl said.

'Miss Harris?' asked Emily, looking at the appointments book. Emily remembered taking the call. Miss Harris's mother had booked her in for a facial, manicure and pedicure as a birthday gift. Emily could see already that the facial was badly needed. A crescent moon of zits adorned each of the girl's cheeks. Her fingernails were bitten. Looking at the girl's scuffed Doc Marten boots, Emily knew she would find the girl's feet and toenails in a similarly unloved state.

The girl looked back at her blankly.

'You're not Miss Harris?' said Emily.

'No,' said the girl. 'I'm Natalie Hill.'

Natalie Hill said her name with a rising inflection that suggested she was just as surprised as Emily was that she was, in fact, that person.

Oh no, thought Emily at once. This wouldn't do. This would not do at all. Natalie stood before her looking expectant. Emily looked back, taking in anew the vile green parka, the filthy knitted hat, the enormous workmen's boots.

'I know you said that I should be here at six o'clock,' Natalie told her. 'But I was already in the area and I thought I might see if you could interview me sooner. Better than spending all afternoon getting nervous, see? I get terribly nervous when I've got to go for an interview.'

Emily continued to look at her.

'So, can you interview me now or not?'

Not, was the word that sprang to Emily's mind. But not just 'not now'. Not *ever*! Emily didn't know what they were teaching at the Welsh National School of Beauty, but it definitely wasn't the critical importance of a good first impression.

'Natalie,' Emily began. 'I'm afraid I can't see you now. The salon is fully booked. My next client will be here in a couple of minutes.'

'Then I'll come back at six,' said Natalie simply.

Emily bit her lip. It wasn't fair, was it, to make the girl come back again when it was already absolutely clear to Emily that she had a snowflake's chance in hell of getting the job? She had to tell her.

'I'm afraid I don't think I can offer you that interview after all,' said Emily firmly. 'I just don't think you're the kind of girl we're looking for.'

Natalie's face fell. 'But how can you tell? You haven't even asked me anything yet! I've got all the qualifications you asked for too.' She dug into her bag – a canvas satchel decorated with the names of heavy metal bands in black felt-tip – and pulled out a handful of crumpled certificates. She thrust them towards Emily.

'Look! I'm exactly what you asked for. City and Guilds. I've got all my certificates. I got a distinction in my level two.'

Emily took the proffered certificates out of politeness but didn't look at them.

'I can't . . .' she insisted. 'Really, it's not worth . . .'

'But you've got to give me an interview. I've come all the way from Wales.'

Natalie's eyes were beginning to fill with tears. Through the glass panel in the front door, Emily could see her next client approaching. A weeping jobseeker was hardly the kind of sight Emily wanted to greet her customers when they arrived seeking relaxation and pampering. It crossed her mind that the best way to get rid of Natalie Hill would be to promise to see her later on, but in the same moment it occurred to Emily that the tears would only continue later on when she stuck by her decision not to give Natalie the job.

'I'll pay your train fare back to Cardiff,' Emily tried. 'I just don't—'

But before Emily could get the rest of the words out, she was interrupted. Chloe practically fell out through the door of her treatment room and lurched into the lobby like a dog that was going down with rabies. She wasn't quite foaming at the mouth but she was as pale as a day-old corpse and she clutched at her stomach as though she were expecting an alien to burst out of it at any moment. She said nothing as she stumbled through the lobby to the staff cloakroom. Emily and Natalie listened in horrified silence as Chloe began a protracted bout of vomiting. It was like listening to the sound-track of one of those horror movies where everyone contracts a hideous disease that melts their livers and turns them into mush.

'Chloe,' Emily rapped gently at the door to the cloakroom, 'is something wrong?'

13

'I'm alright,' Chloe called back from the bathroom. Unconvincingly. 'Be fine in a minute.'

Ten minutes later she re-emerged. She wasn't quite so pale after the exertion of throwing up her internal organs, but she didn't exactly look *better*.

'I threw up,' she said unnecessarily.

'You've got food poisoning,' said Natalie knowledgeably. 'What did you have for lunch?'

'A prawn mayo sandwich from the corner shop,' said Chloe.

'Exactly,' said Natalie. 'Crawling with listeria, I'll bet. You've got to watch out for prawns.'

Emily took Chloe by the arm and drew her into a corner where Natalie couldn't take part in the conversation.

'Who is she?' Chloe asked.

'She's come for an interview. Don't take any notice of her.' Emily body-blocked Chloe from Natalie's view. 'How are you feeling?'

Chloe took a breath and held it for a moment before squeaking, 'I think I'm going to hurl again!'

'You've got to go home,' said Emily. 'I'll call you a taxi.'

'I can't,' said Chloe. 'My next client is already here.'

'You're in no fit state to do a facial.'

'I feel a bit better for having thrown up.' Chloe gave a weak smile.

'No way,' said Emily. 'You're not well enough. What if you pass out? What if you haven't got food poisoning at all but some gastric flu that you pass on to your customer?'

66

Chloe frowned. 'You've got a point.'

'I'm sending you home. I'll let your clients know. You just need to get well.'

Emily and Chloe were suddenly aware that Natalie was standing right next to them.

'You don't have to cancel her clients,' Natalie told them.

'Of course we do,' snapped Emily. 'She's ill.'

'But I could do it. I've got all my certificates,' she said. She pulled out the scruffy certificates again and waved them in front of Chloe. Chloe felt so faint she could barely see, but she nodded vaguely in any case.

'See,' said Natalie. 'Your friend thinks it's a good idea.'

'It is *not* a good idea,' said Emily. 'Would you mind leaving us alone? This is a *staff* meeting. And you are not staff.'

The lobby was getting quite crowded now. Emily's next client was standing at the desk, looking expectant. Chloe's client was hanging her jacket on the coat stand.

'Oh no. It's Laura McKenna,' whispered Chloe, growing even more distressed. 'This facial is really important to her. She's got to go to court to finalize her divorce settlement tomorrow morning. She needs to look her best!'

'We can't let her down,' said Natalie.

'Who's "we"?' Emily asked.

Natalie was already taking her coat off and hanging it on one of the pegs behind the desk reserved for staff. 'Have you got a spare white coat? What's she in for?' Natalie glanced at the appointments book. 'An aromatherapy facial? Oh, you use Natural Goodness products. That's great. I know all about those. We had them at the Pamper Palace. That's where I used to work,' she added for Chloe's benefit. 'Don't worry. I'm totally familiar with this stuff. Which room am I in?'

Emily opened her mouth to protest.

'That one,' said Chloe, raising a weak arm to point Natalie in the direction of her treatment room.

'Chloe!' Emily was stunned.

'Let her do it.'

'Ms McKenna?' Natalie called to the pretty dark-haired woman who was browsing through the back copies of *Get This!* in the magazine stand. 'I'll be doing your facial today.'

Emily was furious. But what could she do? Natalie disappeared into the treatment room with Chloe's client before she could stop her. Chloe said that there was no real choice. It was too late. Too complicated to explain to Ms McKenna that Natalie was a complete stranger who had just walked in off the street and . . . Emily clutched at her head.

'She could be a complete nutter. I should call the police.'

'She'll do OK,' Chloe tried to comfort her. 'She does have her certificates. She had a good reference. You were going to consider her for the job.'

'Before she turned up! Didn't you see what she was wearing?'

'She'll be wearing my spare overall by now. Ms McKenna won't be able to see her boots beneath the couch. Besides, how wrong can a facial possibly go?'

Emily spent the next hour imagining *exactly* how wrong a facial could go. In lurid detail. She'd read the horror stories in the trade magazines. She imagined poor Laura McKenna emerging from her relaxing treatment looking far, far worse than she had done when she went in. Over-exfoliated and bright red, breaking out in a rash that would last well beyond her day in court. She would have to face her soon-to-be-ex-husband looking like freshly grated beetroot. Emily's insurance almost certainly wouldn't cover the subsequent claim she made against her. Even if Laura McKenna didn't sue, she'd tell all her friends about her terrible experience. Laura McKenna had lots of friends who were *habitués* of The Beauty Spot. And doubtless they would tell all the people they knew. In a matter of hours, Emily's carefully tended business would be in ruins. And all because she didn't have the nerve to tell that mad job applicant that she would never, in a million years, give a job to a girl who wore a parka and combat boots to an interview. An interview in a beauty salon! There were few places where first impressions mattered more.

Emily's distress made it difficult for her to concentrate on her own client. She asked her where she was going on her holidays three times.

'Gran Canaria, like I said,' Mrs Griffiths answered patiently. 'We're renting a villa with my daughter and her kids.'

'I'm sorry,' said Emily. 'I'm just a little bit preoccupied.'

Another hideous vision popped up in her mind. Laura McKenna beneath the steam machine, her skin peeling off in strips like old wallpaper.

'Could you turn the steam machine down a bit?' Mrs Griffiths asked. 'Only I don't want to walk out of here looking like a lobster, do I?'

Thankfully Mrs Griffiths had cotton-wool pads over her eyes and couldn't see Emily blush.

The rest of the facial went without serious incident, but Mrs Griffiths tipped a fiver instead of her usual tenner and didn't make another appointment before gathering her coat and heading home.

In contrast, Laura McKenna fished a twenty-pound note out of her purse and slipped it into Natalie's hand as Natalie escorted her back into the lobby to settle her bill.

'That was wonderful,' she said as Emily peered at her face anxiously, looking for steam burns or redness or any other signs of a job done badly. There was no hint of anything untoward. On the contrary, Laura McKenna looked totally refreshed.

'Natalie,' Laura continued. 'You've really cheered me up.

While I wouldn't say I'm exactly looking forward to seeing that swine in the courtroom tomorrow morning, I am starting to feel a lot more optimistic about the rest of my life. You were right. After tomorrow's meeting is over, I can put my "starter marriage" behind me and look forward to *really* living again.'

Natalie touched her arm. 'Just remember you're a wonderful woman. You deserve to be very happy,' she said. 'And I'm sure you'll get to keep the house,' she added. Laura McKenna beamed.

Emily listened in astonishment. She handed over the credit-card machine so that Laura could input her PIN.

'Oh, while I'm here,' said Laura, 'I should make another appointment. What days do you work, Natalie?'

Emily flicked through the book and pencilled in a facial and bikini wax three weeks hence. With Chloe. She'd explain about Natalie next time Laura McKenna came in. Now it was time to deal with the ridiculously pushy girl . . .

But Natalie was already welcoming the next of Chloe's clients into the waiting area.

'Miss Willbourn? Bikini and half leg wax, isn't it?'

Miss Willbourn followed Natalie into the treatment room. As Natalie passed Emily she mouthed, 'I've got my certificates.' Emily could only gape after her in shock.

The rest of the afternoon continued in much the same vein. The salon was fully booked and the timings of the various appointments meant that Emily and Natalie merely passed in the lobby every hour or so. There was never a moment to say, 'What the hell do you think you're playing at?'

On one of her visits to the till, to settle up an account, Emily noticed that Natalie had carefully arranged her certificates along the reception desk. She did indeed have all the qualifications that she had laid claim to in her CV. That assuaged Emily's nerves a little, as did the fact that each client who followed Natalie into Chloe's treatment room came out again looking pleased.

'I have never had such a good facial.'

'Your massage technique is superb. I felt so relaxed, I could have fallen asleep.'

'When can I book in to see Natalie next?' was always their final question.

When her last client asked for another appointment, Natalie raised her eyebrows at Emily as if to say, 'See? They want me here, even if you don't.'

And then the day was over. Emily and Natalie were alone at last.

'Do you want to give me that interview?' Natalie asked. 'It's six o'clock now. We've got an appointment.'

Emily shook her head.

'I don't think that's necessary, do you?'

'You mean, I'm still not the kind of therapist you're advertising for.'

'No,' said Emily, defeated. 'You're exactly the kind of therapist I've been advertising for. You just don't look like I imagined she would.'

Natalie smiled. 'When can I start?'

Chloe had called in confirming that she was still feeling awful and asking Emily to cancel her appointments for the following day. Unless . . .

'Could you do Chloe's appointments tomorrow?' Emily asked.

'You bet!' said Natalie.

14

Less than a day later, practically all Emily's reservations about Natalie Hill were gone. Instead she was starting to view the peculiar little Welsh girl as an angel sent from the Valleys to save The Beauty Spot from disaster. Chloe had been to see her GP and was diagnosed with a particularly nasty and *very* contagious stomach bug. Given the nature of her job and the fact that it involved touching people's faces, her doctor said that it would probably be for the best if she took the rest of the week off. The last thing he wanted was to have to deal with another twenty vomiting women who could all be traced back to the same beauty therapist.

So, Natalie took on all Chloe's clients for the following three days and, like the women she had treated on the first day, they all seemed very pleased with the service she provided. On Natalie's second day at the salon, Emily had taken the precaution of calling a few of the clients she knew well and asking them what they *really* thought of the new girl, but the good news was that they were as positive on the telephone as they had been in front of her.

'Oh, she's fantastic,' they gushed.

Emily sighed with relief.

There was just one small moment of discord in the first week. Matt Charlton arrived for his back wax in preparation for his holiday in Mykonos. As usual, he was accompanied by Cesar. Natalie, rather than Emily, was manning reception at the moment he arrived.

'Get it out of here!' she shouted. 'Get it out! Get it out!'

Natalie climbed up onto her chair.

Matt looked about him in confusion for a moment before he realized that Natalie must be shouting about Cesar.

'Oh, this is Cesar.'

Matt pointed at his dog. Cesar gave a little wag of greeting.

'I don't care what that ratty-looking thing is called, get it out of here. You're not allowed to bring dogs into a beauty salon. They're unhygienic. What are you? Some kind of idiot?'

Matt frowned in confusion.

'But I always bring him in. Emily is fine with it. He's a working dog.'

'Well, you're not blind and you haven't got any sheep. What kind of work does he do? Accounting?'

Matt smiled awkwardly. He didn't really want to have to go through it in front of the yummy mummy who was pretending to flick through *Hello!*, while quite obviously listening to the drama unfold.

'Look, get Emily,' said Matt. 'She'll tell you.'

Natalie remained on the chair while Emily explained the situation in a whisper.

'You mean he's an eppy?' Natalie replied. Not in a whisper. Emily grimaced.

'That's not the correct term for it,' said Matt. 'In fact, that's not the correct term for anything.'

Natalie gave him a look that said, 'Whatever.' Out loud she said, 'Sorry.'

'You'll get used to Cesar,' Emily assured her. 'He's soft as anything. There are dog-chews in the drawer beneath the till. Give him one now. He'll be your friend for life.'

'I'm not putting my hand anywhere near that thing's dribbly mouth,' said Natalie. 'Just keep it away from me.'

She glared at the dog. Cesar glared back and adjusted his posture as though he were preparing for a standoff.

'Come through, Matt. Cesar,' said Emily, before someone got bitten.

Matt seemed somewhat subdued while Emily gave him his back wax. He didn't even shriek as loudly as usual.

'Looking forward to your holiday?' she asked.

'Sort of,' said Matt. 'Gets a bit dull always having to go places by yourself.'

'But then you can please yourself,' said Emily. 'Don't have to go traipsing round any Roman ruins unless you feel like it.'

'I suppose,' said Matt.

'Besides, I don't suppose you'll be on your own for very long. A good-looking guy like you. You'll find some nice boy to hang out with the minute you walk out of the airport.'

'A nice boy?' said Matt. His voice was muffled as he bit the towel while Emily did her worst to his back hair.

'Cesar will help you make friends,' she continued.

'Didn't help me make any friends today.'

'Oh, don't worry about it. She will get used to him,' Emily predicted. 'I always forget that there are people who don't like dogs. I grew up around them. I guess Natalie didn't.'

'So she's the new therapist?'

'Yes. She's very good at what she does. Everyone has been pleased.'

'That's great,' said Matt. 'It's important that you've got someone good on the team.'

Back in the lobby, Natalie pointedly pressed herself back against the wall as Matt and Cesar walked by.

'Have a great holiday, won't you?' said Emily as she sent them off. 'Send me a postcard of all those lovely boys.'

Matt nodded. Though the trip to Mykonos wasn't exactly shaping up to be the holiday of his dreams. What on earth had possessed him to book his trip through a singles specialist?

The last three trips he'd taken had been exactly the same. All the other clientele were sixty-something widows spending the money left behind by the husbands they had lost. He wanted to tell Emily about it. Perhaps make her laugh with how dreadful it would be, but he decided against it. Natalie was looking at Cesar as though he might fly at her throat and rip out her windpipe if she took her eyes off him for a second. He stepped towards the door.

As though she were satisfied that Cesar was on his way out, Natalie nodded to herself and disappeared again, leaving only Emily, smiling from behind the till. Matt hesitated with his hand on the door handle.

'Did you forget something?' Emily asked.

'Actually,' said Matt. 'I wanted to ask you what you're doing on the eighteenth, only I've got a spare ticket to a Barbra Streisand concert. I remember you once said you liked her.'

'Oh,' said Emily. 'I'm busy that Friday. It's my nan's birthday.'

Matt nodded. 'That's a shame.'

'Barbra Streisand concert,' said Natalie when he was out of earshot. 'Could he be any more gay?'

15

Much to Trudy's disappointment, the production team at *Wakey-Wakey* offered Carina Lees the makeover slot. Carina's appointment as the show's new fashion maven was announced on the programme and viewers were invited to send in home videos, Trinny and Susannah style, so that Carina could personally pick out the viewer she considered most in need of her particular brand of makeover magic and a clothing budget of five hundred pounds!

'Five hundred pounds?' said Carina with disdain. 'I can't even find a decent pair of shoes for that.'

Alice, junior staff-writer at *Get This!* magazine, had never owned a pair of shoes that cost more than fifty pounds. The most expensive pair in her wardrobe was from the sale at LK Bennett. They were pale pink suede. Her younger sister had bought them to go with the bridesmaid's dress she made Alice wear at her wedding.

'You can use them again afterwards,' Angela had told her.

Fat chance. Alice had little need for a pair of pink suede kitten heels. They just didn't fit into a life involving the tube and buses and walking for miles when the tube and buses let her down.

'What else did I do this week?' Carina murmured down the phone during their weekly catch-up call. 'Oh, yes. I bought three new pairs of "limo" shoes in Gina on New Bond Street. The silver ones were in the sale at—'

She quoted a figure that was much higher than the fee Alice

would get for writing about Carina's adventures in retail heaven.

'And then I spent the afternoon looking at videos for the *Wakey-Wakey* makeover show. I thought I was going to die laughing . . . Oh, hang on. You probably shouldn't write that down.'

The producers of *Wakey-Wakey* didn't expect Carina to watch *all* the video footage of makeover hopefuls. It would have taken years. Hundreds of tapes had been sent in. Thousands. Two days after the call for submissions went out, the post room at Channel 11 looked as though no one had been working there for six months. There were packages everywhere. They were soon spilling out into the corridor. The mail-room staff were not happy about it at all.

Jenny the producer instigated a very simple policy to cut through the crap. The packages were sorted into two piles. One pile would be viewed. The other pile would be thrown away unopened. (Which would lead to a big scandal about six months later when someone working on a landfill site discovered all the unopened packages while sifting through the rubbish with his digger and put paid to *Wakey-Wakey*'s carefully cultivated image as a show that really cared about its viewers.)

There were still more than a thousand videos left to watch. Jenny had two of her most junior staff go through them. They were given a strict brief as to what they were looking for. For this first show, the makeover victims had to be under thirty years old and over thirteen stone in weight. Preferably, at some point in their footage they should be seen wearing an enormous football shirt and thick-rimmed glasses for a night on the town or to attend a family wedding. They should also be seen standing in a bikini or their underwear, thus indicating that they would be willing to bare all on national television. There simply had to be an underwear shot. Trinny and Susannah had set a very high bar with their embarrassing jug-jiggling.

The two production assistants sat down in front of those packages like the wannabe princess who claimed she could spin straw into gold sitting down at her spinning wheel in the hay-loft before Rumpelstiltskin arrived.

'This is going to take us weeks!' Christian, who had joined Channel 11 straight from three years at Cambridge, protested. Christian further moaned that he had signed up to be a serious journalist, not to spend all day looking at 'fat birds in bikinis'.

'That's what he does in his spare time,' scoffed Maddy, the other assistant, fresh from Oxford, who fancied herself as a future Kirsty Wark.

Jenny told them both to zip it and get to work. Quite why she had employed either of the jumped-up little twerps escaped her at moments like this one. And even though she had specifically asked them to seek out the two worst 'train wrecks' from the thousands of hapless women who had applied, Jenny hated Maddy and Christian even more when she heard the gales of laughter that came from the viewing room later on.

'Oh my god!' said Christian, as he watched footage of one particularly unfortunate woman stumbling across a beach. '*Thar she blows!*'

People could be so cruel, thought Jenny. Sometimes adult life was no better than life in a school playground.

16

A fortnight into Natalie's tenure at The Beauty Spot, Emily was still glad that Natalie had forced her into giving her the job. The spare treatment room had become Natalie's room. The tattered certificates that had been so important to Natalie that first day had been neatly framed (by Emily) and hung in her room above the basin and the hot wax machine. She had her own overalls now, with 'Natalie' embroidered on the breast pocket in bright fuchsia pink thread.

Chloe was fully recovered from her bout of gastric flu but she was very grateful to have Natalie there so that she could work just one less hour per day. So was Emily. It meant that Emily and Chloe could both take a proper lunch break again. Which meant that they could catch up on all those pesky little chores that keep life running smoothly, like going to the bank, or post office, buying food or getting a haircut.

Even better, Chloe and Natalie seemed to get on like the proverbial house on fire. The staff kitchen was always full of laughter. Emily's concern that adding a third therapist to the team might unbalance her little 'family' was assuaged.

There was just one problem . . .

It was the same problem that had jumped out at Emily the very first time she laid eyes on Natalie Hill. The girl just didn't look the part. Even when she was wearing her nice new overall, Natalie didn't have quite the polish that Emily had hoped for. She took out her nose-ring during working hours (way too unhygienic), but she still accessorized her uniform with those horrible black boots. And by the time she'd finished her second appointment of the day, Natalie would usually be covered in smears of face mask or hair-removal wax, like a kid who'd been left unsupervised with a box of chubby crayons. Her fingernails were badly bitten, to the extent that her cuticles were ragged and often bleeding. She wore no make-up, even on those days when her zits punctuated the skin of her cheeks like those ritual scars Emily had seen on the cheeks of the women in a National Geographic show about the Afar tribe of Ethiopia.

And as for her hair . . .

Some days Natalie made Amy Winehouse look like Grace Kelly.

Emily held her breath in horror as she watched Natalie standing at the till one afternoon. While Natalie waited for a printout of a credit-card receipt for one of her customers, she was unconsciously scratching at her head with a pen. Really going for it. It was as though there was something living inside her bird's-nest hairdo.

Nits?

No, they liked clean hair and Natalie's hair was rarely clean.

Fleas?

Emily was reminded of an illustration in a children's history book about the things that lived in Elizabethan wigs. It showed a fashionable sixteenth-century lady with blood from a cockroach bite trickling down the back of her neck. Emily couldn't help looking at Natalie. And neither could the customer. Emily noted the expression of horror creeping across the customer's face.

At last the till finished printing.

'Here's your receipt,' said Natalie brightly. She handed over the pen she had been using as an itching aid. 'If you could just sign it in the usual way. I quite often find that cards from your bank don't work in the PIN machine.'

The customer nodded vaguely and took the pen as though she were being offered a chewed-up chicken bone. She added her signature to the receipt in double-quick time and took off without making a return appointment.

Natalie seemed oblivious to what Emily thought was obvious. She had frightened her client away.

Who knew how many of Natalie's clients had been frightened off by her appearance. Something would have to be said. But where to begin? Emily knew she should have said something there and then – while the incident was fresh in everybody's memory – but, before she could get the words out, Natalie's next customer had arrived. Later, Emily cornered Chloe in the staff kitchen and asked her whether she had any ideas about broaching the subject of Natalie's untidiness and possible lack of hygiene.

'Keep me out of it!' said Chloe, remembering the time she got into a fight for leaving a copy of *Sugar* magazine open to a page discussing a problem about BO on a classmate's desk. Just thinking about that fight made Chloe sweat. The thumping. The scratching. The hair-pulling.

It was a tricky issue indeed. There was little chance that Natalie would welcome Emily's observations on her appearance. How many people *did* appreciate being told they looked a mess? Even if, deep down, they already knew . . .

It would have to be done softly and when there was plenty of time for Emily to introduce the subject with tact and deal with any unpleasant reaction with care.

An opportunity seemed to present itself a week later when Natalie and Emily took their lunch breaks at the same time. It was raining outside, so neither girl was inclined to head off down the high street. Instead, they unpacked their lunches at the table in the staff room and shared a pot of tea. Emily had made herself a couple of delicate little Swedish rye rolls filled with cottage cheese and cucumber. Natalie's sandwiches were like doorsteps of white bread filled with chunks of cheddar. As she ate, a blob of Branston pickle fell onto the crisp, clean tablecloth.

'So,' said Natalie with her mouth full. 'I decided that if I was ever going to get ahead in life, I would have to leave the village . . .'

'Do you miss it?' asked Emily.

'A bit,' said Natalie. She swallowed and wiped her mouth with the back of her hand. 'It's different here. People aren't so friendly in general, though the ladies who come in here seem to be alright.'

'This is a nice area,' said Emily.

'Lots of money,' Natalie observed. 'And free time. Where I come from, most girls our age don't have a lot of either.'

Emily nodded.

'I thought about home the other night when I was watching the rugby highlights, though,' said Natalie. 'They were singing the Welsh anthem. It made my heart swell up. I thought I was going to cry.'

Right then, Natalie looked as though she might be about to cry again. Her eyes glittered.

'Do you know it?'

'Know what?'

'Our national anthem?'

Suddenly, Natalie stood up and placed her hand over her chest. While Emily watched open-mouthed, she launched into a rendition of 'Land of My Fathers'. In Welsh.

It was astonishing. Natalie's voice rang out clear and strong as though she were singing to an entire rugby stadium rather than her boss in a staff kitchen the size of a cupboard. As she sang, she straightened up. She looked proud. She looked strong. It was impossible to concentrate on how untidy her hair looked.

When Natalie finished, Emily broke into applause.

'That was incredible,' she said.

'What radio station are you tuned into?' asked Chloe, poking her head around the door. 'Are you listening to opera?'

Chloe too was slack-jawed with awe when she heard that the singer was Natalie.

'You could have been a professional,' said Emily.

Natalie blushed. 'Do you really think so?'

'Amazing,' Emily confirmed.

'Yeah,' Chloe agreed with her. 'Maybe you should learn a few more modern songs though. Your client's arrived,' she said to Emily.

And so another lunch break was over and still Emily hadn't mentioned the hair. Natalie remained in the staff room for a little longer, practising her scales.

17

Carina's first victim for the 'Makeover Magic' segment had been chosen. Her name was Sarah Lloyd and she was a site manager from Newcastle. A building-site manager, that is. Her 'audition' video hit all the right notes. First there was the opening 'to camera' section in which she explained why she needed Carina's help. For her televisual debut she wore a Newcastle United football shirt that did little for her enormous breasts and left the question as to whether or not she had a waist completely unanswered. Later she posed in her bikini, which looked more like a couple of old garden hammocks than a swimming costume. She hated holidaying on the beach, she explained. Walking in the Lake District provided fewer opportunities for embarrassment.

'But my best friend is getting married,' she explained. 'And she's having her hen weekend in Ibiza. I can't wear my waterproofs for that.'

Sarah Lloyd would not be getting married any time soon. She had no boyfriend. In fact, she'd never had one. Never even been kissed, she added. A shopkeeper had recently addressed her as 'Mr'. Her acne would have inspired topographers. But still she seemed relatively light-hearted as she outlined her plight. She was looking for a bit of help, she concluded, not salvation.

'What she needs is an effing miracle,' said Christian.

On a chilly Friday morning, a week after she was notified that she was the 'lucky winner', Sarah arrived in the studio. She was bundled up in a duffle coat that added fifteen pounds to her weight both literally and visually. On her head she wore a black-and-white bobble hat. On her feet a pair of enormous black trainers. She might have been male or female. Even when she took her coat off, you couldn't quite be sure. Beneath the coat was that beloved Newcastle United top.

'My lucky top,' she explained. 'I was wearing it when I won a hundred quid on the lottery.'

She stuck out her hand towards Carina, who merely looked at it as though surprised that Sarah would even think about touching her.

'Acrylics,' said Carina, fluttering her long fingernails by way of excuse. 'They break really easily.'

Sarah shrugged. 'I don't know how you cope with those things,' she said. 'You're not going to make me have them, are you? I couldn't stand it, not being able to do all the things I wanted to do. Including pick your nose.'

Everyone laughed except Carina.

'I don't think they'd be right on your short fingers,' she said. 'Probably make them look worse.'

Now Sarah wasn't laughing either.

'OK,' said Jenny to break the awkward silence. 'Sarah, I need you to come with me. We're going to do a few "before" shots. They're not going to be very flattering, I'm afraid.'

Sarah was ushered into the studio and positioned in front of a plain white background. The studio lights glared down on her in her Newcastle United shirt, highlighting all the reasons she wanted to be made over, accentuating the greasy sheen on her cheeks and hair.

Carina watched from behind the camera with Christian and Maddy.

'This girl really needs some help,' said Maddy.

'How could she walk around like that, day after day?' asked Christian. 'How could she support Newcastle United, more to the point?'

'Why has it taken her so long to reach out for assistance?' Maddy continued. 'And why has she chosen to reach out on national television, for heaven's sake? Some people have no pride. You've got to feel sorry for her. Can you imagine getting to your twenties without ever having had a kiss, let alone a shag?'

Maddy looked to Carina for corroboration.

Carina shrugged.

Carina's chilly demeanour soon warmed up in front of the camera. When it was time to film the segment in which Carina and Sarah met for the 'first' time, she greeted Sarah like a long-lost friend and talked sympathetically about the difficulty of finding a man.

'You don't know about that!' Sarah exclaimed before following her pronouncement with a honky laugh. 'What with all the lovely men you're seen with.'

Carina thought of Danny Rhodes. Currently in Brazil 'filming a music video'. Or Monkey. Still making like a cactus in The Bakery.

'Well,' said Carina, 'by the time we've finished with you today, you'll be ready to hit the town and pick up your very own hot guy. Now, let's have a look at what needs to be done.'

The show's resident hair and make-up specialist, celebrity salon owner Jamie Wood, stepped in to give his verdict. He pulled at a strand of Sarah's frizzy hair and made a cat's bottom of his mouth. He said he wasn't in the least bit surprised when Sarah admitted that she usually cut her hair herself.

'Do you pluck your own eyebrows too?'

'I don't pluck my eyebrows,' said Sarah.

'Exactly,' said Jamie. 'That was a trick question. I'm going to take this girl backstage and see what kind of miracle I can work in an hour.'

'Well,' Carina concluded. 'I think we can turn you into the sort of woman who can't walk past a building site without bringing work to a complete and total halt.'

'When everyone stops to sing "Who let the dogs out",' muttered Christian from the safety of the producer's office.

'You want to make sure Sarah doesn't hear you. She could easily have you in an arm-wrestling contest,' said Maddy.

And so Sarah Lloyd was ushered away while Trudy and Patrick talked to a former Hollywood wild child who had just released her second biography. She was twenty-four.

'Aren't you coming too?' Sarah asked Carina as they walked down the corridor towards the make-up room. Carina stopped short at a room marked 'private'.

'Oh no,' she said. 'I have to call my agent.'

Sarah nodded with suitable awe.

18

The morning of Carina's debut makeover segment was the first time Emily had watched the *Wakey-Wakey* show in a long time. Ordinarily she would have been at the salon long before the serious business of the morning's news headlines was replaced with sycophantic celebrity interviews, diet tips and phone-ins about the paparazzi or paedophilia. That morning, however, Emily had the luxury of eating her breakfast in front of the telly rather than in front of her appointments book. Since Natalie had joined the salon, the girls were able to take it in turns to have the odd morning off during the week.

Emily was delighted when *Wakey-Wakey*'s Trudy announced that Carina Lees would be joining them after the break. Emily had been singing Carina's praises to anyone who would listen since her second visit to the salon.

'She's so natural,' Emily would say. 'She really seemed interested in how I set my business up. She asked me all sorts of questions.'

And here she was on Emily's television screen, demonstrating just how caring and 'real' she was in an interview with a *Wakey-Wakey* viewer who wanted to become more feminine and perhaps even get a few wolf-whistles from the builders she worked with.

Emily was rapt. Carina tipped her head to one side as she listened to the viewer's woes, just as she had tipped her head to one side while Emily explained how tough it was to run a business all by herself. Seeing Carina taking such an interest in poor, frumpy Sarah, Emily felt the same warm glow she'd felt as she glued on Carina's acrylics and she realized she was in the presence of a really lovely person. It was that which made her feel truly honoured by Carina's patronage, Emily told herself. Nothing to do with anything so shallow as celebrity.

An hour later – during which Emily did a spot of ironing and hand-washed some bras – Sarah Lloyd was back on screen. Hearing Carina's voice, Emily took off her rubber gloves and resumed her position in front of the TV.

In the time-honoured tradition of makeover shows, Carina explained that Sarah had been kept away from mirrors during the transformation and would only discover now, in front of the studio audience, just how well things had turned out.

'Are you ready for this?' Carina asked.

Emily was impressed by the way Carina laid her hand on Sarah's arm to help calm the poor girl down. She was so good at putting people at ease.

'I think so,' said Sarah. She was already dabbing at her eyes.

With a matador flourish (that she had been practising all week) Carina ripped the cover away from the full-length mirror. Sarah's hands flew to cover her mouth before she began to utter the time-honoured response to seeing one's made-over self for the first time: 'Ohmigod, ohmigod, ohmigod.'

Sitting on her sofa at home, Emily nodded in satisfaction. There was indeed reason to appeal to the Almighty.

'Are you pleased?' Carina asked.

Sarah was speechless. But she *was* pleased. Emily could see that. And so she should be. The Newcastle United top and jeans fit only for a builder had been replaced by a pretty pink empire-line dress that accentuated the positive – her breasts

– and skimmed tactfully over her bad bits. The trainers were gone, swapped for a pair of wedges.

'Wedges give you height and a good leg shape but they are easier to walk in than stilettoes,' Carina explained.

'Her feet are so huge I had to get those from a tranny shop in Soho,' said the stylist to Christian and Maddy offstage.

Sarah's previously frizzy brown hair had been washed, coloured with a vegetable tint and lacquered into submission. Now, instead of overwhelming her facial features, her new soft fringe drew attention to her 'beautiful eyes' (Jamie the hairdresser had explained that when there was nothing else to praise, you could almost always fall back on the prettiness of someone's eyes).

'How do you feel?' asked Carina. 'What do you like about this new look?'

'I can't believe I look so feminine,' Sarah managed eventually. 'I'm very pleased. And I'm impressed!' she added shyly.

In her sitting room in Essex, Emily was also very impressed. It was especially hard to believe that the *Wakey-Wakey* team hadn't given up on the hair. She made a note on the back of an envelope of the product Carina had used to tame Sarah's hair, and also scribbled down the name of the boutique that stocked the smock dress. She was sure it would be useful information.

Emily tried to deploy that useful information as soon as she arrived at The Beauty Spot.

'I saw a fantastic makeover on *Wakey-Wakey* this morning,' she told Natalie. 'They found this girl, who actually worked as the foreman – or should that be forewoman – on a building site and turned her into a real princess. You wouldn't have believed it was possible. She turned up at the studio wearing a Newcastle United shirt.'

Natalie pulled a face.

'Terrible, yeah?' Emily asked a leading question.

'Totally,' Natalie agreed right away. 'All that synthetic material. I prefer a rugby shirt, myself. Nice bit of cotton.'

'To snuggle up to, yes,' said Emily carefully. 'Nothing spoils a nice cuddle like getting an electric shock off your boyfriend's outfit. But she was actually wearing the football shirt herself. Can you believe it? She looked like a man.'

'Mmmhmmm,' said Natalie vaguely. She was concentrating on the appointments book.

'Anyway, an hour later she looked totally different. It was gob-smacking what a change you can make with that little time. They smoothed her hair down. She had really frizzy hair.'

Natalie's hand flew to her head as though responding to a subconscious signal, but she said nothing.

'I wrote down the name of the product,' said Emily, sliding the note into Natalie's view.

Natalie scratched her head. She didn't ask what the product was called. She didn't even look at the note Emily had made. Instead, she slid it back out of her view to better see that afternoon's schedule.

'Hmmm. I thought I had two facials and a brow wax this afternoon,' she muttered.

'And they used some really good make-up on her,' Emily continued regardless. 'Made her skin look completely immaculate. Put her in the right outfit – and bingo! She was like another woman. She'd never had a boyfriend, but after that makeover another viewer rang in and asked if she would marry him.'

'I hope she said no,' said Natalie. 'What kind of idiot rings up and says that?'

'I think she knew he wasn't serious,' said Emily. 'But she was very pleased. Not having had much male attention before. She said she'd never been kissed.'

Emily suddenly wondered whether Natalie had ever been kissed.

'Anyway, I think it just goes to show how much happier people are when they make the best of themselves.'

'You're right,' said Natalie, finally looking up from the appointments book. 'I absolutely agree. That's why I like my job. It makes me feel good to make other people feel good about themselves. I'm going to go and turn my wax kettle on.'

She left Emily alone with her helpful notes.

'You got a call this morning,' said Chloe as she bustled past with a pile of towels. 'Some girl from your old school. Said your mum gave her your number. Wants to know whether you're going to the reunion. I wrote her details down on the pad.'

Emily reached for the pad and stared at the name that was written there.

'Are you going?' Chloe asked.

'I don't really have time,' said Emily.

'When are they having it? It'll be in the evening, right? You should go.'

'I don't want to go,' said Emily. 'Who wants to see a bunch of people they haven't talked to in ten years anyway?'

'Don't you want to see how they've turned out?' Chloe persisted. 'I'd love to know what happened to some of the girls in my class. Could be a laugh.'

'No,' said Emily. 'It won't.'

19

A whole month into Natalie's time at The Beauty Spot, Emily still hadn't found the right moment to tell her that fingerless mesh gloves were not a suitable accessory for a beauty therapist. She decided she could wait no longer. At the end of Natalie's fourth Friday in the salon, Emily suggested that the two of them go for a drink. They went to the newly opened Cristal Bar. It wasn't as classy as the champagne it had been named after, but Emily hoped that the clientele would be well dressed enough to do some of her work for her. If Natalie felt a little uncomfortable there in her faded black jeans and baggy jumper, then perhaps Emily's hints might finally have a better chance of hitting home.

Emily remembered one of the books she had read about 'people management'. If you were going to say something difficult to one of your employees, then you needed a soft start-up. In this case, Emily praised Natalie's skills as a facialist to the heavens.

'Every one of your clients drifts out of your treatment room as though they are walking on clouds.'

Natalie seemed very pleased with that. She grinned broadly. Emily was reminded that she needed to pick up some more whitening toothpaste on her way home. And some floss.

'I really love making people look their best,' said Natalie. Then she started to dig around in her teeth with a cocktail stick. She'd been eating peanuts.

'It's important, isn't it?' Emily started again. 'To make the most of your assets.'

'Oh yeah.'

'For example, see that woman over there,' Emily indicated a girl at the bar who was wearing a dress so tight you could see what she'd had for breakfast. 'She probably thinks that squeezing into the smallest dress she can find shows off her figure best, whereas something a bit looser would actually make her look slimmer.'

'Absolutely,' Natalie agreed. 'You see them all the time, people who've practically shoe-horned themselves into a size too small because they think that it's the number on the label that counts. There's another one over there.' She nodded discreetly to a girl who had just teetered in on a pair of vertiginous shoes.

'You're right,' said Emily. 'And her hair doesn't suit her either. She's got a very delicate little face but it's swamped by those platinum hair extensions that just make her look trampy. As do those badly done acrylics.'

'Oh, yeah!' Natalie agreed emphatically. 'Don't get me started on bad acrylics. And novelty painted toenails! I mean, in my opinion, if your toenails are long enough to fit a picture of the Mona Lisa with two diamante studs for earrings, then they're too long, right?'

'Right,' said Emily, chancing what she hoped was a 'meaningful' look at Natalie's own toenails. They weren't overly long, but the red varnish that coated them was horribly chipped and long overdue a touch-up. Her fingernails, meanwhile, were so badly bitten that Emily winced at the thought of how painful they must be. Natalie didn't notice. She was on a roll.

'Some of the girls in here would go up like a Roman candle if you held a match to them. There's just so much fakery around. Fake hair, fake nails, fake eyelashes. And all the fake designer gear of course. They just look like they are trying sooooo hard.'

'There's nothing quite so tragic as grooming overkill,'

Emily concluded. 'But then there are the people who don't try quite hard enough, right? I know that you should never judge people by appearances, and we shouldn't have to resort to artifice to feel ready to face the world . . .'

Natalie nodded again. There was no sign that she had spotted where the conversation was going.

'But if you've got a lovely figure, like you have, you shouldn't go hiding it away under baggy jumpers, should you?'

'Of course not,' said Natalie.

'And if you've got a nice face, then why hide it from the world with a terrible haircut?'

'You're spot on.'

'And if your hands are a lovely shape then perhaps your nails could match them . . . What was it Coco Chanel said?'

Natalie shrugged.

'I think she said, "I don't understand how a woman can leave the house without fixing herself up a little – if only out of politeness. And then, you never know, maybe that's the day she has a date with destiny. And it's best to be as pretty as possible for destiny." That's a good quote, don't you think?'

Natalie looked at her watch.

'It's nine o'clock. I've got to go, Em. I promised my flat-mate we'd watch *Prison Break*.'

'So, you laid it on the line?' texted Chloe later that night.

'I tried,' Emily texted back. 'If I drop any bigger hints, they'll squash her flat.'

The next day, Natalie turned up for work looking even worse than usual.

'Boiler broke. No hot water,' she explained before disappearing into her treatment room.

Emily really thought she might be about to say something when the telephone rang. She picked it up.

95

'Emily,' said the voice on the line, 'this is Carina.'

'Uh,' was Emily's first, deeply uncool response.

'I want to come in and have that facial you were talking about. The aromatherapy one? Can I come in later today? About five o'clock?'

Emily looked at the appointments book. At five o'clock she was due to see a new client. An unknown quantity. Possibly the kind of person who didn't tip and wouldn't become a regular, Emily decided as she crossed the new client's name out and wrote Carina in.

'We've just had a cancellation,' she lied.

20

Carina arrived at the salon in a relatively low-key way this time. That is to say, she was not in a limo. Rather she was in a top-of-the-range Range Rover of the kind that another star had recently been caught driving without road tax or insurance. It was, Emily knew from the press coverage of that incident, a car worth in the region of sixty thousand pounds. She thought about her own Fiat Panda, rusting outside her flat.

Mindful of Carina's last visit, Emily whisked her straight through to the treatment room to avoid any embarrassing scenes with the other customers. Carina was out of their sight before they had any chance to turn their mobile phones to camera mode.

'Thanks for fitting me in at such short notice.'

'I'm glad we had a cancellation,' said Emily.

She felt a little pang of guilt as she remembered the client she had cancelled. 'But I work long hours,' the would-be client had said. 'I can't come in any other time. And I'd been looking forward to it so much . . . Especially since my mother just died.'

Emily shook her head as if to shake the guilt off.

'This is a really relaxing treatment,' she began her spiel.

'Good,' said Carina. 'I need to relax.'

When Carina was settled on the couch, Emily dimmed the lights. She turned on the ambient music (that combination of whale song and pan pipes unique to beauty salons, which is actually more about hiding noise from other treatment rooms than creating an ambience). She scraped Carina's hair back from her face in a clean, towelling hairband and set to work. She whisked off Carina's make-up with a few strokes of cotton wool and cleanser. She warmed the organic aroma-therapeutic (sic) exfoliant in her hands.

'This contains rose,' she said, 'which has been used as an exfoliant since the Middle Ages. If not before.'

Emily had no idea whether that was true, but it was what it said on the product's recycled paper packaging.

'Cleopatra might have used it,' she added.

'Oh,' Carina approved of that, given that she had been an Ancient Egyptian in a past life. 'I think the smell might even be taking me back,' she said.

When she'd finished exfoliating, Emily set about giving Carina a facial massage, but not before she had chinked together the Tibetan bells, which came free with The Beauty Spot's order from the organic cosmetics rep, to 'bless' the 'Mesopotamian' aloe juice she would be using as a lubricant.

'That feels great,' said Carina.

'It's to remove puffiness,' said Emily.

Carina frowned.

'Not that you ever have any puffiness,' Emily added quickly.

'Thanks.'

The whales continued their songs of love.

'I saw you on television the other morning,' Emily said eventually. 'Doing that makeover on *Wakey-Wakey*.'

'Oh yeah? What did you think?' Carina asked.

'I thought it was amazing. Can't have been the easiest of transformations. I mean, a football shirt. What was she thinking?'

Carina smiled faintly.

'And her hair. There are so many good products around, it always amazes me that people still let their hair look like that.'

'That's exactly what Jamie the hairdresser said.'

'And those trainers . . . No wonder she'd never had a boyfriend. She just wasn't helping herself.'

Emily soon found that she was telling Carina all about Natalie. There was something about the reality star that made it seem safe to confide. Perhaps it was because she had been so sweet in the *Living Hell* house. She had never been nominated for eviction. She had been the one who took care of Monkey while he was locked into one of his endless poses.

'Sounds like she needs a makeover,' said Carina when Emily finished.

'That's exactly what I've been thinking. Perhaps I should send a tape of her into your show.'

Carina gave a small, polite laugh. 'We get thousands of tapes.'

'Of course you do,' said Emily, disappointed. 'What else have you got lined up?' she asked. 'I mean, are you going to do more television presenting? You're a natural.'

'Thank you.'

'I probably shouldn't ask, should I? You'll have signed those contracts saying you can't talk about the projects you're involved with.'

'Some of them, yes,' said Carina.

'I'm sorry. Pretend I didn't say anything.'

'No need. Those contracts are standard practice. I think it's mostly to make sure I don't go and blab to other television production companies. But you're not in the business. You're pretty unlikely to have a meeting at Channel Five next week and steal any of my ideas.'

Emily felt comforted and slighted all at once. On the one hand, Carina was absolutely right. On the other hand, Emily suddenly felt out of the club somehow.

'Well, you're not, are you?' said Carina, as though she sensed the hurt in Emily's silence.

'No. Though we do have other television people come in here from time to time.'

That wasn't exactly a lie. Four weeks earlier, a girl who operated a camera at QVC had come in for her first-ever facial. She was getting married the following week. She had blackheads on her blackheads.

'But I do value client confidentiality.'

'OK,' said Carina, 'I'll tell you a bit about what's going on. Promise me it will go no further.'

'Of course,' said Emily breathlessly. Was she about to get an exclusive?

Carina freed her arms from beneath the blankets so that she could count her future work appointments off on her fingers.

'Next week I'm going to do some more ads for that cleaning spray,' she began.

'Whoosh Multi-Surface Cleaner? Whoosh through all your chores?' said Emily, quoting the advert.

'That's the one. Then I'll be doing more makeovers on *Wakey-Wakey*, of course. That segment was really popular. They had loads of emails and texts asking when I was going to be doing the next one.'

'I thought it was brilliant.'

'Well, I'm going to be doing an hour-long makeover special next month. And I'm also working on a new game show called *Confessions*. Now that could be a very big hit.'

'*Confessions*? How does that work?'

'Oh, you'll like this,' said Carina. 'What we're going to do is ask people to write in and tell us about the most evil thing they've ever done. You know, perhaps they killed their sister's hamster and pretended the cat did it, or scratched their brother's car or stole their best friend's boyfriend . . . We'll choose the most evil of the lot – having turned over any murderers to the police, of course – and get them to come into the studio, along with the person they wronged. The person they wronged can then either choose to forgive them or not. If they choose to forgive the confessor then they join forces to compete for a cash prize. If they choose not to forgive, then the confessor and the victim go head to head for the prize instead. It's going to be big money. And the victim gets the opportunity to subject the confessor to all sorts of humiliation too.'

'You could end up with some really nasty situations.'

'Oh no. They've had lawyers check it out. None of the torture actually causes permanent damage. It's just head-shaving, sludge-pouring. That sort of thing.' Carina opened one eye and looked up at Emily.

'Talking of sludge . . .' Changing the subject, Emily took a cosmetic brush and used it to apply a face mask to Carina's skin. 'Mud sourced from the banks of the Danube,' she explained. And chinked her bells for ambience. Then she left her celebrity client alone with the whale music for a few moments while the mask worked its magic.

When Emily came back into the room and started to take the mask off, Carina asked her: 'What about you, Emily? Can we get you on the programme? *Confessions*? Got anything to be ashamed of? What's the most terrible thing you've ever done? You can tell me. What about at school?'

'I was just thinking about that,' Emily admitted. 'And I don't think I have done anything I need to be ashamed of. I've always tried to be good to other people. I'd never commit vandalism. I wouldn't hurt an animal. I would certainly never steal another girl's man.'

'Really? Are you sure about that?'

'Of course I'm sure. That's so unsisterly.'

'Well, good for you. You wouldn't steal another girl's man. But what about anything else? You must have been mean to at least one person in your lifetime. No one goes through life completely blameless. I once stole a Mars Bar from the corner shop,' Carina offered in a bald attempt to encourage Emily to share. 'I was just a kid. About fourteen. But kids can be wicked, can't they? Some say they don't know better, but I definitely did. I was wetting myself walking out of that shop. If I'd got caught, my mum would have killed me. Come on, Emily, you must have done something while you were at school? Everybody did. You mean you never said something bad behind someone's back? You never even borrowed someone's pencil sharpener without asking?'

Emily was silent for a moment then she answered, quite emphatically, 'No. I really didn't. I did my best to get along with everyone.'

'Well,' said Carina. 'I seem to have found the world's nicest girl. You'll go straight to heaven.'

Emily blushed. She was grateful that Carina had her eyes shut.

'Am I nearly done?' Carina asked.

'Just stay put while I apply some moisturizer,' said Emily. Moisturizer on, Carina sat up.

'You know, I had a thought while I was lying there with my face mask on,' she announced. 'It's about that girl who works here. The one who looks a mess.'

'Natalie?'

'Yeah. If you really think she's in need of a makeover, then perhaps I can help you out. It's a brilliant concept for *Wakey-Wakey*: a beauty therapist who spends all day making other women look better but who doesn't have time to fix herself. I'm ninety-nine per cent sure that the producer will go for it. I'll call her when I get out of here and let you know what she says.'

'You'd ask if Natalie can have a makeover on TV?'

Carina nodded. 'Consider it payback for having saved my life on the night of the *Get This!* awards.'

'And if she says "yes", how should I tell her? You were saying that all the people who've applied so far volunteered themselves. Like I was saying, I don't think Natalie thinks there's anything wrong with dressing the way she does. What if she freaks out?'

'You don't have to tell her anything. We'll surprise her. Just say that I've given you some tickets to be in the *Wakey-Wakey* studio audience. You turn up and I'll make it look as though I've just picked her out of the crowd. That way I'll take all the flak. If there is any. Usually, there isn't. Once they hear that there's a five-hundred-pound budget for clothes, most people are willing to put up with a little bit of embarrassment to get their hands on it.'

'She gets to keep the clothes?'

'Of course.'

Emily felt a little more at ease. Five hundred pounds was probably more than Natalie had spent on clothes in her lifetime.

'If it worked, that would solve all my problems. You'd really do that for me?'

'It would be my pleasure,' Carina assured her as she slipped her two-thousand-pound Chanel watch back over her wrist. 'Emily, I feel like you and I could be friends.'

Emily's mouth dropped open. If only a crowd of her clients could have been there to hear the reality star make that pronouncement. Carina Lees wanted to be her friend. Emily's mind fast-forwarded to a day when she would sit in the passenger seat of that Range Rover on a shopping trip to London's best boutiques. It was going to be so amazing.

'Now, how much do I owe you for that fabulous facial?' Carina asked.

'Oh, nothing,' said Emily. 'Nothing at all.'

'Great,' said Carina. 'I'll let you know about those studio audience tickets.' She tapped the side of her nose.

* * *

Carina was as good as her word. She didn't waste a moment. She called Jenny, the producer at *Wakey-Wakey*, as she drove home from the salon, narrowly avoiding an accident as she did so. 'I really must remember to get a hands-free set,' Carina muttered to herself as a Ford Fiesta swerved to avoid her meandering Range Rover and mounted the pavement in the process.

Jenny seemed enthusiastic. She agreed that it was a great angle: a beautician who couldn't get her own look right. Exactly the kind of easy irony the *Wakey-Wakey* audience loved.

Carina called Emily next.

'Jenny thinks it's a wonderful idea,' she said, as a pensioner on a pelican crossing jumped backwards to get out of her way and broke a hip. 'So we'll be sending you three tickets for November the sixteenth. How about that?'

How about that? It would mean that Emily would have to close The Beauty Spot for the whole morning, but it seemed worth it. Carina would almost certainly mention the salon on air again. Emily decided to think of the loss of business as an advertising cost.

'Great,' said Carina. 'Then it's all sorted.'

She waved at a middle-aged man standing on a pedestrian island.

'Fans,' she muttered. 'They're practically throwing themselves under my car these days.'

Carina didn't register the fact that the man had not been waving in ecstasy at seeing a celeb, but shaking his fist at the sight of a Range Rover doing forty-five in a twenty zone.

Emily came off her call to Carina feeling like a kid on Christmas Eve. It wasn't just the thought of having Natalie spruced up that made her feel excited. It was the fact that Carina had made it happen, and so quickly. She had said in the treatment room that she thought they could be friends and now she was proving it by pulling strings to do something nice for her. That was what friends did for each other. This favour was proof that her friendship with Carina Lees was real. It was a feeling as heady as being admitted to the popular girls' gang at school. She wanted to tell everyone.

All Emily had to do now was persuade Natalie to go to the show.

Persuading Natalie turned out to be no problem whatsoever.

When she heard the news, Natalie's mouth dropped open. She was stock-still for a moment before she started jumping up and down on the spot, flapping her hands as though she were a baby bird trying to take off. She was that excited.

'We've got tickets to go to a television studio?' she asked again and again and again. 'A real television studio? Where they make real television programmes?'

'Yes, yes. Yes,' said Emily.

'That's nice,' said Chloe, a little less enthusiastically. She'd grown up in London. The kind of thing that a girl from Wales might find exciting – tickets to be in a studio audience, for example – was the kind of thing that a girl from London might turn down in favour of a nice long lie-in.

'We'll go together,' said Emily. 'I'm going to close The Beauty Spot for the morning.'

'OK,' said Chloe.

'Ohmigod,' said Natalie. 'I've got to phone my mother and let her know.'

Natalie phoned her mother and chatted animatedly for twenty minutes about the treat in store. When Natalie finally finished 'Ohmigodding' down the line to Wales, she went back to bouncing around the lobby and flapping her hands.

'Mum is going to tell everyone in the village. She says she's going to host a special breakfast at her house for all the ladies from the chapel so they can keep an eye out for me in the studio audience. Do you think I should make a placard with "Hello Mum" on it?'

'Er, no,' said Chloe. 'Unless you want everyone to think you're a *retard*.'

Natalie didn't seem hurt. 'This could be it. This could be my big break,' she said suddenly. Her eyes glittered in the peculiar zealous way of someone with a master-plan.

'What do you mean?' asked Emily cautiously.

'I mean, I've been praying for something like this to happen.'

'Really?'

It was true. Though she'd reacted with charming modesty when Emily and Chloe praised her singing, in reality Natalie had long harboured a secret ambition to find a wider audience for her voice. A much wider audience.

'It's a sign. This is my big chance. If one of those television producers hears me singing, they might tell Simon Cowell! If I could just get in front of the camera for a minute. I know it would all fall into place.'

'You're nuts,' said Chloe, who had yet to be filled in on the makeover plan.

'It happens!' Natalie insisted. 'I promise I'll forgive you for saying I'm nuts when I have my first number one single.'

Emily felt a little twinge of guilt. But then she told herself that perhaps Natalie was right, though for the wrong reasons. She was going to get her moment in front of the camera. And the people at *Wakey-Wakey* would probably be delighted to let her sing a snatch of 'Land of Our Fathers'. It would make the makeover more interesting.

'Just so long as you give me a month's notice when you leave The Beauty Spot to become the next Mariah Carey,' Emily said.

That evening Natalie exited the salon singing.

* * *

The news about those *Wakey-Wakey* tickets put Natalie in such a good mood that she forgot to overreact when Matt and Cesar dropped by the salon. (Cesar, however, did find it in himself to growl as Natalie skipped by him.) Matt didn't have an appointment this time. Instead, he was carrying a small-business magazine for Emily. She was very pleased to receive it.

'You need to keep abreast of this sort of thing now you're a proper businesswoman,' said Matt.

'How was your holiday?' she asked him. Matt was looking very well. He was sporting a light tan that looked particularly good against his pastel pink shirt.

'Excellent choice of colour,' Emily told him.

His tan made it less obvious when he blushed.

'So, tell me,' Emily leaned over the desk and adopted a conspiratorial look. 'Did you meet anybody nice?'

'Well,' he said. 'There was one person that I got on pretty well with. Chris, the archaeologist who was leading our tour. Knew such a lot. It's really inspiring to be in the company of people who know their stuff.'

'Any . . . er, romance?' Emily asked.

Before Matt could answer, they were interrupted by Chloe, who erupted from her treatment room in much the same way as she had done the day that Natalie arrived. This time, however, it wasn't her stomach that was giving her problems.

'I dropped a bloody hot stone on my foot!' she said.

Emily was immediately distracted. 'Ice. You need ice.' She hurried away to find some.

Matt hung around for a couple of minutes before he gave up.

'Bye, Emily,' he called in the direction of the staff kitchen, hoping that she would hear it. She didn't reply.

As he was walking back to his office, Matt's phone vibrated to let him know that he had a text message. It was from Chris, his holiday friend. She'd promised that they would stay in touch. The text said simply: 'Did u ask her out?'

'Didn't get a chance,' Matt replied.

'Shame,' Chris texted. 'But you'll get another opportunity. I'm sure.'

Matt managed a little smile as he imagined Chris sitting across a table from him in Mykynos, talking about how she had gone back to university to become an archaeologist after her children left home, and listening so patiently when Matt told her about his unrequited love for Emily Brown.

21

The morning of the television show recording arrived. The Beauty Spot girls were used to early starts. The first appointment of the day at the salon was at eight o'clock, in the hope of catching ladies on their way into the office, and that meant arriving to prepare the treatment rooms at least half an hour before that. But getting to the *Wakey-Wakey* studio would require the kind of wake-up call that even Emily thought unreasonable.

Emily's Fiat Panda drew up outside Chloe's house at five a.m. Chloe staggered out of her flat like a sleepwalker. She said she would apply her make-up in the car. Actually, she fell asleep on the back seat and had to apply it in the loos at the studio instead.

Natalie, by contrast, was wide awake and raring to go when the other girls parked up outside the house where she lodged with a fellow refugee from the Valleys.

She looked, for Natalie, remarkably well groomed. She had abandoned the combat trousers for a skirt (albeit a skirt in the same utilitarian military colour and stiff material). Instead of the black cardigan with the droopy pockets, she was wearing a slightly smaller black sweater with no pockets. She had pinned a silver brooch in the shape of a Welsh dragon to her breast.

'My great-grandmother's,' she explained. 'For luck.'

She was wearing make-up. Well, lipstick. Most of it on her teeth.

Emily smiled at her encouragingly, if a little nervously. After all, Carina had explained that the success of a makeover segment was largely dependent on the degree of the transformation from minger to goddess. For that reason, Emily was greatly heartened when Natalie opened the passenger door and Emily saw that she was still wearing those enormous, nasty boots.

'I am so excited,' said Natalie. 'I've phoned my mum. She's set up the video.'

'We're not going to be at the studio for half an hour and the show doesn't start going out until eight.'

'I told her that. But she doesn't want to miss any of it. She's got to put the finishing touches to the breakfast buffet. Oh, please God, let it happen.'

'What?'

'That I get a chance to sing. They sometimes do that, Mum said. They go into the audience with a microphone and invite people to ask the guests questions and sometimes afterwards they get a chance to do their party piece.'

On the back seat Chloe stirred and opened one eye.

'Just don't start singing until we get there,' she warned.

A queue of people was already forming outside the studio when the girls arrived. A production assistant walked down the queue, checking people's tickets. When she saw Emily's tickets, she nodded.

'Friends of Carina Lees? Come with me,' she said.

They were shown to three seats in the third row from the stage, in the middle of the three seating blocks.

'I'm surprised we're not sitting in the front,' said Natalie.

'I suppose Trudy and Patrick's friends will be sitting in front of us,' said Emily.

Once the entire audience was seated, Jenny the producer stepped out onto the floor and explained how the show would proceed.

'As you know, the studio portions of *Wakey-Wakey* go out live,' she said. 'So once the camera starts rolling, I'd appreciate it if none of you move from your seats until I come back out here to tell you that you can. That means there will be no toilet breaks for the first hour and a half, so if you need to go . . .'

'I think I need to go,' whispered Natalie to Emily. 'I'm so nervous,' she explained. 'Excuse me.' She had to clamber over five people to get to the end of the row. Jenny smiled benevolently as she watched another seven people follow Natalie's lead. This always happened.

Finally, everyone was back in their seats and it was time for the show to begin. The audience waited in silence until the familiar *Wakey-Wakey* music began and they were given the signal to applaud. They were rewarded by the sight of themselves, as recorded by one of the four cameras, on a screen to the side of the stage. Catching a glimpse of herself, Natalie applauded uproariously. She just about managed to remain seated.

The stage was fitted with a sort of turntable that swivelled around during the opening credits to reveal a pseudo-sitting-room set with two big sofas and a coffee table. Patrick and Trudy were seated on one of the sofas, each holding a pile of newspapers, as though they had been catching up on the morning's news to be better able to inform their audience of the most pressing issues of the day. When the revolving set came to a standstill, Patrick and Trudy put their papers to one side and smiled broadly, as though surprised to find the audience in their home. The applause grew louder. To the side of the stage, an assistant producer gave the signal for 'stop'.

'Good morning,' Patrick and Trudy chimed simultaneously.

'We've got a wonderful show for you this morning,' Patrick continued. 'Unfortunately, our scheduled guest, Academy

Award Winner Helen Mirren, has been stranded in Los Angeles by bad weather, but in her place we have another Helen – Helen Burrows, star of Channel 11's inner-city dentist drama, *Veneered* . . . I know I'm looking forward to that.'

'And of course,' said Trudy, 'as it's Friday, we're looking forward to sharing the sofa with *Living Hell*'s Carina Lees, who will be performing yet more miracles in her morning makeover . . .'

Natalie leaned forward in her seat. Rapt. In the seat beside her, for the first time in her lifetime, Emily Brown was tempted to bite her fingernails.

Helen Burrows of *Veneered* was an excellent *Wakey-Wakey* guest. She answered all Patrick and Trudy's questions with great aplomb and paid tribute to the brave men and women at the forefront of dental science. She confirmed that she had indeed spent an afternoon with a dentist while honing her on-screen performance as Jacqueline Dufort, orthodontist and part-time psychic detective.

At the end of her interview, Helen Burrows revealed that she was dashing straight to Bristol to start recording a new series.

'We'll look forward to seeing it,' said Trudy.

'All we really want to know is, will Jacqueline Dufort ever give in to her feelings for Michael Foster?'

'Only if he remembers to floss!' Helen Burrows quipped.

After that, there was a brief break in proceedings while the channel aired a news update. House prices. Climate change. Three men arrested for stealing pub urinals to order . . . And then, at last, it was time for Makeover Magic.

The studio audience applauded on cue as the revolving stage turned around again and, this time, Carina Lees was sitting next to Patrick and Trudy on the sofas.

'She looks lovely, doesn't she?' whispered Natalie to Emily.

Carina did indeed look lovely. She was wearing a tight pink sweater and white Capri pants. Her hair was freshly extended. On her feet she wore a pair of white patent wedges. It was the stuff of a WAG's dreams.

Carina chit-chatted with Trudy and Patrick for a little while, filling them in on her week (which she would talk about at length in her column in *Get This!* magazine). She'd attended a premiere. The opening of a boutique. An Italian footballer's twenty-first birthday party.

'So not much time to visit Monkey in the hospital this week?' Trudy threw in.

'Carina doesn't want to be spending her time visiting hospitals,' said Patrick, in a misguided attempt at support.

From the sidelines, Jenny the producer made the signal for 'move it on'.

And so, with the camera focused squarely on her face, Carina started to talk about that week's project.

'Today's makeover is going to be a little different from anything we've done before,' Carina began. 'This time, we haven't chosen our lucky victim from the tapes you've been sending in by the lorry-load. Instead, we're going to surprise somebody in the studio audience.'

Camera four panned across the audience. There was a collective gasp. Half the audience shrank back into their seats as though to make themselves invisible, hoping *not* to be picked. The other half subconsciously sat a little straighter, hoping *to* be picked, though they, for the most part, were the people who least needed help.

Natalie shrank into her seat.

'As you know,' Carina continued, 'this morning we asked everyone in the audience to fill in a questionnaire so that we could find out a little bit more about them.'

The questionnaire had concluded with a very subtly worded release form.

'You probably thought that we were just doing some audience research, but we actually wanted time to get a good look at you as you waited in the queue and work out which one of you needs the most help.'

There was nervous laughter.

'So, it's time to put you out of your misery as you wait to find out who is the most fashion-challenged person in the studio audience today.'

Carina gave a traditional, results-reading pause, before saying quickly, 'I've chosen Natalie Hill.'

A cameraman carrying a mobile camera was already positioned in the aisle next to The Beauty Spot girls to catch Natalie's reaction.

Natalie pulled the traditional 'fish gasping for air' face.

'Oh no,' breathed Chloe.

'I can't believe it,' Emily lied.

'Why me?' Natalie managed eventually. Miserably.

She was about to find out.

22

A production assistant took Natalie by the arm and led her down onto the studio floor, where she was positioned, blinking like a rabbit that had just been whacked on the back of the head, right next to Carina.

'Now Natalie,' said Carina. 'You're a very unusual girl. You work as a beautician, am I right?'

Natalie nodded.

'So you spend six days a week helping other women to look their best?'

Natalie nodded again.

'And that obviously leaves you with very little time to pamper yourself. Or even get to the shops and buy yourself some new clothes. Or shoes.'

Natalie automatically looked down at her Doc Marten boots. Though she had cleaned them specially that morning, there was no doubt they still looked a mess.

'I mean, how long have you had those boots, Natalie? Doc Marten's haven't been fashionable since the mid-eighties. Before I was born.'

'I got them last year,' Natalie squeaked.

'Wow. You must walk a *lot*,' said Carina.

In the audience, Emily covered her mouth with her hand and closed her eyes.

Carina had been joined on stage by her makeover accomplice, Jamie, celebrity hair-stylist.

'Split ends,' he announced. 'Uncontrollable frizz. Yet quite remarkably greasy at the roots.'

Marcia, celebrity make-up artist, was similarly damning. 'Shine where there shouldn't be. Blackheads. Isn't that big red boil by your left ear quite painful?'

They soon had Natalie wilting beneath the combination of their criticism and the hot studio lights.

'Make them stop,' murmured Chloe.

'Well, today, Natalie Hill,' said Carina eventually, 'you're going to have a little bit of "me-time". We're going to pamper you with all the treatments you usually give to your clients. We're going to fix that terrible barnet.' Carina picked up a strand of Natalie's hair, pulled a face and dropped it. 'Marcia will give you a new face. And then we're going to give you five hundred pounds' worth of new clothes to take away with you today. Isn't that great?'

The studio audience applauded.

Natalie said nothing.

'She doesn't look happy,' Chloe whispered to Emily.

'She's getting five hundred pounds' worth of clothes,' said Emily. 'She'll be fine when that thought sinks in.'

'Take her away!' said Carina.

Linking their arms through hers, Marcia and Jamie whisked Natalie off for her transformation. Not that they would have anything to do with it . . .

Backstage, Natalie was handed over to a team of junior stylists, cutters and make-up artists. They stripped her of the clothes she had come in and made her change into a robe. They washed her hair and cleansed her face. Her eyebrows were plucked into something resembling submission.

For the first half-hour, Natalie was still in shock. She wondered how many people she knew had seen her dragged from the studio audience and picked over on-screen by Carina Lees. She wondered how many people she knew agreed with Carina that it was 'about time' she did something about the way she looked. What did Chloe and Emily think? Why hadn't they said anything to her before it got so bad?

Eventually, however, she started to feel a little better. There was something rather wonderful about having so many people work on her at once. She felt like a Formula One car taking a pit stop as they moved around each other in a well-choreographed beauty dance.

And the clothes were lovely. They came from shops that Natalie had never dared enter for fear that the shop assistants might smell how little money she had in her purse and laugh her straight back out of the door. She stroked the gunmetal velvet skirt lovingly. It would be the perfect outfit for Christmas day, even if the shoes the stylist had paired with it were a little impractical for her grandmother's farm in Wales.

Natalie decided to shake the cloud of embarrassment off and concentrate on the silver lining. There was one, she was certain. All week long she had been looking forward to this morning in the hope that she would get a chance to sing in front of someone influential. Now that dream seemed a little nearer.

'I don't see why you shouldn't be able to sing something,' Maddy, the lovely production assistant, had told her. 'We love that kind of thing on *Wakey-Wakey*.'

Natalie became convinced that she was going to have her fifteen minutes. If she could just find the courage to open her mouth and sing, she could turn them into fifteen years.

The hairdresser stood back and surveyed his work. A make-up artist stepped into his place and started to transform Natalie's face. She applied thick foundation to Natalie's skin. It was way more make-up than Natalie wanted to wear, but the make-up girl explained that she needed more than usual to counteract the studio lights.

'It looks a bit much in here but once you're in front of the camera you'll look perfectly natural. You've got nice eyes,' she continued. 'You should wear a bit of mascara to make the most of them.'

'Making the most of things' seemed to be the theme of that morning. Natalie thanked the make-up girl for her compliment and vowed to make the most of the opportunity she was about to be given!

'Close your eyes,' said the make-up girl, as she pressed powder all over Natalie's face to give the make-up staying power.

With her eyes tight shut, Natalie could see stardust.

'Ladies and gentlemen!' announced Carina. 'Here comes the new Natalie Hill!'

Natalie stepped out into the spotlight to a warm and heart-felt round of applause. As she had been instructed by Maddy the production assistant, she walked across to the sofa where Patrick and Trudy held court, then did a little twirl in the space right in front of them. Carina and Trudy looked on indulgently. Patrick did a comedy double-take.

'Can it really be the same girl?' he asked.

'Doesn't she look fabulous?' said Trudy, clapping her hands almost spontaneously. 'Carina, will you tell us what you did back there?'

Carina ran through the mechanics of Natalie's transformation as though she had wielded the straightening irons herself. She explained how the nipped-in waist of the gunmetal grey skirt made the most of Natalie's figure, in sharp contrast to the shapeless black jumper the audience had seen before.

'Natalie was making the mistake that lots of women make. Because she was feeling self-conscious about weight-gain, she started to dress in baggy clothes but, as we say in this makeover slot every week, big clothes actually add pounds. They don't disguise anything.'

Carina and Trudy moved on to a discussion about Natalie's new shoes. It was always best to wear a heel if you could.

It made the most of a shapely calf. Patrick interrupted with his own reverie about the shape of Trudy's calves. She shot him 'the look'.

Natalie was pretty much oblivious to the banter taking place on the sofa behind her. She stood in the centre of the studio like a prize cow while Carina pointed out various aspects of her attire. Inside, she was buzzing with excitement.

'This is what it's like,' Natalie thought, 'to have the eyes of the world upon you. I could do this. I could totally do this.' Natalie was surprised to find that she wasn't in the least bit afraid. All those years of singing in the shower had been building towards this moment. She couldn't wait to let fly. She was going to ace it.

Carina stood up and crossed the floor towards Natalie. She put her arm around her waist.

'So, what do you think?' she asked Natalie. 'Are you going to go back to your old frizzy-haired ways?'

'Oh no,' said Natalie, 'I'm going to buy some straighteners on the way home.'

'I'm sure we can find her a pair of straighteners,' piped up Patrick from the sofa.

'Glad to hear it,' said Carina. 'After all, your job title is *beaut*-ician not *beast*-ician,' she added.

'Thank you,' said Natalie. 'For everything you've done.'

'Well, that's it from me until next week,' said Carina. 'Next week I'll be back with a Makeover Magic special, turning two new mums from slummy to yummy—'

'Excuse me,' Natalie interrupted.

'Yes, Natalie.'

'I'd just like to sing a little bit of the Welsh National Anthem, if I may.'

Carina seemed not to hear. She didn't respond, just smiled more broadly. The camera zoomed in on Carina's face, cutting Natalie right out of the frame.

'Over to you, Trudy,' Carina said.

On the other side of the set, Trudy and Patrick were shuffling their papers again. Keeping abreast of those current affairs.

'Thank you, Carina,' said Trudy. 'Another miracle makeover.'

'Wasn't it just?' said Patrick. 'I think that our Natalie might just have been Carina's biggest challenge yet. That hair. Frightful.'

Trudy shot Patrick 'the look' again. He could be remarkably tactless. And while she knew that his awful off-the-cuff remarks and her careworn reactions were part of their appeal for Middle England, she couldn't help worrying that one day he would go too far and public opinion would swing against them. She had insisted that they turn down the chance to appear on *Celebrity Big Brother* for exactly that reason. He could be an idiot when the camera was on him. If he forgot it was on him . . .

'Well, I think Carina just brought out Natalie's *natural* beauty,' said Trudy in an attempt to close the conversation.

Patrick pulled a face. Fortunately, the camera wasn't on him this time.

Just as the camera wasn't on Natalie. Her fifteen minutes were over before they began.

'Is that it?' Natalie asked as she was escorted back out into the corridor.

Carina had disappeared.

'Yes,' said Maddy the production assistant, as she unhooked Natalie's mike, 'that's it.'

'But I didn't get to sing.'

'I'm sorry. I did tell them that you wanted to. I guess we just ran out of time. I think there are some more *X Factor* auditions coming up soon. You could give them a try.'

Natalie was taken back to the green room to collect the

clothes she had arrived in. They had been neatly folded and placed in a big, string-handled carrier bag from one of the forbidden boutiques.

'Do you want to change back into them?' Maddy the production assistant asked.

'I better had,' said Natalie. 'Don't want to get this skirt creased on the way back home.'

When Natalie had finished changing back into her old clothes, she came out of the green room to see Carina Lees standing in the corridor with Emily. Natalie ducked behind the corner to gather herself. She wanted to say thank you to the star but she didn't want to come over too gushy. She would catch her breath and . . .

'I wanted to say thank you,' Emily was speaking.

'Really, it was nothing. She was a good sport, wasn't she?'

'Here's hoping she keeps it up when we get back to Blountford,' said Emily.

Natalie felt a growing sense of discomfort and stepped out from her hiding place before Emily said anything more. She plastered on a smile.

'Thank you, Carina,' said Natalie. 'I never would have believed I could look this good.'

Carina gazed at her creation like a benevolent Madonna. 'I must be off,' she said. 'We're doing a pilot for that other show I was telling you about. Sure you've got nothing to confess?' she asked Emily.

Emily laughed at their shared joke.

'Come on, Nat,' she said. 'Let's go and show off your new look at the salon.'

Natalie was trying to keep up the good work, Emily told herself a week later. The Doc Marten boots had been retired for good in favour of the pretty ballet flats, though they quickly started to get scuffed. And she did try to keep the frizz out of her hair. Sometimes.

'I just didn't have time this morning,' she wailed every other day. At least it looked clean. Emily decided she should be grateful for that. And her guilt about setting Natalie up in front of the Great British Public had definitely subsided. Natalie didn't seem unduly scarred by her experience. She still burst into song at every opportunity.

It was during that week after the makeover show that Carina Lees made her fourth unexpected visit to the salon. It put Emily into a fluster. She would have liked to have told her next client that their appointment was cancelled, but Mrs Hinton was already inside the salon and stood behind Carina, waiting her turn to be checked in.

'I'm just after a facial,' said Carina.

'I . . . I . . .' Emily glanced at Mrs Hinton, half-hoping that the middle-aged woman would disappear. She didn't.

'I can't fit you in,' said Emily in some distress.

'That's OK. How about Natalie?'

It was time for Natalie's lunch hour. She hadn't had a break since eight a.m.

'I'll do it,' Natalie said. 'She's our VIP client, right?'

Emily nodded, though everything inside her was saying 'no'. What if Natalie did something wrong? The chances are she wouldn't – she'd never cocked up before – but Sod's law meant that today would be the day if she did.

'Besides,' Natalie concluded, 'I feel like I sort of know Carina now.'

'I'll be using the aromatherapy products you had last time,' Natalie said as she began the treatment. 'Emily has written out a sort of "prescription" for you so I know exactly what to do.'

'I'm sure you'll do great.'

'You know, I'm so grateful to you for what you did for me on the makeover show. It was a bit embarrassing to be picked from the studio audience at random, but—'

Carina laughed. 'Natalie,' she said, 'don't be so naive. Nothing ever happens randomly on TV.'

23

When Natalie and Carina reappeared an hour later, Emily breathed a sigh of relief. Carina looked happy enough, even if Natalie looked a little tense. That was to be expected though. It wasn't every day you got the chance to work with a celebrity.

'This girl is fantastic,' said Carina to Emily as she slipped Natalie a tenner.

Natalie folded the note into the pocket on her overall.

'I can't think when I last had such a nice time in a beauty salon. Now, you'll remember what we spoke about, won't you, Nat?'

Glancing quickly in Emily's direction, Natalie nodded, 'I will.'

'What did you speak about?' Emily asked as soon as Carina was gone. She had to know at once. She couldn't bear the thought that anyone might usurp her position as Carina's new best friend.

'Nothing important,' Natalie shrugged. 'Just motivational stuff. She was trying to encourage me to make the best of myself, I suppose. Like she did when she made me over on *Wakey-Wakey*.'

'She's good like that,' said Emily, satisfied with Natalie's answer. 'Very inspiring.'

'She is,' said Natalie. 'She's left me feeling *very* inspired.'

A few weeks later, Matt was back in the salon. This time he was having another manicure. He was going to a wedding.

'It's usually the bride who gets her nails done!' Emily laughed.

'I just want to look, you know, nice,' said Matt.

As Emily worked, she talked about how business had been doing since Matt had last been in. The salon was still pretty much booked out a couple of weeks in advance. Emily had abandoned her plan to take a summer holiday. Chloe and Natalie both needed time off. If she took any time herself, it could cost too much in lost revenue.

'Have you considered moving into a bigger premises?' Matt asked suddenly.

'A bigger place?' Emily shook her head.

'It might be time,' said Matt. 'I know it's probably come around a bit more quickly than you expected, but I don't see that you have any other choice. The three of you are always bumping into each other as it is. You can't take on any extra staff without more treatment rooms, and there isn't the space here for those.'

'But it's such a big step. It could all go wrong,' said Emily.

'It could all go right,' smiled Matt.

Emily didn't really think she could take Matt's suggestion seriously. By the time she was buffing his nails, he was talking about taking out a loan twice as big as the loan she had originally taken out. That first step had given her sleepless nights. Double the loan would only give her double the worry, right?

And yet she couldn't help thinking that it might be fun. Her wildest fantasy had been that she would one day have a whole chain of spas and perhaps even her own cosmetics range, like Marcia Kilgore, who set up Bliss. Marcia Kilgore didn't get where she was by being timid, Emily reminded herself.

And there was no harm in looking. Emily's route to work took her past an estate agency that specialized in commercial premises. She didn't often have time to stop and look through the window, but now she made time. The estate agent saw her peering in and came to the door to ask whether she might be able to help.

'I'm not sure,' said Emily.

'Try me,' said the estate agent.

Emily left the office with a fistful of property specs. She spent her tea break leafing through them, dreaming of how she might decorate each of the different spaces if money and confidence were no object.

In the end it was Carina Less, not Matt, who swayed Emily's opinion. Matt might be a whiz with figures, but Carina was a woman and, as such, Emily reasoned, she knew what other women wanted. And if she thought that what the women of Blountford wanted was a bigger and better beauty salon, then Emily would take the chance.

'You should definitely expand,' said Carina, when she came in for her second appointment with Natalie. According to Carina, Natalie had a magic touch when it came to facial massage. 'I've got every faith in you, Emily,' she continued. 'Look at this place. You've built it up from nothing and now it's impossible to get an appointment less than two weeks in advance.'

'Unless you're a VIP,' said Emily.

'Exactly.'

Emily went straight from The Beauty Spot to the estate agency that lunchtime and expressed her interest in taking over the lease of a former hairdressing salon near the town library.

'I think this place would make a fabulous beauty salon,' said the estate agent. 'I don't think you'll regret it.'

'I hope not,' thought Emily, as she sanctioned the transfer of an enormous deposit from her business account.

* * *

As soon as she left the estate agency, Emily called her parents to tell them she'd done the deal. They sounded pleased.

'You're a proper businesswoman these days, love,' said her mother. 'That'd be something to tell them at the school reunion. You have phoned that girl about the school reunion, haven't you?'

The very word 'school' made Emily feel slightly sweaty. Why was that girl still hounding her to go to the party? They'd never really been friends. The thought of walking into that assembly hall again made Emily feel dizzy with fear. The confidence she had felt when the estate agent shook her hand and wished her well had all but evaporated now.

'I'll call her, Mum,' Emily lied. 'Soon as I get home.'

24

It took two months for the old hairdressing salon to be refitted as The New Beauty Spot. During that time, Emily, Chloe and Natalie worked hard on ensuring that the new salon would open with a full appointments book. Though the salon had five treatment rooms, to begin with the staff would comprise just the three of them and a new part-timer on reception.

The pink theme of the original Beauty Spot was echoed in the new place. It had the same gingham accents on the upholstery and the same fluffy pink towels. The lettering above the door was also identical to that on the first sign, which Emily had hand-painted herself. Most excitingly, The New Beauty Spot had a steam room and a jacuzzi that clients could use before they had their treatments. It was a proper 'day spa' at last.

Still, saying goodbye to the old salon was an emotional moment for Emily. On the day that the first Beauty Spot finished trading, she couldn't help but shed a tear.

'But this isn't a sad occasion,' said Natalie. 'Think of it like a child leaving primary school. Next year he's going to secondary school. It's all progress, isn't it?'

Emily thanked Natalie for her understanding. And she was right, of course. The closing of the tiny salon was not a sad occasion. So, locking the door of her first place behind her, Emily went straight to her second launch party.

* * *

'I'm so proud to be standing here,' said Emily's father. 'Just a year since my darling girl opened her first salon, we're already toasting the opening night of salon number two!'

'I'm crying with happiness,' Emily's gran insisted once again as she chucked down a Bacardi Breezer.

It was a magical evening. Everyone who had celebrated the opening of the original Beauty Spot was back. Surrounded by her family and friends, Emily couldn't help but feel uplifted by their support.

The most magical moment of all, however, was when Carina Lees stopped by. She was on her way to the opening of a new bar in Chelmsford, but she had her driver make a special detour and she joined the crowd as they raised a glass to Emily's future success.

Afterwards, Emily paraded her celebrity best friend around the room, introducing her to aunts and uncles and next-door neighbours.

'You look familiar,' said Grandma Brown when Carina was quite formally presented to her. 'Do I know you from somewhere? Didn't you used to live round here?'

'No,' said Carina quickly, 'I'm from Colchester.'

'No, you're not. I definitely know you.'

'You know her off the telly, Gran,' Emily interrupted. 'She's famous.'

'But she looks like that girl you went to school with. The one with the funny eyes.'

'Ignore her,' said Emily, taking Carina by the arm and leading her towards the local news reporter. 'She's so embarrassing. Nearly eighty. And going round the bend.'

Carina graciously posed for a couple of photographs alongside Emily, Natalie and Chloe. The journalist affected not to know her name. He hadn't spent two years at journalism college so that he could cover nobodies turning up for the opening of nothing much in nowhere. He wanted to be a serious journalist, in the vein of A. A. Gill. Writing about important things. Like himself.

And then Carina had to leave. Her car was waiting to take her to the new bar in Chelmsford, where she would twirl on the red carpet in front of more local hacks. Emily escorted her to the door.

'Thank you so much for coming tonight. It's so good to have you here. I mean, we wouldn't be here if it weren't for you being so supportive and mentioning us on TV that night all those months ago.'

'One good turn,' said Carina.

'I just fixed your nail. But you . . . You've made it possible for me to realize my dream. I've wanted to have my own beauty salon ever since I was a tiny little girl. I had this really glamorous auntie who used to let me experiment with her make-up. She got me into it. And all through school I used to beg my friends to let me try out my skills on them. It's the only thing I've ever been interested in. Good job, really, because I wasn't very academic or anything.'

Carina nodded sympathetically. 'I know what you mean.'

'Setting up my own business was the scariest thing I ever did. It must have been like that for you going into the *Living Hell* house. It was like a fork in the road of my life. If it worked, I would be heading towards the life I'd always dreamed of. If it didn't . . . Now I'm in the same place again. If this bigger salon works out then maybe one day I'll be as successful as that woman who set up Bliss in New York. But if it goes wrong, I've got nothing. Literally nothing. Everything I own is mortgaged against this business. I don't even own the place where I live. I'd have to move back in with my mum and dad. I don't think I would ever recover if I had to go bankrupt or something like that.' Emily took a deep breath as a picture of that future – the unhappy one – danced in her brain.

'Don't even think about it. You've got to be positive,' said Carina. 'That's what I always say.'

'You're right.' Emily plastered on a smile. 'Anyway, I don't know how to thank you. The broken nail that brought you into my salon was the luckiest break in my life.'

'Then I'm very glad it happened,' Carina laughed. She bestowed a couple of air kisses to Emily's smiling cheeks and was gone.

Emily waved until she could see Carina's car no longer. The reality star was such an inspiration. Sometimes Emily felt that destiny had brought Carina into her life.

Finally seeing his moment to catch Emily alone, Matt followed her out onto the pavement where Emily remained. He was still holding the bunch of roses he had brought with him. He'd been holding them very tightly for the best part of two hours. It was hot inside the new salon. The roses were looking the worse for wear.

Emily didn't notice Matt was beside her until Cesar put his wet nose on her leg.

'Oh! Hi,' she smiled.

'For you,' Matt handed her the flowers.

'Yellow. They're nice,' she said.

'Have you been having a good evening?' Matt asked.

'Yes. But I'm tired,' she said. 'Getting this place together has really taken it out of me.'

Matt nodded in agreement. It had been hard work for him too, helping Emily to get her business plan straight and ensure that her contractors weren't ripping her off. Emily had transferred her banking to the branch where Matt worked, but he certainly wasn't treating her like any other client. For the past two months he had spent his evenings and weekends living and breathing The Beauty Spot. He'd even started subscribing to beauty trade magazines to make sure he knew what he was talking about when Emily called to ask whether she should buy this particular electrolysis machine or splash out on something more special.

'Well,' said Matt, 'you're up and running now. I see a great future ahead.'

'The one thing setting up this second salon has shown me is what good friends I have,' said Emily, reaching down to scratch Cesar between the ears. 'I mean, can you believe Carina Lees actually came here tonight? To my opening night? She is such a good friend.'

Matt nodded, though personally he wasn't quite sure what Carina's motivation was – hanging out at The new Beauty Spot when she could be somewhere much grander. Still, Emily would hear nothing bad about her.

'Emily!' Eric Brown called out from inside. 'Come and say goodnight to your gran. She's going.'

'Excuse me.'

Emily stepped back into the shop. Matt remained outside, watching Emily through the window as she weaved through the crowd. He watched her lean over her diminutive grandmother and give her a kiss goodnight. He was still watching when Emily handed her grandmother the bunch of roses Matt had given her. And then he lip-read, 'You can have these, Gran. I don't really want them.'

25

The New Beauty Spot got off to a flying start. It was close enough to the old salon that most of the regular customers were very happy to transfer their business to the new premises. In fact, they were more than happy. The parking was much easier and that was extremely important to the yummy mummies who had a limited amount of time between dropping their kids off at school, stretching at their private Pilates classes, doing lunch with the girls and picking the kids up again.

The added attraction of the steam room and Jacuzzi meant that the appointments book was quickly full, and Emily placed an advertisement for a fourth therapist in all the trade magazines. She would not have believed the market for manicures and pedicures. At last it seemed the British women were taking grooming as seriously as their American counterparts. Not a moment too soon, thought Emily.

She even took a day off and visited a trade show to find out what was new and exciting in the beauty trade. Matt had suggested to her that having exclusive treatments should be a big part of her expansion plans, because, as the salon grew in size, people would expect a wider range of services.

Then Emily started to interview hopefuls for the new job. Maybe it was the size of the new salon that did it – the slightly slicker approach – but, for whatever reason, the applicants for this job were of a far higher quality than the applicants for the position that Natalie had eventually taken. Emily interviewed fifteen girls. Natalie and Chloe were in attendance when Emily recalled her favourite three. Between them, they settled on a girl from Krakow called Nina.

'She'll fit right in,' said Natalie, noting that Nina had listed 'singing' as a hobby. Chloe groaned at the thought of the potential for duets.

A month after The New Beauty Spot first opened its doors, Emily found it hard to believe that she had ever been nervous about the venture. It seemed to be working perfectly. She started to say proudly that she was glad she had taken the risk.

'It's important to stretch yourself,' she explained to one of her clients, 'before you get too comfortable with the status quo.'

Soon the staff of The Beauty Spot numbered five. They had been joined by a full-time receptionist called Kathy, returning to work now that her children had started school. The somewhat scruffy appointments book was replaced with a smart new PC, which enabled Kathy to input appointment details and email confirmation to clients who were technologically inclined. Emily put the old book away in a drawer. Part souvenir of her early days as a salon owner, and partly because it contained so many contacts that Kathy would need to transfer onto the new computer system.

Meanwhile, Matt helped Emily set up a proper payroll scheme and guided her through the maze of National Insurance documentation for her new employees. The most important thing now was to ensure that the new appointments spreadsheet remained full.

Emily arranged for a meeting with Matt to discuss progress. He had become, without any formal announcement, Emily's official small-business advisor. She was very happy with that, since Matt always seemed so pleased to help.

'These figures are excellent,' he said when The New Beauty Spot had been trading for six weeks. 'But I think it's time you did a bit of serious promotion. Some special spring offers, that sort of thing.'

At Matt's suggestion, Emily called her first-ever staff meeting. She'd had meetings before but, when there were only three staff members in the entire business, it had seemed a little pretentious to give the gathering official status. Now, however, there were five staff and Matt. Emily had Kathy pick up some cream cakes and a bottle of Chardonnay on her lunch break. All the better to encourage lateral thinking.

When the salon closed for the evening, the girls and Matt gathered in the little kitchen and opened the bottle of wine.

Matt outlined the plan. The salon needed to attract business outside its usual catchment areas. The first thing was to decide what kind of customer was walking on by rather than coming in and making an appointment, or even just picking up a leaflet.

'That's easy,' said Natalie at once. 'It's men.'

'I mean,' Natalie elaborated, 'we have some men. Mostly gay men,' she nodded slightly towards Matt. He shifted in his seat. 'But we're completely off the radar when it comes to straight guys. Wouldn't you agree?' she asked her fellow therapists. 'I think we've got just about everyone else covered.' She counted them off on her fingers. 'We get young single women preparing for their big dates. We get yummy mummies recovering from the stress of dealing with their families. We get older ladies after a bit of pampering but, apart from the gay guys and the odd hairy husband, we get no male customers at all.'

'It's a waste of time,' said Chloe, as she reached for her cake. 'They don't want to come to a beauty salon. Simple as that.'

'I disagree,' said Natalie. 'I think it's more the case that they're *afraid* to come to a beauty salon. In the same way that any of us girls might be worried about having to take the car into a garage.'

'I'm not,' said Nina. In addition to her beauty certificates, she had the basic qualifications of a junior car mechanic.

'Well, I am. It's frightening because we think we don't know what to do. We're not sure what to ask for. We don't want to get ripped off and we don't want to look silly.'

'I don't see where you're going?' Emily admitted.

'We've got to make our salon accessible to men. We should offer specific treatments targeted at the boys. Now we girls and the gay guys,' she looked at Matt again, 'know that all the treatments on this list are suitable for either sex, but the average man on the street doesn't. They see a pink leaflet and assume it's not for them. So I think we need to produce a treatment package that is just for them. A facial, a massage and a pedicure, say. All for a hundred quid.'

'Can you do that?' Matt asked Emily.

'I suppose the treatments would cost you one-twenty if you bought them separately,' said Emily.

'Yes,' said Natalie, 'but we don't even have to give them the full-length treatment each time. We can do a fifty-minute massage instead of an hour. A twenty-minute pedicure instead of half an hour. After all, they're unlikely to be wanting nail polish.'

'I think Natalie may be on to something,' said Matt.

'What should we call it?' asked Emily.

'Oh, I've already thought of that,' said Natalie proudly. 'I think we should call it "Man-tenance". Get it?'

It turned out to be the best idea of the meeting. All the other strategies mooted were variations on a similar theme but, as Natalie pointed out, they were offers that would appeal to existing clients, not to a whole *new* set. And the potential catchment for 'Man-tenance' was huge. To prove her theory, Natalie had Emily stand at the window and watch the people walking by at the end of the day. There were literally hundreds of young men in suits, walking back from the station after their commute to Essex from the City.

'These are the chaps we should be targeting,' said Natalie. 'Look at that one!' She pointed out a man whose shoulders were up around his ears. 'Now there's a man who really needs a massage. He'd love it.'

As if on cue, the stressed-out City boy glanced in the direction of The New Beauty Spot and seemed to hesitate, as though he were seriously considering stepping inside and stretching out on a couch beneath Emily's capable hands.

'How are we going to advertise it?' asked Chloe.

'We'll have big notices in the window and take out some ads in the local paper,' said Natalie. 'I'll help you word it.'

'What do you think?' Emily asked Matt.

'I think it's a good idea. I would definitely sign up,' said Matt.

They took a vote and decided unanimously to go with Natalie's idea. She grinned.

'This is going to be great,' said Natalie. 'Just wait and see.'

Emily couldn't wait to put Project Man-tenance into action. Natalie was equally keen to see her idea brought to life, so, when the others had gone home, the two girls stayed in the office and mocked out their ideal advertisement on the salon laptop. Natalie found a clip-art picture to illustrate the ad. It was a silhouette of a good-looking (in so far as you can tell someone is good looking from a silhouette) bloke, running his hands through his hair.

The wording: 'Summer's coming. Make sure you're ready for the beach, boys!'

'I like that,' said Emily. 'Beach, boys. Makes you think of The Beach Boys. Very summery music.'

'That's exactly what I was thinking,' said Natalie. 'Clever, eh?'

Below that they listed the specifics of the offer.

'We should play up the fact that we've got a Jacuzzi,' said Natalie. 'Men like that.'

'You do realize what you're letting yourself in for?' Emily asked her. 'Pedicures. I don't think I've met a man with nice feet in my life. Not even a gay one.' She cocked her head to one side as though hearing her thoughts. 'Except Matt.'

Emily saved the advertisement onto a CD.

'I'll take this to the local paper,' said Natalie. 'It's on my way. I'll drop it off tomorrow morning.'

'Would you do that? You know,' said Emily, 'I can't tell you how glad I am that you refused to go away the day I was supposed to interview you. You're such a valuable part of the team. I can't imagine what I'd do without you.'

'Oh, thank you.' Natalie gave Emily a brief hug. 'I don't know what you'd do without me either,' she added with a wink.

So, the ad went in to the local paper. It was supported, as per Natalie's suggestion, with a big banner across The Beauty Spot's window. Emily was slightly disappointed that the banner didn't generate a lot of new male footfall, but Natalie explained that simply wasn't the way men operated.

'They won't just walk in,' she said. 'But you have to believe that the banner is working. They'll memorize the number and think about it for a bit. Then they'll call up and make an appointment. They don't want to have to cross the threshold of a beauty salon any more often than necessary. What if they were to be seen by one of their mates?'

Natalie was right. Not a single new male customer walked in off the street but, after a couple of days, they did start to telephone, and they were all very keen to get appointments. When the first of them called, Emily shook Natalie by the hand and tried not to let her expression betray her surprise. That became harder when the next guy called for an appointment. And the next and the next. Over the following seventy-two hours, The Beauty Spot signed up twenty-five 'Man-tenance' clients, representing two and a half thousand pounds' worth of business! Emily stared in amazement at a particular fully booked day in the diary two weeks' hence, which contained not one *female* client.

'Natalie,' she said, 'you are clearly an advertising genius.'

'I'm working on my next campaign already,' Natalie replied. 'Maybe we could even convert one of the treatment rooms into a special "man's room". You know, paint it blue. Hang a few pictures of glamour models on the wall.'

'I don't think we need to go that far,' said Emily.

When she heard about the exclusively male day ahead, Chloe joked, 'Perhaps we will meet some decent men through this job after all.'

26

Chloe wasn't the only one on the lookout for a decent man. Mickey Shore had called a crisis meeting at the offices of Shore Thing PR. Danny Rhodes had announced that he wanted to come out. He was tired of squiring Carina around town. More importantly, the Brazilian boyfriend was threatening to go back to his ex if he had to see one more picture of Danny with 'that woman' in the tabloids.

The situation had to be spun. Mickey calmed Danny down by promising that he would be able to come out soon but, for the time being, he begged his 'favourite client' to remain discreet. It was decided that the press release would explain that Carina had instigated the split, due to a realization that her ongoing devotion to Monkey was more than just friendship.

'We'll have to have you photographed coming out of The Bakery again,' Mickey told her.

Carina was furious. The last thing she wanted to do was to have to go back to The Bakery. But there was no choice. It would look far better, she knew, if the public thought that she was in charge of her romantic destiny. And perhaps it would stop Trudy from snidely mentioning Monkey at the end of every Makeover Magic segment on the *Wakey-Wakey* show.

Get This! magazine ran a big article about Carina and Monkey's enduring love. *Wakey-Wakey*'s resident psychic, Liyo Aslan, looked into his crystal ball to see what the future had in store for the starry pair. He also delved into Monkey's past life and revealed – to the delight of *Wakey-Wakey*'s viewers – that, like Carina, Monkey's past life included a stint in Ancient Egypt.

'His present-time paralysis is related to the fact that he was mummified alive,' said Liyo knowledgeably. He even offered to visit The Bakery and release Monkey from his still and silent hell with the laying on of hands. Dr Forrest, Monkey's chief physician, politely declined.

But Dr Forrest said that he was sure Monkey would welcome a visit from Carina and Carina dutifully appeared at the clinic in her Range Rover a couple of days later. Once again she followed Dr Forrest through the chic lobby to the bleak corridors that rang with the unmistakable sounds of unhappiness. And this time she managed to get through the door.

Monkey didn't even turn to look at her.

He wasn't standing like a cactus this time. He was sitting in the plain leather armchair with chrome arms in front of the window. He was looking out into the grounds but, when Carina stepped in front of him and waved her fingers at him, it was clear that he wasn't actually seeing anything.

'It's Carina,' she said, 'your girlfriend.'

Outside in the corridor, someone sniggered audibly. It was either Dr Forrest or the nurse who had been tidying Monkey's room when they arrived.

'I've brought you your favourite crisps,' Carina continued. 'Everyone's been asking after you.'

Monkey did not stir. Outside, a blackbird flew across the garden, chattering loudly about a cat on the prowl. His eyes flickered briefly in the direction of the bird's flight but otherwise he remained quite still.

'OK,' said Carina. 'I'm going. See you soon.'

She exited smartly. By the time she was halfway up the corridor, she was practically running. She was still breathless when she reached her Range Rover and drove, very slowly, out through The Bakery gates to give the paps long enough to catch her looking the part of the dutiful girlfriend. As soon as she was past the photographers, she put her foot down.

'I never want to go back to that place,' Carina told Mickey's assistant Lucy over the phone.

'Why does it freak you out so much?' Lucy asked.

'It just does, OK,' said Carina. She hung up.

'Brings back memories. I reckon she was sectioned,' Kenny, Lucy's colleague, concluded.

'No. I don't think so. What for?' asked Lucy.

'Anorexia?'

'Bulimia,' Lucy countered.

'Bet you a tenner it was anorexia,' said Kenny.

'No. She's a puker,' said Lucy. 'Definitely. I'll find out.'

They shook hands on their horrible bet.

27

On the morning of the first Man-tenance customer's arrival, The Beauty Spot girls were full of excited anticipation. An array of men's fashion magazines was spread out in a fan on the counter. Emily sent Chloe to the supermarket to buy some 'man-friendly' drinks and snacks for the complimentary corner.

'What's a man-friendly drink?' Chloe pondered. 'Full-fat Coke? Tizer?'

At eleven o'clock, the tinkling of the little bell above the front door announced 'Mr Smith's' arrival. Emily, Natalie, Chloe and Nina were all congregated around Kathy at the front desk, eager to see what this brave man looked like. Natalie had even prepared a little exit questionnaire. She wanted to ask him what in particular had made him decide to visit The Beauty Spot. It was the kind of information that could help them tailor future marketing initiatives more successfully, she explained. Question one: had he come to the decision to try the Man-tenance package alone or had he, as Chloe still suspected, been volunteered by a caring girlfriend?

It quickly became clear that there was no caring girlfriend in Mr Smith's life. Or sister. And a caring mother certainly wouldn't have let her son out of the house looking quite so . . . well, *manky*.

At first, the girls assumed that the man who shuffled through the door at eleven o'clock precisely must be a down-and-out, coming in to ask for a couple of quid to put petrol in an imaginary car. That happened quite a bit. Emily automatically checked that the cash drawer was locked and prepared to usher the poor old guy out, gently but firmly. But he didn't seem at all confused about what he was doing there.

'Can I help you?' Emily asked, praying that he didn't really have a reason to be there.

'I'm here for the Man-tenance package,' said the old guy with a wink.

Chloe pulled a face at Natalie and Nina. Their annoyance at missing out on a potential husband dissipated immediately.

'Are you sure?' asked Emily, hoping against hope. She took in his straggly grey hair. His unshaven chin. The old overcoat with the greasy sheen of a garment that hasn't been washed in a very long time. After a minute Emily realized she could actually smell it. All the girls could. The others backed away, leaving their leader to deal with this unpleasant development on her own.

'That's right. I'm Mr Smith,' he said. 'Eleven o'clock. I've got an appointment.'

He delved into the pocket of that horrible coat and brought out a roll of banknotes.

'It's all there,' he said, handing the money to Emily.

'You don't have to pay until afterwards,' Emily told him, pushing the money away. 'I really don't like to take a client's money unless I'm sure that they've been satisfied.'

'Oh, I'm sure I'll be *very* satisfied,' said Mr Smith, placing the money on the counter and rubbing his hands together. 'Can I choose which one of you does it?'

'Er . . .' Emily hesitated.

Mr Smith looked from Chloe to Natalie. Both girls took another step back. Nina had already scarpered to the bathroom.

'I want that one,' he said, pointing at Chloe.

Chloe's mouth dropped open in horror. She shook her head most vehemently.

'I'm afraid Chloe already has a client at eleven,' said Emily.

'Thank god,' Chloe mouthed to Natalie.

'You're booked in with me,' said Emily.

'But I prefer blondes,' said Mr Smith.

'Well, you won't be able to tell the difference when you've got your eyes closed,' said Emily.

Mr Smith gave a faintly amused snort. 'I suppose not. Bet you're all the same underneath anyway. Know what I mean?'

Emily wasn't sure she did.

'Can I take your coat?' she asked.

Mr Smith shrugged the coat off and handed it over. Holding it between her thumbs and forefingers to minimize contamination, Emily went to hang it on the client coat pegs but decided against it. The other girls weren't too impressed to see Emily hang the coat next to their jackets instead, but they had to come back the next day. The customers didn't, and Emily wasn't going to risk scaring anybody off.

'Follow me,' she said brightly.

Emily led Mr Smith through to her treatment room, ready and waiting for him. The aromatic candles were already lit and the whales were gently crooning their songs of love. Emily gave her new client the spiel she gave all her clients. She explained that the lavender scent of the candle was supposed to aid relaxation. The subsonic sound of the whales was intended to do the same but she could switch that off if he found it annoying.

'Whale music isn't for everybody,' said Emily.

'Don't care,' said Mr Smith as he loosened his tie (which was shiny with grease, like the coat). 'I'll let you know if I'm finding it hard to concentrate.'

'Fine,' said Emily, though she couldn't imagine what concentrating he thought he would have to do. 'In that case, I'll step outside for a moment while you get undressed and hop onto the bed.'

She waved him in the direction of the couch. 'Just shout when you're ready.'

Back in the reception, the other girls were laughing about something.

'He really needs some man-tenance,' said Natalie. 'Who do you think sent him? His wife?'

'Wife! No way. He looks like a widower to me. Or a plain old bachelor,' said Chloe. 'Definitely smells like one.'

Emily noticed that the girls had removed their coats from the pegs next to Mr Smith's overcoat, which now hung alone, looking, Emily thought, almost as though it did feel lonely.

'Well, he certainly needs a facial,' said Natalie.

'He does seem quite excited by the idea,' Emily confirmed. 'He asked if we could do that last.'

'I don't envy you having to deal with his feet,' said Nina. 'Judging by the rest of him, I think you're going to have a really big job on your hands.'

'Don't be silly,' said Emily. But inwardly she was absolutely in agreement with Nina. Being a beauty therapist wasn't all glamour and the perverse joy of squeezing someone else's blackheads. Sometimes you just didn't want to touch a customer. It happened with women as much as men. There would be something about them that made you recoil. For Emily, one of the worst things she had to deal with was an aversion to Miss Dior perfume. The smell of the stuff made her gag. Fortunately, it wasn't as fashionable as it had been and she didn't encounter it half so often as she had done when she was first starting out.

But the issue with Mr Smith was not going to be his after-shave.

'Good luck,' said Natalie as Emily prepared to do battle with whatever Mr Smith kept in his socks.

Emily knocked gently on the door to the treatment room.

'Come in,' said Mr Smith, with what was almost a growl.

Emily slowly pushed open the door. Her steadiness was less in anticipation of something awful than because it was what she always did. From the moment her clients entered the salon, they were treated to the perfect relaxation experience and that meant low noise and slow movements from the therapists.

'Think of yourself like a Buddhist monk,' she'd once told Chloe. Chloe had looked at her as though she were mad.

But Emily was playing the Buddhist monk role now. Though Mr Smith most certainly wasn't.

'I'm ready for you,' he announced from the couch.

Emily glanced in his direction.

He wasn't joking.

28

From the second Emily walked back into the treatment room it was obvious that Mr Smith had never been to a beauty salon before and had no idea of the proper etiquette. Emily had left a carefully folded blanket on the end of the bed. Ordinarily, people understood that they should undress and lie down on the bed with the blanket lying over them, protecting their modesty. Mr Smith was lying on the bed with absolutely nothing protecting anything. And what wasn't protected was pointing straight up at the carefully dimmed spotlights.

Emily's hands flew to her eyes.

'Mr Smith. You're supposed to be underneath the blanket.'

He'd thrown the blanket onto the floor.

Making sure she didn't look directly at her client, Emily picked the blanket up and waved it in Mr Smith's direction. He took it.

'I suppose it is a bit nippy in here,' he said.

When Emily dared open her eyes, the blanket was draped over Mr Smith's lap, but his anticipation of what must have been his first massage was still all too obvious. Ah well. Emily had been warned about this sort of thing at beauty school. She decided that her best tactic was to proceed as usual. She would get Mr Smith to lie on his front to start with. That would probably calm things down.

'Roll over, please,' she told him. 'There's a hole for your face.'

Mr Smith snorted with amusement. Emily didn't know what he had found funny.

'Aren't you going to take your clothes off?' Mr Smith asked.

'What?'

'For the facial? Don't want to get them dirty, do you?'

'Oh no,' said Emily brightly. 'These are overalls. They're supposed to get dirty.'

'And I'm sure they will. But if I'm paying a hundred pounds, I expect you to get your clothes off too.'

'You what?' said Emily.

The penny dropped.

'Mr Smith,' said Emily quickly. 'There seems to have been a misunderstanding. I think you ought to put your clothes on. It's best if we don't go any further. You won't be charged for a cancellation, of course.'

'Come on now,' Mr Smith mumbled from his face-down position on the treatment bench. 'I didn't ask for coy.'

'Mr Smith, I am not being coy. I'm being direct with you. I'm going to step outside. I'm giving you three minutes to get dressed and vacate my treatment room.'

'I didn't ask for a dominatrix either,' Mr Smith complained.

'And you're not getting one!'

Emily fled the room and shouted from the other side of the firmly closed door.

'Mr Smith! Please do as I ask. Don't make me call the police!'

It took a while, but eventually Mr Smith was convinced. No matter what he said or offered, Emily was not going to give him what he'd come for.

'What kind of establishment is this?' he muttered as he stepped out into the lobby and retrieved his horrible coat.

'It's a beauty salon,' Emily told him.

'Funny sort of set-up if you ask me.'

As Mr Smith exited the salon he passed another customer

who had booked a Man-tenance package. Chloe's eleven-thirty. This man, like Mr Smith, was wearing a long grubby coat. He had his hands in his pockets but he wasn't jangling his change.

'I'm not doing it.' Chloe covered her eyes and made a bolt for the staff room.

'I'd like the happy ending,' the man announced when Emily asked how she could help him, knowing at the very same time that she absolutely couldn't.

'Out,' was all she said to him, pointing him straight to the door.

The afternoon progressed in much the same vein. The shiftiest men in Essex appeared one after another at The Beauty Spot's door and were turned away disappointed. By the end of the afternoon, Chloe refused to be anywhere near the lobby, so traumatized was she after four of the men had walked in, pointed straight to her and said, 'That one.' Emily had to spend half an hour convincing Chloe that she didn't look like a hooker.

'You could try to take it as a compliment,' she said unconvincingly. 'All it means is that they thought you were the most beautiful girl in the place.'

'One of them said I had blow-job lips!' Chloe wailed.

Natalie and Nina couldn't help smirking.

Emily was dismayed. How on earth could so many men have misunderstood her advertisement? 'Will you bring me the ad?' she asked Natalie.

Natalie duly placed a copy of the newspaper in front of her. All five girls peered closely at the little square Beauty Spot advertisement in search of clues. There had been no misprint. The ad was exactly as Emily had last seen and approved it.

'How on earth could so many people have misinterpreted what was on offer? It's perfectly clear that we're a beauty salon and we're offering beauty treatments. Not hand relief!' Emily shuddered.

The others agreed that there was no obvious reason for the mix-up. Especially since the very same page carried an advertisement for The Beauty Spot's female clients that quoted from a review calling The New Beauty Spot 'Blountford's premier beauty salon'.

'There's no knowing what goes on in the minds of some people,' said Natalie. 'There are people out there who can see an innuendo in anything.'

That didn't help Emily. That week's schedule was full of potential Man-tenance clients. Having to turn them away, leaving empty spots in the diary, was a disaster.

'Girls,' Emily set her damage-limitation plan in motion. 'I need you to call up all the men who have made appointments for the Man-tenance package and make certain that they know we are a respectable business and do not offer "happy endings".'

Natalie and Chloe paled at the thought. But they needn't have worried about how one broaches such things in a telephone conversation because, of course, not one of the guys who had made appointments had left a bona fide telephone number. In all likelihood, they hadn't even left their real names. Emily berated herself for failing to notice that nearly all her new male clients were called Mr Smith or Mr Jones. There was no way of getting hold of them and yet she didn't dare cancel their appointments without giving them notice in case that day's disaster had been an aberration and she ended up offending genuine new clients.

Over the next couple of days, a dozen more 'Mr Smiths' turned up at the appointed time and were quickly turned away again. It was a complete debacle. From the happy prospect of two and a half thousand pounds' worth of new business, Emily suddenly found herself with an empty diary and an empty till. She attempted to fill the holes in the salon's schedule by texting some of her regulars, offering them lovely big discounts if they just popped in on the spur of the moment, but not enough of them took her up on her offer to make up the shortfall.

Ordinarily, The Beauty Spot's weekly turnover was in the region of five thousand pounds. That week it was closer to one.

Emily knew she mustn't panic. This was just a blip. In the big scheme of things, it wouldn't matter, she assured her staff. But her distress was obvious to everyone. Even without them knowing that she would have to dip into her own savings account to find money for the girls' wages that week.

'I blame myself,' said Natalie, when they found themselves alone in the staff room.

'It's OK,' said Emily. 'There was no way you could have known that this would happen. We took a chance but it seems Chloe was right. Men just don't go to beauty salons. Not straight men.'

'I should have known that. But instead I made you waste all that money on an ad and we ended up with no real customers all day today.'

'Really. It's OK. You were trying to help.' Emily gave Natalie a big hug. 'And we've learned a big lesson. We need to concentrate on the customers we have and not try to work against human nature. Besides, next week is really busy. We'll be back to normal in no time.'

Natalie seemed happy with that. It really wasn't her fault, Emily said to herself once everyone else had gone home and she was left looking at the paltry number on her spreadsheet that should have represented an excellent week. Natalie was totally dedicated to The Beauty Spot. It was important that she didn't lose confidence in her ability to bring something new and exciting to the place.

Things could only get better.

29

'I'm sorry,' said Carina when Emily told her about the Man-tenance debacle over a manicure. 'But I can't help finding it funny.'

'I'm sure I will eventually,' said Emily. 'When I've recovered some of the shortfall in takings.'

Carina's face grew grave. 'Oh. I didn't even think of that. Did you lose an awful *lot* of money?'

'It probably cost me five thousand pounds altogether. And I'm worried that some of the people I couldn't accommodate because we were so busy trying to please our new male clients, won't come back.'

'Surely they'll be more loyal than that?' said Carina.

'I hope so. But you know what people are like. They want instant gratification, which is why I expanded the salon in the first place.'

'They'll come back,' said Carina. 'Plus, it's just five thousand pounds. It's not like that could sink the business or anything . . . Is it?'

Emily looked at Carina. Around her wrist, the reality star was wearing a diamond-encrusted Gucci watch that had probably cost close to five grand. She had probably forgotten what it was like to earn just enough to get by, so that fifty quid was not the cost of a couple of quick cocktails in a West End club but the difference between paying the gas bill and being cut off, or the difference between paying your rent or having to move back in with your parents.

Emily wished she had the guts to ask Carina for a favour.

If Carina would agree to plug The New Beauty Spot again then the customers would come rushing back. But Emily decided she couldn't ask. She would have to wait for Carina to offer her help.

When her manicure was finished, Carina disappeared into Natalie's treatment room for an aromatherapy facial.

Emily was glad that Carina approved of Natalie's skills, but she found herself feeling strangely unnerved whenever she heard the laughter that escaped from Natalie's treatment room while Carina was in there. They sounded like a couple of schoolgirls driving each other into more and more hysterical giggling. She had to turn the whale music up to cover it. Hearing them laugh made Emily blush, as though they were laughing about her. Which was ridiculous. Why on earth would they be doing that? Still, Emily found it hard to concentrate on her own work while Carina was in the booth next door.

'I swear,' Carina said on her way out of the salon, 'this girl,' she pointed at Natalie, 'is a miracle worker.'

Natalie beamed.

Certainly it seemed that Carina could work miracles on Natalie. Later that afternoon, Natalie took a moment to slick back her unruly hair into a neatish ponytail and asked Chloe if she would help her tidy up her nails.

'Carina hinted that I've been letting things slip,' she explained. 'And there can be no slacking on the road to your dreams. You alright, Em?' she asked suddenly. 'You're looking a bit stressed out. Still thinking about the Man-tenance thing?'

Emily shook her head but she knew she wasn't fooling anybody.

'You've got to stop worrying about it,' said Natalie. 'Tomorrow will bring something different, I promise.'

30

Natalie was right. The next day did indeed bring something different. But it was hardly a welcome development.

Emily knew the moment she turned the corner into Longbury Road that something was not quite right. When she got within twelve feet of The Beauty Spot, she knew for certain. She could see that the salon door was not quite shut. When she got right up to it, she saw furthermore that it had been *kicked* open.

They'd been burgled.

Emily felt short of breath. She slumped down onto the pavement outside the salon and had to wait, sitting on her bag, until Natalie arrived before she dared go inside. When they went inside together, Emily's suspicions were immediately confirmed.

'Oh, Em!' cried Natalie. She even tried to shade poor Emily's eyes from the scene that greeted them. The hat stand had been knocked over. The magazine table had been upturned, scattering glossies all over the floor. The beautiful jasmine plant that Emily had tended so carefully had been swept from its place on the windowsill onto the floor. The ceramic pot the plant lived in was broken, spilling dirt onto the white painted floorboards.

The PC that usually stood on the reception desk was gone, of course, leaving nothing but a square outline in the dust. The till drawer built into the reception desk, precisely so no one could lift it up and carry it off, had been forced open and ransacked. Fortunately, there had been little inside but some loose change and several gift vouchers.

Emily started to cry again.

'Wait outside,' Natalie instructed her. 'You can't take any more of this. You're in shock.'

While Emily obediently waited outside on the pavement with her head in her hands, Natalie bravely headed for the treatment rooms armed with a huge golf umbrella left behind by a client.

Seconds later Natalie was back. White faced.

'You really don't want to go in there,' she said.

'Is it . . . ?'

'A mess,' Natalie nodded. 'There's hot wax all over my couch.'

'What have they taken?'

'I can't tell,' said Natalie. 'Everything's on the floor.'

Emily grimaced.

'Did they leave anything extra?' she asked cautiously.

Natalie dropped her eyes. She knew what Emily was thinking. They'd both read a recent report in the local paper about a burglar who liked to leave an all-too-human 'calling card' to add insult to the injury of nicking his victim's valuables.

'Oh no,' Emily's face took on the expression of a tragedy mask.

'No. It's OK. There was nothing extra,' Natalie promised.

'Well, I suppose that's a small mercy,' Emily said. 'I can't believe this has happened. I always close this place up so carefully.'

'No amount of care on your part was going to stop someone with a crowbar,' said Natalie, as she inspected the splintered wood of the doorframe.

'I can't believe that someone would be so . . .' Emily paused. 'Wicked.'

'People can be very cruel,' Natalie agreed.

* * *

Emily was still in shock. It was Natalie who took control and called the police while Chloe sat with Emily in the staff room and made her a cup of tea.

Within minutes a police car was drawing up outside the salon. Natalie walked Constable Garfield, their local community officer, around the premises, and with his help she produced an inventory of missing items. Surprisingly, the burglars had not taken much. The treatment rooms were a mess but valuable items of equipment such as the electrolysis machine had been overlooked. The expensive aromatherapy products were still safely tucked away inside the storage cupboards.

'It's just the computer and the cash,' said Natalie at the end of Constable Garfield's tour of the crime scene.

'No,' said Chloe. 'I can think of one more thing.'

The old black appointments book from the original salon was gone.

Constable Garfield didn't seem to see the significance, though Natalie understood at once. That old appointments book was more than a diary. It contained the names and numbers of everyone who had ever stepped through the door. It was the original customer database. Kathy had been saying for months that she would transfer all the information it held onto the computer, but she'd never had the time. And anyway the computer had been taken too.

Natalie seized on this new turn in events like Sherlock Holmes. 'The burglar must have been someone who knows what that book is worth,' she told Constable Garfield. 'So I think you should start by questioning all the local salon owners.'

'Nah,' said Constable Garfield. 'You're making it too complicated. There's been a spate of burglaries around here. Got to be the same chap. We already have someone under surveillance.'

'You mean the one who . . .' Emily couldn't bring herself to say the word.

'That's the fella.'

'But we didn't find his calling card here. Which suggests to me that our man isn't the same burglar at all. I'm telling you,' said Natalie, 'this has the hallmark of a burglary done to order.'

Constable Garfield still wasn't convinced. 'The missing appointments book is a red herring. Whoever it was probably just came in here and swept everything off the desk into a bin-liner. They didn't know what they were taking.'

'The appointments book wasn't on the desk,' said Natalie. 'It was kept in a drawer.'

'Alright then,' said Constable Garfield, clearly growing ratty. 'They opened a drawer and swept the contents of that drawer out into a bin-liner.'

'But that's clearly not what happened . . .'

Chloe put her hand on Natalie's arm and pulled her away from the policeman. Emily stepped forward.

'Thank you, Constable Garfield,' she said. 'We're all just a bit shocked.'

His face softened.

'I understand. We'll catch whoever did this,' he promised her. 'Don't you worry yourself.'

'I'm not so sure,' said Natalie, behind his back. 'Not if he doesn't follow up all the clues.'

31

The next week was chaos. Without the computer, the girls had no idea who was supposed to be coming in and when. It made it impossible to set up the treatment rooms properly. And, of course, it was impossible for anyone to take a proper break in case they missed a client.

The customers didn't seem to mind but Emily felt embarrassed. She was sure they must be irritated when they had to fill out their details for the database again.

And, gradually, Emily became more unsettled about the loss of the appointments book. Natalie was right. A secondhand computer was worth next to nothing. Maybe fifty quid if the burglar got lucky. But the old appointments book was very valuable indeed, to someone who knew what to do with it. Slowly, Emily had come to share Natalie's view. Constable Garfield was wrong. She was increasingly concerned that the salon had been robbed to order and that, right now, some other salon owner was sending out special offers to all Emily's clients. Whereas, without her computer or the addresses and numbers in the appointments book, Emily most definitely could not.

Emily went through a list of the other salons in Blountford in her mind. It had to be someone local. Not much point having a list of clients in the Blountford area if your salon wasn't within a couple of miles.

Over tea and biscuits at break-time, Natalie helped Emily with her hypothetical investigations.

'Have you made any enemies?' Natalie asked dramatically. Emily shook her head. 'No.'

'You say that,' said Natalie, 'but I think I saw the woman who owns Me-Time looking in through the window the other day. She's got a mean face if you want my opinion. And her eyes are very close together.'

'I don't think that's enough to get a conviction,' said Chloe.

Emily nodded, but inwardly she couldn't help but agree with Natalie. That woman from Me-Time *did* have a mean look about her. She had been polite enough when she and Emily were introduced at a local business networking night, but she wasn't exactly what you would call friendly. And, since moving premises, Emily was even more directly her rival. Their salons were closer together now. The big New Beauty Spot had to be hurting Me-Time's business. The woman from Me-Time had every reason to hope that The New Beauty Spot would fail.

'Or how about Herr Kutz?' suggested Natalie. 'When I was in there the other day, I overheard Malcolm the head stylist telling a customer that they were planning to convert one of their back rooms into a treatment room for facials and the like. Our client list would be very useful to them.'

'Malcolm definitely has criminal connections,' said Chloe, suddenly perking up. 'I once heard him say he met someone who knew Ronnie Biggs on the Costa Del Sol.'

'Oh my God,' said Natalie. 'Then he would have had no trouble arranging a burglary.'

'Everyone who's ever been to the Costa Del Sol claims to have met someone who knows Ronnie Biggs,' Emily reminded them.

She hated the thought that her salon had been deliberately targeted. It was bad enough that The Beauty Spot had been burgled at all. The odd theft was a fact of life for most shop owners. Some might think she had been lucky to get so far without being hit. Industrial espionage, however . . .

* * *

That night Emily took a circuitous route home that took her by Me-Time and Herr Kutz. It so happened that, as Emily was passing by, Maria of Me-Time was locking up her own salon for the night. Seeing Emily approaching, Maria nodded curtly.

'How's it going?' she asked in a tone that made it clear she wasn't bothered about the answer.

'You might want to think about improving your security system,' said Emily. 'The Beauty Spot has just been burgled.'

Maria paused in her lock-up routine.

'No,' she said. 'That's terrible. What did they take?'

'The computer. Some cash. Luckily the till was pretty much empty.'

Maria nodded sympathetically. 'That is lucky.'

'They also took our old appointments book.'

As she said that, Emily watched Maria closely for any hint of a guilty reaction.

'What would they want that for?' Maria asked.

'That's what I thought, but Natalie, who works for me, said that she'd heard of that kind of thing before. She thinks it might have been stolen to order by someone who wanted access to our client list.'

'Blimey,' said Maria. 'Do people really do that?'

'Apparently so,' scowled Emily.

'In that case, I'm glad I just backed up my client list on the computer. I keep it on here as well.'

She showed Emily the little silver flash-drive that dangled from her key ring. 'Don't you have one of these?'

'No,' said Emily tightly. 'I don't.'

'You want to get one,' said Maria. 'I'm sorry to hear about your trouble, Emily. I hope they catch the buggers. I really do.'

Maria finished locking up her business and gave Emily a little wave 'goodbye'.

Emily wasn't sure what to think of the exchange. Maria hadn't looked guilty when Emily mentioned the appointments book. Likewise, when Emily passed his salon a few minutes later, Malcolm from Herr Kutz didn't look the least bit shifty. In fact, he abandoned a client and raced out onto the pavement, scissors and comb still in hand, to talk to her.

'Constable Garfield dropped by for a short back and sides and told me all about your burglary,' said Malcolm, laying a hand on Emily's shoulder in a gesture of perfect concern. 'How are you bearing up, my love? It leaves you with the most terrible sense of violation, doesn't it? When my flat was burgled last year, I couldn't sleep there alone for six months. It was a terribly difficult time. Not least because I didn't have a boyfriend and I had to find someone new to bring home every night!' He laughed at the memory. 'Anyway, sweet pea, I just want you to know that I'm there for you. If there's any way at all I can help, you let me know. If you find out who nicked your stuff and you want them taken out, I could call up that gangster I met in the Costa Del Sol.'

'Thanks, Malcolm. But I think I'll let the police handle the case.'

'Tchah!' Malcolm rolled his eyes. 'Constable Garfield is an absolute sweetie but he's no Inspector Morse, my dear.'

Alas, Emily had to agree.

'Remember, if there's anything I can do . . .'

Malcolm kissed Emily on both cheeks and scuttled back inside Herr Kutz to finish attending to a trim.

If Malcolm had ordered the burglary, he was pretty bloody blasé about it, thought Emily. He would have to be a psychopath to find it in him to be so friendly if he had been involved.

* * *

A few days later, Constable Garfield dropped into The Beauty Spot while making his rounds of the area. He accepted a cup of tea and a milk chocolate HobNob but, alas, he admitted, he was no nearer to solving the crime than he had been the last time he popped in.

'There are so many fingerprints in a place like this,' he explained. 'It's next to impossible to narrow the suspects down.'

'You could start by working out who might have something to gain from our contact list,' Natalie said again.

'I've ruled out that line of inquiry,' Garfield told her.

'How?' Natalie insisted. 'The way I see it, it's the only real line of inquiry you have.'

Constable Garfield blushed.

'It's OK, Nat,' said Emily. 'I'm sure Constable Garfield knows what he's doing. The insurance will pay out.' The last thing Emily wanted was for Natalie to get arrested for harassing a cop. Though, as far as she could tell, Constable Garfield did his utmost to avoid arresting anybody. Especially if it was nearing the end of his shift and the paperwork might take him into unpaid overtime.

Two weeks after the burglary, Emily was starting to get over it. The salon had been fitted with a new front door with a very complicated locking mechanism – one that would have outfoxed Houdini. The insurance company had confirmed that they would pay for a new computer and for repairs to the cash box. It was time to start counting her blessings again, Emily decided. Things were just things. No one had been hurt. The missing appointments book had no significance. Natalie's idea that it had been stolen to order was the result of an overactive imagination. She watched way too many police procedural shows. Emily decided she was satisfied that the burglars had no motive other than to take what they could carry and use the resulting cash to buy drugs. She should only feel sorry for the kind of people who had no greater ambition than finding their next fix.

It didn't matter if the burglars were never caught. Really, Emily told herself, it didn't.

32

Chloe Jones, Emily's colleague from the very beginning, had always been as interested in fashion as she was in beauty. Whenever she had a spare moment, she could be found poring over the fashion magazines that the salon provided for waiting clients. She was *au fait* with every hip designer, every hot new boutique, every trend from bubble skirts to turbans.

'Not that I can afford to keep up with them,' she moaned.

Chloe had been moaning about the amount of money she *wasn't* making quite a bit recently. Emily had promised that she would do her best to find a decent pay rise for her longest-serving staff member but, for the time being, with the new salon still in its infancy, there was very little to spare. Chloe claimed she understood. She said that she was happy with the status quo. She knew that Emily would reward her loyalty as soon as she could and, in the meantime, it wasn't as though Emily was swanning round in Jimmy Choos and driving a new Mercedes.

So Emily was quite surprised when Chloe came back from a shopping spree one lunchtime carrying not a bag from her usual haunts – New Look or Topshop – but a swanky, rope-handled, stiff cardboard bag from Diva, the expensive new boutique that had recently opened in the mini shopping complex that had once been the town library.

The coveted black bag with its gold-embossed lettering immediately drew the attention of the other girls, who wanted to know, at once, what Chloe had been buying.

'Just some jeans,' she said, putting the bag underneath the counter without letting anybody see inside.

'What kind of jeans?' asked Natalie. She wasn't about to let Chloe get away with that.

'Straight ones,' said Chloe.

'What brand?'

'They're just jeans,' said Chloe, leaving the bag unopened as she took off her coat.

'Are they Sass and Bide?' Natalie asked. 'Citizens? Rock and Republic?'

'They're Sevens,' said Chloe eventually.

'Were they in the sale?'

Chloe looked at the floor. She blushed. Chloe wasn't a girl who blushed easily.

'They weren't in the sale!' Natalie translated.

'No. They weren't.'

Natalie's eyes grew wide.

'Let me see them.'

'I want to see them too,' said Nina.

'And me,' said Emily.

Chloe reluctantly pulled the jeans out of the bag. They had been carefully wrapped in tissue paper, fastened with a small gold sticker that was also embossed with the familiar Diva logo. She unpicked the sticker carefully, as though she were planning to save it.

It was actually Emily who shook the jeans out, pretending to look at the cut, but secretly much more interested in the price tag. One hundred and fifty pounds! One hundred and fifty pounds? For a pair of jeans? This was quite a departure from Chloe's usual shopping habits. Emily knew what Chloe was paid, of course, and very much doubted that her tips would have allowed her to upgrade to a pair of jeans that cost more than a week's rent on Chloe's studio flat.

Emily handed the jeans to Natalie, who also went straight for the price tag. As did Nina. As did Kathy.

'Very nice,' said Natalie, raising an eyebrow.

Kathy handed the jeans to Chloe who frowned and stuffed them back into the bag.

'Do you mind if I get on with my work now?' Chloe asked.

'I think I know what you're thinking,' said Natalie when Chloe was back at work and she and Emily were alone at the front desk.

'What?'

'You're thinking it's strange that Chloe has got money to spend on designer jeans all of a sudden.'

'I'm sorry.'

'I saw the look on your face, Em. You're wondering where she got the money from.'

Emily shook her head. 'I wasn't thinking that at all. Is that what you thought I was thinking?'

Natalie nodded.

'Well, I admit I think that more than fifty quid is too much to spend on denim, but . . .'

Natalie nodded again. 'You're right. It is way too much. Chloe doesn't usually have that kind of cash to spare. And so you're wondering where the money came from, right?'

'No,' Emily lied.

'You're wondering if someone gave her a really big tip in return for her services?'

'No. Natalie, you're being weird. What are you getting at?'

'I'm not getting at anything. But there's no need to hide what you really thought when you saw that bag from me. Where did she find the cash?'

Natalie didn't need to say anything more.

'Chloe has been with me from the very beginning!' Emily

protested at the unspoken implication. 'She wouldn't do that to me.'

'Even Jesus had to lash himself to a rock in the face of temptation,' said Natalie. 'You know how hard it is, seeing all these yummy mummies with nothing to do all day but have facials and go shopping. They come in here, flashing their money around. They've got wardrobes full of jeans that cost more than a week's rent. I can see why Chloe might think she deserves something more. So if someone offered her some money in return for something as simple as—'

'You really think she arranged the burglary?'

'I'm not saying that as such . . . . Perhaps the door wasn't properly locked,' said Natalie. 'Can you remember exactly who locked the salon up that night?'

Emily's brow wrinkled as she thought back to two weeks ago. 'Well, I thought it was me but—'

'Though if you were going to arrange for somewhere to be burgled, you wouldn't actually need to leave it unlocked. You could just get a set of keys cut . . .'

'The top lock was busted open,' said Emily.

'The bottom lock wasn't.'

'You're right!' Emily exclaimed. 'That was weird!'

Suddenly Emily's mouth dropped open, as if shocked by the thought that had just hit her.

'What is it?' Natalie asked excitedly.

'There was a day a couple of weeks ago when Chloe arrived at work without her keys . . .'

'I remember that,' said Natalie. 'Where do you think those keys were?'

'I left them on my kitchen table. Like I said I did.'

Neither Natalie nor Emily had noticed that Chloe had walked into the reception and was standing right behind them.

'The CD player in my room keeps skipping,' she explained. 'So I turned it off. And I heard everything you said.'

Emily's hand flew to her mouth as though to contain the words that had already done their damage.

'Thanks very much, is all I can say. Is that what you think, Emily? That I would take money to help someone steal your client book?'

'No! No!' Emily said at once. 'I didn't . . . It was just—'

'You've got to admit it's strange,' Natalie jumped in. 'One minute you're complaining you're completely skint like the rest of us. The next minute, we've been burgled and you've got a new pair of jeans. Jeans that cost hundreds of pounds! It's quite a coincidence.'

'How about this for a coincidence?' said Chloe. 'Last Thursday was my birthday. My gran, my mum and dad and my brother all chipped in to buy me the pair of jeans I have wanted for approximately eighteen months and this lunchtime I went to pick them up.'

Emily closed her eyes in shame. She had forgotten all about Chloe's birthday.

'Last Thursday?' she echoed.

'Yes. I turned twenty-five.'

'And you got the jeans.'

'I got the jeans.'

'Oh Chloe,' Emily cried. 'Can you forgive me?'

'I had no idea it was your birthday,' said Natalie, somewhat indignantly.

'Yeah, well, I might have mentioned it, but since it fell on the day that the salon got burgled, I didn't think it would be particularly appropriate to make a fuss.'

'Chloe, I am so sorry,' said Emily. 'We didn't even get you a card. We'll go for a drink after work tonight, eh? To celebrate.' She reached out to touch Chloe's arm. Chloe didn't exactly shake it off, but she didn't call for a quick group hug either.

'I can't go for a drink tonight,' she said. 'I'm busy.'

'Tomorrow then?' Emily tried.

'Perhaps.'

'What doesn't make sense to me is why you tried to hide the jeans when you came into the salon,' Natalie persisted.

'It's not because I bought them with blood money!' Chloe exploded. 'Didn't it occur to you that I hid them because I was slightly embarrassed by how expensive they were? It *is* an extravagance and I didn't want to have to justify it to the rest of you. But I wanted a pair of jeans that would make my bum look good and a hundred and fifty pounds is what they cost. That's all.' Her voice trembled. She started to well up. 'Now, I hope you're both happy,' she said. 'You've completely ruined my special treat.' She pulled the jeans out from beneath the counter and shook them in Natalie's face. 'I'm going to take these bloody things back to the shop. Alright?'

'Do what you want,' said Natalie coolly.

Emily was horrified.

'No, Chloe, don't do that!' she pleaded. 'You've wanted them for ages.'

'And I don't want them any more. Now, if you'll excuse me, my client is waiting,' she said. 'I'd keep your voices down in future. Noise travels in this place.'

Emily didn't find herself alone with Chloe for the rest of that day. Chloe left for the night before Emily finished treating her final client. On the way home from the salon, Emily dropped into the newsagent and bought a belated birthday card and a box of Roses chocolates. The following morning, Chloe opened the card in front of her and managed a wan smile when she read the message of congratulation and apology. Emily dared to think that perhaps she had been forgiven.

But at the end of the day, Chloe asked for a quiet word,

and the second she heard the request, Emily knew that the news was not going to be good.

'I'm going to come straight out with it,' said Chloe. 'I'm leaving.'

Emily dropped one of the mugs she'd been carrying into the empty sink. The handle fell off.

'You're what?'

'I'm leaving, Em. I've decided I don't want to work here any more.'

'But . . .'

'When I first started working with you, it was such a laugh. We used to have a good time, you and me. But I've seen a different side to you over the last few weeks. I know you've always been the boss, but back in the old days, it didn't feel like it. You never made me feel like I wasn't your equal in the salon.'

'That's because we are equals,' said Emily.

'Yeah. Right.' Chloe shrugged. 'I never thought you would talk about me behind my back. I thought we were friends. Proper friends. I thought you trusted me. To think it even crossed your mind that I would nick the appointments book and betray our friendship for a hundred and fifty quid.'

'You've got to understand I was confused. Natalie and I were just thinking out loud. I didn't know who to trust.'

'Well, if you don't know to trust me after everything we've been through together since this place opened, then that's pretty sad for both of us.'

'I do trust you. I promise I never really believed what Natalie was suggesting. And even she was just throwing thoughts out there, I'm sure. She didn't mean it. Don't go,' said Emily. 'I'll put your wages up,' she added.

'You can't afford to put my wages up,' said Chloe sadly. 'I know what the takings have been since the Man-tenance disaster. Look, it'll be better this way. There isn't enough work for four therapists here. With me gone, you, Nina and Natalie will have enough clients to do pretty much a full day each. You won't have to worry about finding my wages.'

'But I want to worry about finding your wages! I want you to stay!'

'My mind is made up. I know I should probably work out some notice, but I'd rather not come in again if that's alright with you.'

Emily's shoulders slumped. She knew that Chloe was not about to change her mind.

'I'm sorry things have turned out this way,' said Emily. She opened her arms for a hug. Chloe didn't step into them.

'I'm sorry too,' said Chloe. 'I really am. You're a good person and I wish you luck.'

Chloe handed Emily her neatly folded overall and her keys.

'Of course, I haven't made any copies,' she said with reference to the keys. 'Just one more thing . . .'

'What is it?'

'If I were you, Emily, I would keep a close eye on Natalie. I don't think she's quite the naive kind-hearted girl you think she is.'

'Of course she said that,' Natalie snorted when Emily relayed Chloe's accusation. 'You know what it looks like to me? It looks like Chloe has been offered big money to sell you out. Why else would she be happy to leave without working out her notice? Wake up, Emily! It's because she doesn't need the money. She could easily get a couple of grand as a sign-on bonus for taking your entire client list to another salon.'

'Do you think so?'

'Oh yes. I mean, I can almost understand it. She saw how things have been getting here – losing a lot of custom – and she started to fear for her job. In the same circumstances, wouldn't you be tempted by a nice lump sum for going else-where?'

Emily couldn't help but nod.

'She's like a rat leaving a sinking ship.'

'Do you think The Beauty Spot is sinking?' Emily asked in distress.

Natalie's eyes widened. 'Oh, Emily. Of course I don't! I have every faith in you. I can see the bigger picture.' She gestured as though drawing Emily's attention to that bigger picture. 'Trust me, Em, I'm with you till the very end.'

33

Emily was miserable that evening and for the next few days. Either Chloe really had betrayed her, as Natalie insisted was the case, or Emily had thrown away Chloe's friendship. Whatever the truth of the matter, it was not a happy situation.

Neither were things improving. Emily simply couldn't understand why The New Beauty Spot was experiencing such a sudden and dramatic downturn in the number of clients. Whereas previously clients had to make appointments weeks in advance, now there were days in the diary where the girls had nothing to do but file their own nails for hours on end.

Emily called a staff meeting. Matt and Cesar attended.

Natalie suggested that they line up some more special offers.

'Maybe it's because interest rates have gone up,' she said. 'With bigger mortgage payments, people can't afford to spend money on treats like they used to. But I'd rather work for half my usual fee than not work at all.'

Natalie further suggested that they take out another advertisement in the local press, but Emily was concerned that even that might be too expensive.

It was almost a relief when Nina quit. She had gone back to Poland for a holiday, but called two days before she was due to return to the salon to say that she and her boyfriend had decided to try to make a life for themselves in Krakow rather than continue to live in a hovel in Essex. The weather wasn't any better, Nina joked, but at least they would be able to swing a cat while they had to stay indoors.

Kathy followed soon afterwards. She'd been offered a better hourly rate as a receptionist for a building company.

'I'd rather be here,' she told Emily. 'But I've got to go for the money. The kids seem to need something new every week!'

And so The Beauty Spot was down to just two staff again. Just Emily and Natalie. Whenever both girls were busy giving treatments, the front door of the salon had to be locked shut to safeguard the till, which meant that anyone who wanted to walk in and make an appointment could only do so in the brief periods when the desk was manned. Likewise, all phone calls now went straight to answer-machine. Emily had recorded what she hoped was an upbeat message, asking clients to leave their name and number so that she could call them back, but she could tell by the number of messages that began with the click of a phone being put down that customers were turning away. Her clients had become used to the convenience of getting straight through to a full-time receptionist and thus being able to plan their beauty treat the moment the notion popped into their heads.

The gaps in the diary grew bigger.

'It's going to be OK,' Natalie assured her. 'It's a bit quiet now because the school holidays have started. That's all. As soon as the kids are back at school, the yummy mummies will be back in the salon.'

But the kids went back to school and the yummy mummies continued to stay away. Not even the approach of the summer brought the usual influx of women keen to depilate and exfoliate before they swapped their opaque tights for fake tan.

Still, Natalie remained optimistic.

'It's been a bad summer so far,' she said. 'But the weather forecast is for a brilliant September, so we'll make up for this quiet time then.'

* * *

Matt wasn't quite such a Pollyanna, but he too tried to persuade Emily that there was no need to despair. He went through her books for her again, looking at every single item of expenditure, ensuring that she wasn't paying over the odds for anything. He helped her to switch the salon's utility bills so that they were as low as possible. He suggested that the Jacuzzi and sauna were kept out of operation for a while. Not much point having them burning up electricity while there was no one to use them. And at last he persuaded her to source cheaper beauty products, reasoning that she could still offer the full organic aromatherapy experience but at a slightly higher price.

'Research suggests that people are actually happier to pay higher prices,' he informed her quite seriously. 'I read something about it in the *Economist*. It makes them think they're getting something really special. You can even lower the prices on your other facials if you like. I bet you your customers will go for the most expensive.'

Emily agreed to give it a shot but her face betrayed her unhappiness.

Matt longed to take her in his arms and give her a hug but, every time he thought of that, the memory of Emily passing his roses straight to her gran popped into his mind. She didn't want the roses. She definitely didn't want him to give her a hug.

'You'll be fine,' he said instead.

One customer who had remained absolutely loyal to The Beauty Spot was Carina Lees.

'I think your friend Matt is right about putting your prices up,' she said, while Emily gave her a pedicure. 'Doesn't mean you have to do anything different. It's all about image, isn't it? See these shoes? They cost me the best part of five hundred quid and they rub my feet the same as any fifteen-pound pair would do.'

'That'll be because you keep your feet so soft,' said Emily. 'You've got no hard skin to protect you. They look lovely though.'

'They do, don't they?' said Carina, stretching out her right foot so that she could admire it and accidentally kicking Emily in the chin as she did so. 'Whoops!' she apologized. 'I'm sorry.'

'It's OK,' said Emily, sitting back on her pedicure stool and holding the bridge of her nose in an attempt to stop the tears. 'That happens all the time. Especially if you're exfoliating someone ticklish.'

'In that case I won't feel so guilty,' she said. 'Is Natalie ready for me yet?'

These days Carina always booked her facial treatments with Natalie. Emily had been relegated to nails alone.

'You'll be alright,' Carina promised Emily with a light squeeze on the shoulder. 'Things will start looking up. They always do. You'll get what you deserve in life,' she added.

Then she disappeared with Natalie. Hearing their laughter punctuating a conversation she wasn't in on, Emily finally succumbed to the tears that had been welling up since Carina accidentally booted her in the chin.

34

A few days later, Emily visited her parents' house for Sunday lunch. She told them about the worrying downturn in business since the new salon opened. They were concerned for her, of course, and did their best to cheer her up. Emily told them how hard Natalie had been working and how supportive Matt had been.

'Then you should do something nice for them,' said Emily's mum. 'Make sure that they know they're appreciated. Besides,' she added, 'doing something for somebody else will help take your mind off your problems.'

By the end of that afternoon with her parents, Emily felt much lighter. They always offered her good advice. She spent a couple of happy hours looking through her father's cookery books (her mother hated to cook) and decided that a dinner party would be the perfect way to let Matt and Natalie know that she was grateful for their continued support. A much-needed morale boost. She asked Natalie first thing in the morning, then she called Matt.

'Of course,' she said, 'I'll understand if you're too busy.'

'No,' said Matt. 'I mean, I'll make a space in my diary. I'd love to.'

The date was set for the following Thursday.

Even the prospect of a day at the office could not dampen Matt's spirits that Thursday morning. Emily had finally invited him to her house. They had known each other for almost two years, but this was the first time she had ever

asked to see him outside the beauty salon after hours. And
she was going to cook for him. Matt recalled a conversation
he had overheard in the men's room at work. Two of the
younger guys were discussing their love lives.

'She's invited me over to her place for dinner,' said one.

'You know what that means?' said the other.

'No. What does it mean?'

'It means she wants to get it on! You're in there, mate.
Don't forget your condoms.'

Matt blushed with guilt as he replayed the conversation
with Emily in mind.

'Well, Cesar,' he said. 'I think we're going to have to get
you a new collar.'

Emily began to prepare for her dinner party the moment she
decided to throw one. Together with her father she had chosen
a three-course menu. They would start with filo-wrapped
prawns (she checked that neither of her guests was allergic,
of course). After that, lamb with minted potatoes. For dessert,
a pavlova. She made the meringues the night before. They
were more like cowpats than the fluffy white tutu layers in
the cookery book, but she was sure they would taste fine.

To go with the food, she sourced the perfect wine. Well,
as perfect as you could buy in the off-licence at the top of
her street, which specialized in bottles for less than a fiver
called names like 'Cat's Pee Pinot' and 'I Can't Believe It's
Not Chardonnay'.

On the day of the dinner party itself, Emily shut the salon
at half past four (it was hardly as though they were turning
away custom, alas) and raced home to finish cooking. She set
the table using the linen she had inherited from her great-
aunt. All that was left after that was to prepare herself.

Emily pulled out the little black dress she'd bought for the
launch of her first tiny salon. It hadn't had much wear since.

The woman in the shop had said that it was the 'perfect date dress'. Over two years later, there had been no time for the perfect date.

'Ah well,' thought Emily as she pulled it on. At least it still fitted.

Half a mile away, Matt was preparing for that evening's dinner party with equal diligence. He had spent the previous evening trying to decide what to wear. He'd pulled everything out of his wardrobe and laid it across his bed. Emily had rarely seen him in anything but a suit. It was easy to get dressed for work. The only possible room for error was in choice of tie or socks. But casual dressing was a minefield. How casual should he go? Chinos? Chambray shirt? Should he wear a jacket? Were jeans appropriate? He longed to ask the lad in his office what one wore to have dinner at a girl's house, but decided that they would take the mickey and perhaps even stitch him up.

Matt decided on a pair of black jeans (not even slightly faded since he always got his jeans dry-cleaned) and a casual pink shirt. On his feet, a pair of shoes by Prada that weren't quite trainers but were cooler than the 'school shoes' he wore for work.

By lunchtime on the day of the dinner party, he decided that he had chosen the wrong outfit altogether. He dashed out to Ted Baker and bought himself a different shirt. This one was stripy, silky, slightly more festive. It showed he'd made more of an effort, he thought.

Matt's lunchtime panic was rewarded.

'You look really lovely,' said Emily as she opened the door to him. It wouldn't be until much later that evening that Matt noticed he had neglected to remove the sticky label that announced he was a size large.

But for the moment he was happy. Emily had appreciated his outfit and it was clear that she had made an effort too. It hadn't occurred to him until then that, apart from at the launch of The New Beauty Spot, he had never seen her in anything but her overalls. Now here she was in a dress. A beautiful little black dress of the kind Audrey Hepburn wore in *Breakfast At Tiffany's*. It was the sort of classy dress Matt always imagined when he thought about the sort of girl he would marry.

'You look nice too,' he said.

'Thank you,' Emily smiled. 'Shall I take your jacket?'

Matt followed her into the house, wishing he had managed a slightly more poetic compliment. 'Nice' was rubbish. 'Nice' was the kind of thing you said when you couldn't think of anything *really* positive. He wondered what the guys at work would have said in the same position.

Cesar was much more at home. He charged ahead into the kitchen and set about sniffing out this new territory. Matt was very glad that Cesar was well trained enough not to have to mark it, though he was embarrassingly interested in the flip-top Brabantia bin.

'I didn't know whether or not you would have fed Cesar, so I bought him this,' said Emily, going into the fridge and bringing out a steak. 'How does he like it cooked?'

'Wow. I don't think he's ever had steak,' said Matt.

'Then I'll just sear it on both sides. Wine?'

'Oh no. No need to cook it in wine. That'll give him the squits.'

'I meant for you. To drink.'

'Oh. Yes.' Matt nodded.

'Red or white?'

'Whatever's open?'

'I'll open whatever you choose.'

'Well, what are you cooking?'

182

The house smelled delicious.

'Prawns, then lamb. And garlic bread for you to eat while we're waiting,' Emily explained, 'for Natalie.'

Matt's heart sank as though someone had cut the strings to its parachute.

'Oh,' he said, 'I didn't know she was coming.'

'Didn't I mention it?'

She hadn't.

'I wanted to cook something special for the pair of you,' she explained. 'To show how much I appreciate all the support you've given me over the past few months.'

Emily led Matt through into the sitting room where the little round dining table was indeed set for three.

'It'll be nice to see Natalie outside the salon,' said Matt.

Even Cesar seemed disappointed.

Cesar managed a desultory wag of the tail when Natalie walked into the room. Emily recognized the outfit her friend was wearing at once. It was the skirt and top combo she had been dressed in for her *Wakey-Wakey* makeover. She was even wearing the shoes, though she took them off the moment she stepped over the threshold.

'Feet are killing me,' she explained. 'How do people walk in these all the time?'

She sat down on the sofa and rubbed at her stockinged toes. Cesar chanced a sniff in the direction of her feet. Natalie scowled at him.

'Hey, Matt. How's it going? Nice shirt,' she added.

'Thanks.'

He poured her a glass of wine.

'What's up with this?' she said, looking at the glass in disgust. 'I'm not driving. Fill it up to the top.'

Matt obliged. Natalie drained half the glass in one long gulp and held it out for more.

'I should go and put the prawns on,' said Emily, disappearing into the kitchen.

'Can I help?' Matt called after her hopefully.

'It's all under control,' she assured him. 'You and Natalie can just chat and relax.'

Relax? That wasn't the first word that came to mind when Matt thought of Natalie. Though they had met each other on several occasions and she no longer jumped onto a chair every time Cesar walked into the salon, Natalie hadn't exactly warmed to Matt or his dog. She could usually be relied upon to say something slightly snide. Still, Matt knew he had to make an effort. He couldn't ignore the only other guest at the dinner party. And if he wanted to make a good impression on Emily, then it was important to be the perfect guest – and that meant making witty conversation.

'How was your day?' he began.

'Alright,' said Natalie. 'How about you?'

'Alright.'

There was silence. Then Matt had a unwitting stroke of genius.

'Did you watch the rugby last weekend?'

'I get goosebumps when they play my national anthem.'

'I don't know it,' said Matt.

'Then I'll sing it for you,' Natalie replied.

In the kitchen, Emily smiled to herself as she heard Natalie break into song. That meant that all would be well. Her guests were relaxed. The prawns were done to perfection. The lamb too would be a triumph. And the pavlova . . .

'I could live on pavlova . . .' Natalie announced. 'And white wine.' She poured herself another glass. By half past ten, she was well into her second bottle.

* * *

At eleven o'clock, Emily yawned quite ostentatiously and commented on the early morning she had ahead of her. Matt recognized the 'closing time' signals at once.

'I should get going,' he said.

'Really?' said Emily. 'It's not that late.'

'It is,' he said. Emily rewarded him with a grateful nod.

'I'll call you a taxi,' said Emily. 'Shall I call one for you too?' she asked Natalie.

'Nah,' said Natalie. 'No need. I'll walk.'

'You can't walk home at this time of night.'

'I won't be on my own. Matt can take me.'

Matt hadn't counted on that. He looked at Cesar. Cesar looked up at him as though he didn't relish the idea of walking Natalie home either. Matt started to formulate an excuse. They lived in opposite directions, didn't they? And he had a very early meeting to prepare for, too. He would, of course, be perfectly happy to give Natalie the cash to take a taxi instead.

'Would you?' Emily interrupted Matt's excuse-making process. 'Only,' she added with a whisper, 'she's a little the worse for wear and I would never forgive myself if she didn't get home in one piece.'

When Emily looked at him with those big soft eyes of hers, there was nothing Matt could do but agree.

'I'll make sure she gets home safely,' he said gallantly. As though no other thought had ever crossed his mind.

'Thank you,' said Emily.

'Let's go, Lover-boy,' said Natalie, lurching to her feet.

Matt tried to help Natalie put on her coat. In her drunken state she kept missing the armholes. It was like wrestling with an octopus.

Afterwards, alone in her kitchen with only the washing-up for company, Emily thought about her life. It was at moments like this that she felt especially lonely. She'd spent the evening with friends. There had been good food, faintly drinkable wine and laughter.

But the warmth of the evening soon vanished. How nice it would have been to be washing up with her lover, dissecting the evening together, rehashing the conversation and reliving the jokes. Then she found her thoughts wandering towards Matt. He'd looked especially great that night. She hoped he'd had a good time. Had she imagined that he was disappointed when she told him that Natalie would be coming for dinner too? There was something in the way he had looked at her . . . Emily drifted off into remembrance.

Of course he wasn't disappointed that Natalie was there, Emily concluded. Why would he be? Men like Matt loved hanging out with the girls. All the gay guys she knew did. And Matt was gay . . . wasn't he? The attention he paid to his appearance, the musicals, the holidays in Mykynos . . . Emily sighed and climbed the stairs to bed.

35

On the other side of Essex, Carina Lees was also going to bed alone and thinking about how nice it would be to be sliding under the covers with the warm, comforting body of a lover. Like Emily, she longed for a companion to share the day's events with. Particularly at the end of a day such as the one she'd just had.

Carina had been fifteen years old when *Titanic* hit the screens. She saw the movie with her mother and spent most of the film feeling acutely embarrassed. She'd fallen in love with Leonardo DiCaprio the moment he first appeared on-screen and was certain that everyone must be able to see it on her face, though of course in the dark cinema it was next to impossible to see her blushes.

Carina's crush on Leonardo DiCaprio endured for the next decade. She saw every movie he ever starred in. Whatever role he was playing, Carina loved it. She even adored his Afrikaans accent in *Blood Diamond*. Her fondest wish was that one day she would get to meet him. She practised the scenario a thousand times over in her head. What she'd be wearing. How her hair would look. Leonardo's face when he saw her. What he would say to her. The ring he would buy to celebrate their engagement . . . Her wedding dress.

Well, that night it had happened. The first part of the dream, at least.

Carina had been a celebrity guest at the opening of Leonardo DiCaprio's new movie: a British gangster flick called *EC1*. At the after-party, Mickey had told her that there was

someone special he wanted her to meet. She had followed
Mickey into the VIP room and there he had been. Leonardo
himself.

Even Mickey – the man who once went jogging in
Brentwood, Los Angeles, with Steven Segal – seemed slightly
overawed. With anyone else, Mickey would have stormed right
in there, interrupting a conversation or even a kiss if he had
to, in order to introduce one of his charges to someone useful.
But he hung back. Almost reverently. Still, he recovered enough
professional poise to introduce his number one client to the
most important man at the party. And Leonardo was gracious
enough to stand up and shake Carina's hand.

'Hello,' said Leonardo.

'Er . . . ttt . . . hi.' Carina tittered.

They hadn't exactly had a conversation, but Carina was
sure she felt a warm connection in the way they exchanged
their hellos. And it might have developed into a proper
conversation had they not been interrupted by the Brazilian
supermodel Leonardo was rumoured to be dating.

'Darling,' said the supermodel, 'our car is here.'

'Excuse me,' said Leonardo. Then he left.

Carina wished she had someone to call. Someone with
whom she could share the moment.

'I was so star-struck I almost fainted,' she wanted to say.
'Can you believe it? Leonardo DiCaprio! Leonardo DiCaprio
shook my hand! He said, "Excuse me".'

But there was no one to call. At least no one she could call
sounding as breathless and excited as she felt right then. She
opened her mobile phone, as if to check for certain. She
scrolled down through the numbers. There were hundreds.
Possibly more than a thousand. Some of the numbers were
attached to names she barely recognized. Some were attached
to names any woman in the UK under the age of thirty-five
would have recognized from the gossip mags. But they weren't

exactly friends. She and Caprice had swapped numbers at some new Chelsea striker's eighteenth birthday party. They'd clicked and bonded over tales of hair-extension horror. They'd promised to call and do lunch. But she couldn't call Caprice at two in the morning to gossip about Leonardo. How uncool would that be? Hadn't Caprice actually slept with him?

But Carina couldn't sleep. She had to talk to someone. Her mum, she knew, was unlikely to be alone. And if she was alone, she was unlikely to be happy to chat at this time of night.

Carina opened her phone again. She found a number. She closed her phone. No, it was too late. She opened her phone. She closed it. She opened it.

She dialled Alice. The journalist from *Get This!* magazine.

'Who is it?' Alice groaned when she took the call. It was clear that she had been asleep, but Carina didn't feel too bad. As far as she was concerned, if people really didn't want to be disturbed, they should switch their mobiles off, shouldn't they?

'Doesn't my number come up on your mobile?' Carina asked.

'You called my landline,' said Alice with a sigh. 'Is that Carina Lees?'

'Of course it is,' said Carina. It was a phrase that echoed with rather different intonation in Alice's mind.

'What's the matter?' Alice asked at last.

'I've got the best bit of celebrity gossip for next week's column. I want you to take it down before I forget all the gory details.'

Alice put her hand to her forehead in dismay.

'Hang on a minute,' she said.

Carina could hear Alice shifting in her bed as she sat up and reached for the notepad she kept on her bedside table.

'Are you ready?' Carina asked.

'Fire away.'

'So, right, anyway . . . Tonight I went to the premiere of *EC1*, the new gangster movie from that hot British director who's married to that old woman who used to be a pop star in the old days. Anyway, Leonardo DiCaprio was there. And we were dancing. But then we were interrupted by his super-model girlfriend, Nicosia Albarino, who's not all that super if you're asking me and—'

'Spell the supermodel's name for me,' said Alice.

'Oh, ha ha. Very funny,' said Carina. 'Anyway . . .'

36

The following morning, Natalie was not at work on time.
Emily didn't know whether she had any right to be disgruntled, given that her dinner party was almost certainly the
reason why Natalie was still asleep when she should be setting
up her treatment room for Mrs Howell's upper-lip wax.

When Natalie eventually appeared at nine o'clock, she
looked as though she was still sleepwalking. She had dark
circles under her eyes. Her brief period as a paragon of great
grooming was definitely over. She was back to the Natalie
Emily had worked so hard to tidy up. She was wearing her
combat boots and carrying that horrible canvas bag like a
comfort blanket. It was clear that all was not well.

'Natalie, are you OK?'

Natalie burst into tears and ran into the kitchen.

Emily dismissed Natalie's client with an apology and a
handful of gift vouchers and followed Natalie to her hiding
place.

'What's wrong?' Emily asked. 'Whatever happened?'

'Matt Charlton is most definitely not gay!'

The smile that had automatically sprung to Emily's face upon
Natalie's revelation was very quickly dismissed.

'He is nasty!' Natalie began. 'When we got back to my flat,
he practically pushed his way in. I told him that I had an early
start in the morning but he said that, since he'd walked me
home, and it was much further than he had expected, the very
least I could do was offer him a cup of coffee. Well, when he

put it like that, I didn't see what choice I had. It seemed like it wouldn't be polite to tell him to go. So, I thought I would be able to make him some Nescafé and get rid of him after that. While he was drinking his coffee, he asked about the people I live with. And stupidly I told him that my flatmate is working nights restocking the shelves at Waitrose to pay for his interior design course. And when he asked what time he'd be back, I stupidly told him that he didn't get off until four. And so he knew that we were in the house on our own. Just him, me and his horrible dog. I know he'll come in here and try to tell you a completely different story. And you'll probably believe him.' Natalie gave a dramatic sob.

'Natalie,' said Emily. 'What exactly are you saying? Did he try to . . .'

Emily couldn't bring herself to complete the sentence.

Natalie just nodded, as though she couldn't say it either.

'Matt?' Emily murmured. 'Our Matt? I can't believe it.'

'You see!' Natalie pounced on Emily's words. 'I knew you wouldn't! That's the thing, isn't it? Nobody ever believes a girl like me!' she wailed.

'Of course I believe you,' Emily tried to calm Natalie down. 'And if you're saying he . . .' Emily choked on the words again. 'If you're really saying that . . . Perhaps we should call the police.'

'No!' Natalie insisted. 'I don't want to.'

'But . . .'

'If we go to the police, it will just get messier. It could end up in court and then it would be his word against mine. Who's going to believe a girl who grew up on a council estate against him? Mr City Money-bags?'

'But if we don't go to the police, then . . .'

'Maybe I'm overreacting.' Natalie backtracked hastily. 'Maybe it was just a misunderstanding. Perhaps I did give him reason to think I wanted him to try it on with me.'

Emily found herself thinking back to the laughter she'd heard while she was putting the finishing touches to her pavlova and Matt and Natalie were alone in the other room. She could see why perhaps Matt might have thought Natalie liked him 'that way'. Emily brought herself up short. That was the kind of thinking that led to chauvinist judges announcing that girls had asked to be assaulted because they were dressed provocatively. And yet it was so hard to believe that Matt would have done something so crass. He was always so nice. So shy. After all, he was so far from even being a flirt that they'd assumed he wasn't into girls! Was it all just an act? Had Emily assumed that Matt was sensitive and caring just because he had a seizure-alert dog? Had that made him seem somehow different from the average guy? More vulnerable?

'What do you want me to do?' she asked Natalie.

'Nothing,' Natalie told her. 'I'm OK. Right now, I'm just angry. He didn't hurt me. He had a fit before anything really bad happened.'

'A fit?' Emily was shocked but she tried not to look concerned for him.

'God, it was horrible. He just fell over and started twitching. But it got me out of trouble. As soon as he came round, he went.'

'But if he . . . I still feel like we should make a complaint.' Emily thought that was what she was supposed to say.

'No. Don't do that.' Natalie looked anguished. 'I just want you to ban him from The Beauty Spot. That's enough for me.'

'It doesn't seem right . . .' Emily murmured. 'I'm your boss. I asked Matt to walk you home. I feel responsible. I should make a proper complaint.'

'It's not what I want you to do,' said Natalie. 'I was tipsy too last night. There's a chance I did send out the wrong signals. And I was so drunk I can't be sure that I'm remembering everything right. I'm fine. Really. I want you to give Matt the benefit of the doubt, but I don't ever want to have to see him again.'

As though his ears were burning, Matt called the salon just fifteen minutes later.

'I don't want to hear anything you've got to say,' Natalie told him before he had a chance to say anything. 'You're just lucky I've decided I don't want to call the police.'

'What? Why? I don't understand,' said Matt. 'I was just calling to thank Emily for dinner and to apologize to you that you had to deal with me having a fit.'

'Emily's insisted I give you the benefit of the doubt.'

'For what?'

'You're probably going to tell me you had some kind of blackout when you collapsed and I'm sorry for you if you did.'

'Are you going to tell me what I'm supposed to have done?'

'Absolutely not. You'll probably get off on having me tell you.'

'Eh? But . . .'

'We don't want you to come here ever again. Emily has banned you.'

'Natalie. At least tell me what's going on?'

'That won't be necessary. Goodbye.'

Natalie cut short the conversation. 'That was Matt,' she told Emily.

'I guessed that.'

'Thanks for agreeing to ban him from the salon, Emily,' said Natalie. 'If you hadn't agreed, I would have had to quit.'

Emily had guessed that was the only other option.

'No one has ever stood up for me like you do. I feel like

you're my very best friend. We girls have to stick together, don't we?'

In his office, Matt stared into space, still holding the phone. He sat there for such a long time that his assistant came in to check he wasn't having a fit. She'd read somewhere that epilepsy could take all sorts of forms. Perhaps he wasn't just thinking. Perhaps he was having the type of episode that involved staying very, very still. Like that Monkey bloke off that reality programme. What was it? Oh, yes. *Living Hell.*

'I'm alright,' Matt insisted, somewhat testily. But even Cesar looked at him with concern.

What on earth did Natalie believe had happened the previous night? It was clear that it was something terrible. But what? He remembered walking back to Natalie's house. They'd been getting on pretty well. In a friendly sort of way. That had been a surprise to Matt. He hadn't been certain that Natalie liked him at all when he saw her at staff meetings at The Beauty Spot. But that night, after Emily's dinner party, she was very friendly indeed. And by the time they got to her house, she was on the point of being what one might refer to as 'touchy-feely'.

When they got to her house, she had invited him in for coffee. Matt had refused, citing an early start as his reason. He worried that, if he did accept, it might lead to an ugly moment if Natalie tried to make a pass at him. Natalie had insisted. She said that if he refused a cup of her best freshly ground coffee, she would take it as a personal insult. And she had pouted. Matt had given in. They'd been arguing about coffee for so long that he needed to use the bathroom anyway.

It was quite hot inside Natalie's house. She had said that she was going to change out of her outfit, because she didn't want to sweat on it. 'Dry-clean only,' she explained. When she came back into the kitchen she was wearing another 'dress' that was little more than a slip. Matt didn't think she was wearing a bra but was too embarrassed to look again. Instead, he very deliberately kept his gaze to Natalie's face.

When she handed him his coffee, her fingers had touched his hand. He remembered thinking that she'd done it on purpose. He excused himself to the bathroom again.

What had happened after that? What had he done? All Matt could remember was coming to on the sitting-room floor. When Matt had a fit, occasionally he lost the preceding half-hour or so. Sometimes, memories of that lost time would come back to him a few days later. Sometimes they never came back. Right then, what had happened with Natalie was staying firmly out of his mind. Had he done something wrong before having a fit?

He called The Beauty Spot again. Once again Natalie picked up the phone. When Matt announced himself, she just shouted, 'You pervert!' and cut him off. He tried again. This time no one picked up. It went straight to the answer-machine.

Natalie had told him never to darken The Beauty Spot's door again, but Matt was determined to find out exactly what was going on. Most importantly, he wanted to know what she'd told Emily. Perhaps he'd just said something insulting. He'd heard that sometimes happened while a fit was taking place. If he could just explain that it was due to his condition and not to anything else . . .

'Come on, Cesar.'

Cesar got to his feet.

'We're going to get to the bottom of this.'

It had been a difficult day at The New Beauty Spot. Quiet. There had been a couple of no-shows. Natalie had gone home. Emily was alone when the doorbell rang. She had a sense, before she opened the door, that it would be Matt.

'Hello,' she said.

Matt smiled shyly. He looked his usual tidy, friendly self. It was hard to believe that this was the man who had made Natalie so upset. But he had. Natalie had looked preoccupied all day. And so Emily didn't fully open the door.

'Am I really banned?' Matt asked.

'It's what Natalie wants,' Emily confirmed.

Cesar, who obviously hadn't understood the ban, was already stepping over the threshold into the salon. Matt used Cesar's harness to pull him back onto the pavement outside. Cesar looked up at his master, hurt at the intervention. The look of confusion in the dog's eyes made Emily feel bad too.

'I can't let you in,' she said.

'Is Natalie still here? Perhaps I could talk to her too?'

'She's gone home.'

'Emily, you've got to tell me what happened. I really don't know what I did. That fit last night was the first one in ages.'

'I know.'

'Well, when I have a fit, sometimes it sort of wipes my short-term memory clean. So I can't remember what went on last night. At least, not the very last part of the evening. I can remember coming over to your house. I can remember how beautiful you looked . . .'

Emily felt a flutter in her chest. She quickly put paid to it. She subtly shook her head to let Matt know she thought any reminiscences of that kind would be inappropriate.

'The thing is, I cannot remember a thing. If you told me I was dancing naked on Natalie's coffee table, singing "Livin' la Vida Loca" and waving my boxer shorts over my head, then I would have to believe you. I wasn't singing "Livin' la Vida Loca", was I?' he asked in an attempt to raise a smile.

'No,' said Emily. 'You weren't.'

'Then what was I doing? Please, Emily, you have to tell me.'

'It's not my place. I wasn't there.' Emily's eyebrows were raised in anguish.

'But Natalie must have told you what I did. I don't believe you would have banned me from the premises unless she gave you the details. She wouldn't talk to me. I'd go round to her place and confront her, but I don't even remember where she lives.'

'That's probably a good thing,' said Emily.

'Then she must have told you something very bad. Emily, please. Whatever you think of me now, I hope you believe that we were friends. I valued our friendship enormously. And I deserve to know what's broken it.'

'Matt,' said Emily. 'It sounds like you tried to molest her.'

'What?'

'She said you walked her home OK but when you got there you insisted that she invite you inside for a coffee. She didn't want to because she had an early start, but she thought, because you were The Beauty Spot's business advisor, that that made you one of her bosses. So she let you in. Because she felt obliged. And you started making suggestive comments. And when you finished your coffee and she asked you to leave so that she could get some sleep, you made a lunge at her. The only thing that saved things from becoming worse was that you had a fit.'

'I don't believe it.'

'Well, I wouldn't have believed it of you either, but what am I supposed to do? It's her word against yours and you, by your own admission, have no idea what went on between midnight and one o'clock last night. It would be irresponsible of me not to act on her accusation. In fact, I told Natalie that she should file a proper complaint against you. With the police!'

'Emily,' said Matt. 'You have to believe that, if I did act inappropriately, I would not have done so consciously. It's just not in my character. I'll go to my doctor right now and ask him to look at my medication again. He did give me some new tablets last month. Perhaps they don't agree with me. I'll find out. They might have turned me into some kind of Jekyll and Hyde.'

'I'm sorry, Matt. You better go.'

'Emily . . .'

She was already closing the door.

'Emily, please say that you trust me.'

'I don't know if I can any more,' she said, finally closing the door altogether. She leaned against it, as though he might force his way in. Matt stood outside for a moment or two, but eventually she heard the sound of him and Cesar walking away.

Emily knew she had done the right thing. Ninety-nine per cent of her wouldn't have believed that Matt was capable of the kind of behaviour that Natalie had implied, but on this occasion the other one per cent of her had to have veto. There was a possibility that Natalie was overreacting, but perhaps her reluctance to go into any real detail about what had happened the previous night was a sign of just how serious the matter was. A sign of trauma. Emily had to side with Natalie: her colleague, her friend and her fellow woman. It was the only course of action to take. Emily spent all day every day with Natalie. She believed that she was a trustworthy person. Emily didn't know Matt half so well. And yet . . .

As Emily locked up the salon for the night, she prayed that Natalie would decide that she had overreacted to a clumsy pass and accept Matt's apology so that all could be well again.

On the other side of town, Matt was furious with himself. How had he turned into such a dick-head? How much had he drunk?

He hadn't even wanted to walk Natalie home that night. He would have been more than happy for her to take a taxi. He'd walked Natalie home because he wanted to impress Emily. And now everything was ruined. Emily didn't even want to see him any more. All Matt cared about was that he had disappointed her.

37

By the end of that week, Natalie seemed to have recovered altogether from her alleged trauma at the hands of Matt Charlton. She was her usual cheerful self, joking with the clients and delivering her top-notch beauty treatments without complaint. From time to time, Emily asked her how she was coping and even suggested that she might like to take a long weekend to recuperate – 'because these things can creep up on you' – but Natalie refused.

'There's no way I'm going to let that stupid man ruin my life,' she said in one of her more vociferous moments. 'I'm over it. I don't need to take time off. In fact,' Natalie continued, 'I'm much less worried about myself than I am about you.'

'Why are you worried about me?' asked Emily.

'Isn't it obvious?'

It wasn't.

They were sitting at the kitchen table. Natalie reached across and took Emily's hand. She patted it gently.

'Anyone can see that you're suffering from upheaval as a result of Matt's actions too,' she said. 'You're a victim by extension.'

'I am?'

'Oh yes. I've noticed how strained you've been looking.'

'I don't feel like a victim.'

'You say that to me, but you're clearly wracked with guilt at the thought that your bad judgment, in associating with a scumbag like Matt Charlton, could have cost me my mental and psychological health.'

Emily nodded slowly as she followed Natalie's train of thought.

'This is what happens when someone commits a crime. It's like throwing a stone into a pond. The ripples go on for ages. You need to accept that you're going to have to deal with quite a bit of mental anguish as you readjust your own world-view. It might take you quite some time to trust in yourself as a person in a position of responsibility towards others. Your faith in your people skills has been severely shaken. As it should be. Some people in the same position might have considered quitting rather than put someone else in danger again. But of course, you can't quit. You're the boss. This is your salon.'

Emily nodded along.

'So you need to take steps to work through this difficult situation with the least disruption possible.'

'What exactly are you saying, Nat?' Emily asked at last. 'Do you think I should get counselling?'

'Not exactly. I'm saying you need to get a new business advisor right away,' said Natalie. 'But you probably can't trust in your ability to pick the right guy, can you? I wouldn't in your situation. Luckily, I know someone.'

'You know a business advisor?'

'Don't look so surprised!'

'I'm sorry, I didn't mean . . .'

'My cousin's cousin's boyfriend Evan is an accountant. He works for this big firm in the City, but he says as a special favour to me he'll take a look at your books on the side. I think you ought to call him as soon as you have a spare minute. Given what we've found out about Matt Charlton already this week, I wouldn't be at all surprised if we find out that he hasn't been entirely honest in his accounting.'

Emily felt her throat tighten at the very idea.

'Here's Evan's card,' said Natalie, handing the little white oblong over. 'Remember to mention my name and he'll give you a discount off the usual fee.'

Even with a discount, Evan's fee was ridiculously high. When Emily questioned Evan about that, explaining that Matt had been their consultant in return for free treatments, he told her ominously, 'Oh, yeah. We hear about those dodgy bartering situations all the time. But what you save at the outset, you'll pay for twice over when the Inland Revenue does an investigation. Think about it, Emily, if you were a dodgy accountant, wouldn't you offer to work for nothing to stop your clients from getting upset about anything else that didn't seem quite right?'

Emily murmured her assent. He had a point.

'I'll be over this evening to collect all your paperwork,' Evan continued. 'And stop worrying, Emily. You're in safe hands now.'

Emily wished she felt as confident as Evan sounded. The truth was, Evan's brusque tone had set her on edge. Ordinarily, she would have made her excuses not to use him but, with Natalie's suggestion that Emily lacked insight into other people's motivation still at the forefront of her mind, Emily sat on her doubts. And she continued to sit on them even when Evan turned up looking and talking more like an estate agent than an accountant. She knew she mustn't let his slickness count against him. It was no reflection on his character at all.

As Natalie had explained over lunch that day: the least trustworthy people were without doubt the most highly skilled at making you trust them.

Sitting alone in her little flat the week after Natalie had told her the horrible truth about Matt, Emily opened up the diary she had kept – somewhat sporadically – for the past few years, since her time as a beautician on that cruise ship, when there was sometimes little else to do. She knew which page she wanted to look at. One of her fellow beauticians on the cruise ship – a girl called Louise from Cape Town – had been passionate about the power of creative visualization and cosmic ordering. She had all the books – Jonathan Cainer, Noel Edmonds – and was convinced that, if she just thought about it hard enough, the universe would deliver her the perfect rich husband. When she announced that she was going to marry a wealthy widower who had joined the cruise to recover from his grief and found solace with Louise in the salon, Emily couldn't help but wonder if the visualizing had done the trick. And so, with Louise's help, she set out a cosmic vision for her own future, drawing the life she wanted to have in the centre pages of her diary.

Emily looked at that picture now. She wasn't terribly skilled as an artist, but her request to the benevolent universe was still pretty clear, she thought. She had drawn herself standing outside a beauty salon that was called, of course, The Beauty Spot. The colour scheme wasn't quite the same – the actual pink paint she'd used was a little lighter – but the script of the name was very similar. And the Emily of the future was wearing a white overall with her name in pink on the breast pocket.

There was more than the salon in the picture. On a table beside Emily was a little row of bottles. They represented her very own cosmetics line. Beneath the picture she had written: in five years' time, I will be the head of my own beauty empire!!!!!

How foolish that picture seemed now. Those optimistic exclamation marks! Her dream was further away than ever.

For the next week, The Beauty Spot would be running at less than half its capacity. For the first time since Emily threw open the doors on her new business venture, the appointments spreadsheet had more empty white boxes than boxes containing names and numbers. The phone had simply stopped ringing. The previous afternoon Emily had sat on reception for three hours straight and hadn't taken a single call. Not one. Emily couldn't understand it. And it was frightening. Especially now that Evan was on-board. He demanded that Emily pay his consultancy fee up front.

'Standard practice,' he assured her.

Emily had to make the payment with her own debit card, plunging her personal bank account further into the red. She'd have to do the same again later in the week, when it was time to pay Natalie's wages.

With that thought going through her head, Emily started to nibble on one of her cuticles.

38

Mickey was very pleased with the latest deal he'd struck for Carina. Her makeover section in the *Wakey-Wakey* show had been a great success. Together with the production company, he'd forged a deal with a big publisher for a book to accompany the makeovers. It was to be written by Alice the journalist who wrote Carina's column in *Get This!* magazine. She'd seemed pretty pleased with the news that she would get ten per cent of the advance for her troubles. Possibly because she didn't actually know that the figure Mickey had quoted her represented only ten per cent of the ridiculous number he'd thrown at the publishing house. She thought it must be about half.

Now, thought Mickey, it was time to branch out. Think laterally. He was entering into negotiations with a number of health-and-fitness-based companies. Also, he'd been approached by a cosmetics giant that produced perfumes and marketed them under the names of the hottest celebrities *du jour*. If Jade Goody, a woman who had never looked particularly fragrant to Mickey, had managed to successfully promote a scent (at least for a while), then for Carina it should be a piece of cake. She was still a favourite on the nation's most exclusive guest lists (if you took 'exclusive' as a rather loose term).

Carina had been in a bad mood all evening. The newest star in *EastEnders* had chatted her up at the launch of a new cocktail bar, but she had had to tell him that she couldn't follow him to a nightclub – since her 'fairytale romance' with Monkey was still a large part of her appeal for the general public, Mickey had warned her that she must not be seen in a compromising situation with any Tom, Dick or Soap Star.

So Carina spent the rest of the night in a hotel room watching QVC. She happened to turn on during an hour whose focus was on exercise equipment. That just depressed her even more. Six hours a week with a personal trainer and she still didn't look like Victoria Beckham. Possibly because she was still eating one square meal a day. No discipline, Carina berated herself.

Mickey called first thing the following day.

'I've got some news that will cheer you up,' he said.

'What?' Carina sat up in bed. The possibilities ran through her mind. Judy Finnegan had left Richard and he wanted Carina to take her place on the coveted sofa? Victoria Beckham had developed a stye on one of her eyelids and Carina had to rush to Milan to do a photo-shoot for a sunglasses manufacturer?

'You have been chosen as the new face of . . .'

Mickey paused dramatically. He had developed the terrible habit of conducting his conversations with clients as though he was announcing the results on *Pop Idol*. Though, to be fair, most of his clients acted as though they were on *Pop Idol* at all times.

'What? What?' Carina squeaked. 'What am I going to be the new face of?'

'*Cellulite!*' said Mickey proudly.

Cellulite!

Carina sent up a wail like an air-raid siren. She threw her mobile phone across the room, breaking the enormous wide screen of the television. Then she threw herself down on the bed and pummelled the mattress with her fists and feet, like a five-year-old who had just been denied an extra half-hour on the swings. Then she flopped over onto her back and wailed at the ceiling. Anyone walking in at that moment might have assumed that Carina had just lost her parents, or a million pounds. Or both.

In his office in central London, Mickey stared in bemusement at the suddenly blank screen of his own telephone. Why on earth had Carina hung up on him? He called her back.

Carina snatched up the phone.

'Is this some kind of joke, Mickey? Because you can tell them exactly where to stick it!' she screamed. 'Bastards.'

She cut him off again.

Mickey called back.

'But Carina, this deal could be worth five hundred thousand pounds over the next three years.'

'To be the face of *cellulite*! No money is enough.'

At last it dawned on Mickey where the conversation had gone wrong. 'Not cellulite, Carina. Did I say that?'

'Yes, you bloody did.'

'Slip of the tongue,' said Mickey.

Freudian slip, thought his PA Lucy, who was waiting on the other side of his desk to hand him a contract that needed a signature.

'I meant to say "Cellusmite".'

'What?' Carina sat up again. She wiped her nose on the back of her sleeve. It didn't sound that much better to her.

'Cellu*smite*,' Mickey repeated, 'is a fabulous new technique from Germany.' He picked up the brochure and started to read. 'It's a machine that breaks down fatty deposits in the thighs, lower abdomen and buttocks using ultra-high frequency vibration. It's been shown to have ninety-three per cent effectiveness in point two per cent of people in clinical trials. Everyone is talking about it. And you're going to be there when the first Cellusmite machine comes to the UK.'

'Why? Because I need it? Because I've got a fat arse? Is that what you're telling me?'

'No. Of course not,' Mickey tried desperately to calm her down. 'No one is saying *you* need it, Carina. Quite the opposite, in fact. You're going to be promoting this machine so that your clients can be more like you. As the face of Cellusmite, you're an example of how good anyone's thighs could be if they were prepared to fork out sixty quid for thirty minutes three times a week for four months.'

'Oh.' Carina was a little happier with that. 'How much are they going to pay me?'

By the time Mickey had broken down the details of the deal for her, Carina was very happy indeed.

39

Emily was expecting a genuine Man-tenance client that morning so she wasn't surprised when a man walked into the salon at eleven o'clock. Her heart sank a little when she saw that he was wearing a buff-coloured mackintosh, but she tried to suspend her judgment. It was, at least, a clean mackintosh.

'Mr Merchant?' she asked.

'Mr Smith,' he said, putting his briefcase down on top of the desk.

Oh no, thought Emily. Another Mr Smith. She put on her best stern face.

'Mr Smith,' she said, punctuating his name with little air commas to let him know she knew it was a *nom de guerre*. 'I suspect there has been some kind of misunderstanding. We are, as you can see, a beauty salon. And as such we offer beauty treatments. We do not offer any services that you can't find on the menu here.' She handed him a leaflet. 'No extras, no *special* massages, no happy endings. And absolutely no *loving you long time*.'

Mr Smith frowned.

'I hope that's straightened things up,' said Emily. 'Now, if you'd like to tell me your real name and whether you're genuinely interested in a manicure or pedicure . . .'

'My name *is* Mr Smith,' he repeated. He reached into his breast pocket and brought out a small black leather wallet. He flipped it open in the manner of a television detective. It contained his identification. 'I am here to see Ms Emily

Brown on behalf of Blountford Council's Department of Environmental Health.'

'Are we due an inspection?' Emily asked. She couldn't understand how she'd been taken by surprise. She was normally so good at checking her diary. Perhaps she'd lost track of this inspection when the salon computer was stolen.

'You're not due an inspection, no,' said Mr Smith. 'Though I will be carrying out a general inspection while I'm here. I'm afraid I have to tell you that we've had some complaints.'

Complaints. The word went straight to Emily's heart. She clutched at the edge of the counter as though to steady herself. When she was eventually able to talk again, the words came out in a croak.

'Someone has complained about my salon?'

'Yes.'

Mr Smith had opened his big black briefcase and pulled out a buff-coloured folder. On the outside, a sticker announced that this folder concerned 'The New Beauty Spot.' Mr Smith leafed through the thick pile of papers inside.

It got worse.

'In fact, we have received here a number of calls,' he said.

'But I don't understand. Nobody has complained to me. Not one person. Surely if anyone had a problem with my salon they would let me know right away.'

'Well, perhaps they felt intimidated,' said Mr Smith.

'By me?' Emily's eyebrows were raised in disbelief.

'Or perhaps they didn't realize they had grounds to complain until they got home. Like this lady, who reported the development of an unsightly and uncomfortable rash in her, ahem, pubic area after visiting your salon for a . . .' Mr Smith squinted at the file. '. . . *Brazilian* wax.'

'Some people are very sensitive to the waxing process,' Emily started to explain. 'Rashes may develop but they usually go away very quickly. I tell all my clients that. And I always recommend a patch test!'

'We had five other complaints along similar lines,' said Mr Smith. 'That seems to be an unusually high incidence of sensitivity to me. Far more likely that these unfortunate women picked up some kind of infection from dirty equipment.'

Emily gasped. It was as though he had accused her of killing kittens for kicks.

'But I don't have dirty equipment,' she said firmly.

'I'll be the judge of that,' said Mr Smith.

'Who made these complaints?'

'I can't tell you that. The ladies in question all chose to remain anonymous.'

'Then perhaps they were prank calls?'

'Perhaps. At this stage I still need to take them seriously. Miss Brown, I'm afraid I'm going to have to ask you to close the salon for the rest of the day while I investigate these claims.'

'But we're fully booked. I've got eight people coming in.'

'That's none of my concern,' said Mr Smith. 'And I'm sure that the last thing you want is for another eight of your customers to pick up infections and make a complaint. Please turn the sign on the door to closed. I will go out to my car and fetch the rest of my equipment.'

What else could she do? Emily did as she was told. She walked to the door on automatic pilot and flipped the sign from open to closed. Her next client – the genuine Man-tenance client – had already arrived. Emily stepped out onto the street to talk to him. She decided that the best strategy was to lie.

'We've had a power cut,' she said, before realizing that the lights were still on. 'In the treatment rooms,' she added hurriedly. 'They're on a different circuit.'

'Have you taken a look at the fuse box?' the client asked.

'Not yet.'

'I could take a look for you.'

Damn, thought Emily. Why did men always think they could fix things?

'It's not the fuse,' said Emily. She needed to get rid of this client before Mr Smith came back. She could see him a little further up the street, unloading yet another ominous black suitcase. He also took off his mac, laid it carefully in the boot of his car, and replaced it with a white overall. He had one of those paper masks favoured by Japanese cyclists hanging around his neck. He did not look like an electrician.

'Mr Merchant,' said Emily, taking her client by the arm and bodily turning him so that they were facing in the opposite direction to Mr Smith. 'I'm really sorry we won't be able to do your treatment today. I'm going to make a note in the book that your next treatment is to be on the house. Perhaps you could call later today and rearrange?'

'I can come in and rearrange right now,' said Mr Merchant.

'No can do,' said Emily. 'Can't let you inside the door while there are electrical issues. Health and safety.'

'Oh well,' said Mr Merchant. 'I hope you get it sorted out soon.'

'Miss Brown?' Mr Smith was upon them. 'I'm ready to start my tests.'

'Electrical tests,' Emily mouthed as she ushered Mr Smith inside, leaving Mr Merchant on the pavement scratching his head.

Mr Smith was kind enough to let Natalie finish the treatment she had already begun but, after that, he was adamant that neither Natalie nor Emily were to touch anything until he had finished his inspection. While they sat on their hands on the comfy chairs in reception, Mr Smith spent at least two hours going over The New Beauty Spot with his swabs and his test tubes, taking samples of water from the hot tub and wiping surfaces for the germs that he would take back to his lab and culture.

When he had finished, his face was grim.

'Some of my instant tests are already showing unacceptably high levels of bacteria,' he told the girls. 'You'll have to remained closed until further notice.'

'Don't let him close us down!' Natalie begged as Mr Smith started to load his equipment back into his briefcase. 'Please.' She hung onto the inspector's jacket sleeve. 'Whatever went wrong was probably my fault. I haven't been a beautician for very long. I've been doing my best but I'm bound to make the odd mistake. How about if I resign? Will you let Emily keep the salon open then?'

'I'm afraid I can't,' said Mr Smith. 'It doesn't matter what you have or haven't done. It was Miss Brown's responsibility to ensure that all health and safety regulations were being followed to the letter. In effect, your actions might as well have been her actions. Whoever breached the regulations, the manager of the salon ultimately takes the blame.'

'But that's so unfair!'

'The law is the law,' the inspector said flatly. 'Now, I'll have to ask you to properly close the premises down while I'm here watching. You'll need to write a notice for the door.'

As if on autopilot, Emily followed his instructions. Meanwhile Natalie continued to cajole, to coax, to wheedle.

'What if we just don't do any waxing?' she suggested.

Mr Smith would not budge.

'I can't allow you to do that.'

'Just manicures?' Natalie begged.

'Don't even think about opening the salon back up without my say-so,' Mr Smith warned her. 'If you do, we shall have to get the police involved. There are very strict penalties for non-compliance.'

'I won't reopen,' Emily promised him.

'Good. Thank you very much for being so cooperative, Ms Brown. Enjoy the rest of your day.'

Natalie almost flew at him.

'Enjoy the rest of the day? How can we enjoy the rest of the day? You're a dick-head. You're a bloody jobsworth.'

Mr Smith stepped backwards, holding his briefcase across his body as if for protection, but his face remained passive. He had heard it all before.

'Natalie.' Emily held her employee back to give the inspector time to escape. 'Natalie, this isn't making things any better.'

Still, Natalie followed him out to his car, shouting abuse all the while.

When Mr Smith was gone, Natalie slumped down onto the front step of The Beauty Spot. She put her head in her hands and started to cry.

'This is all my fault,' she snorted loudly. 'I feel so guilty. It must have been me who got the wax machine all contaminated. There's no way that any of *your* clients would have complained.'

'We don't know that,' said Emily.

'Of course we do. It was all my fault. But I'll make it up to you, Emily. Tell you what – you can keep my week's wages. A month's!'

'Don't be ridiculous,' said Emily. 'How will you live?'

'I'll manage,' said Natalie bravely. 'You're going to need every penny to fight this ban. I know a lawyer,' she added. 'I'll call him and get him to come over and tell you what can be done. He'll have this place open again by the end of the week. I know it.'

'I'm not so sure,' said Emily, glancing at the wedge of

paperwork the inspector had left behind for her perusal. 'We have to wait until we pass another inspection.'

'That could take ages!' Natalie raged.

Emily enfolded Natalie in a big hug. She almost felt more sorry for Natalie than she did for herself. Natalie had shown such incredible loyalty and she was taking the closure so badly. So personally. It was flattering that Natalie didn't believe Emily could have cocked up, but, if she was honest, Emily wasn't sure she hadn't.

It was almost eleven o'clock at night when the Range Rover pulled up outside The Beauty Spot and Carina Lees stepped out. The Beauty Spot was completely dark, of course. There was no chance of an emergency facial. Still, when she was certain that nobody was looking, Carina Lees crossed the road to the salon. She read the notice that had been taped to the door.

'*Dear Customers*,' it began. '*We regret to have to tell you that The Beauty Spot is going to be closed for a little while. We apologize for any inconvenience to our loyal customers. We hope to be up and running again as soon as possible and, when we are, you can bet that we will make it up to you! With best wishes, Emily and Natalie.*'

Emily had added a kiss below her name. Below Natalie's name was a row of kisses and hearts in the style of a twelve-year-old schoolgirl. It was an upbeat sort of notice. There was no mention of why the salon had closed down. Carina exhaled slowly. She nodded to herself, then she walked back to her car, jumped in and drove back to her exclusive executive home.

40

Now that she no longer needed to get up early to open The Beauty Spot, Emily was in serious danger of not getting up at all. For a few days after the environmental inspector announced that he was closing The New Beauty Spot down on the grounds of public safety, Emily was in shock. How was it possible that her salon wasn't up to the strict hygiene standards he imposed? Emily had always been so careful and she'd instructed everyone who ever worked for her to make sure that they always used clean waxing spatulas for each client. They had to wash their hands before and after every treatment. There were notices all over the staff bathroom insisting the same. Even the shelves in the staff refrigerator were carefully labelled to ensure that no one's chicken sandwich contaminated someone else's fat-free yogurt.

But still, Mr Smith insisted that he had found traces of the kind of bacteria Emily couldn't even spell in the wax heaters, in the hot tub, on the counters and even on the brochures on the front desk.

It was a disaster.

When she took on the new bigger premises, Emily knew that she was taking a big financial risk. Her margins were tighter than a glamour model's trousers. The Beauty Spot could have weathered a fifty per cent drop in bookings, but the hundred per cent loss of income caused by having to close the salon until it passed the health and safety checks was a blow it couldn't withstand. Maybe for a week. But one week dragged into two. Two weeks into three. Three into a month . . . And then Evan announced that Emily owed the Inland Revenue ten thousand pounds!

It wasn't only the tax bill and the salon rent she couldn't afford to pay while the salon wasn't open for business. Without any income whatsoever, Emily could no longer afford the rent on the pretty little flat she had called home for the past two years. She gave her landlord a month's notice and prepared to go back to her childhood bedroom at her parents' house. What she saved on rent could help her hang on to the salon.

But it wasn't enough, and as the month stretched into six weeks and the break point in the lease grew nearer, Emily's father took her aside for a serious talk.

'I think you're going to have to let the salon go, love,' he said. 'You don't know how long it's going to be before you're able to reopen. If you let the salon go now, you'll immediately save that wasted rent and, while the salon equipment is so new, you could sell it on and recoup some more money there.'

Emily couldn't speak. She knew her father was being pragmatic, but it was the biggest heartbreak of her life. When she eventually opened her mouth to let him know what she thought, the only thing that came out was a sob.

'It's OK,' said Eric Brown, wrapping his arm around his daughter's shaking shoulders.

'That place was my entire world! My life is over!'

'Rubbish. You've got a lot of life ahead of you,' said her grandmother. 'If you live to be as old as me, you're not even a third of the way through.'

But Emily didn't want to hear that kind of platitude.

'You do it, Dad,' she said. 'You tell the landlord I want to end the lease. Can you ask him to try to sell the equipment too?'

Her father nodded and went to make the call straight away.

It was for the best. Allowing Emily to sleep on the decision was pointless. There was no real choice to be made. Every hour that passed represented a footstep further into debt.

'Good news,' said Emily's father later that same day. 'The landlord was completely fine about ending your contract. He said you don't even need to worry about the notice period. Won't be any problem at all getting the place rented out again. In fact, he said that a couple of people had already made enquiries.'

'Really?' That didn't sound like such good news to Emily. 'Vultures,' she said. 'They must have been watching. Waiting for me to fail.'

It was a terrible thought.

But as the days passed, Emily began to feel something that was almost like relief. Well, not like relief. More like the absence of pain. She felt as though she had fallen off a bucking bronco she had been riding for two months and now lay sprawled on the crash mat staring up at the strip lights. She was shell-shocked. Pole-axed. The only real consolation was that things could not possibly get any worse.

Emily had to adjust her whole life to try to stave off the pain of losing her beloved salon. First, like a heartbroken lover trying to forget an unfaithful ex, she gathered together every little piece of Beauty Spot memorabilia – her white overall with the pink embroidery, her headed notepaper, her specially embossed Beauty Spot biros – and packed them into a cardboard box which she got her father to stow in the attic.

Next, she decided that she had to take a different route into town – a much longer route – to avoid walking past the old place. She couldn't bear to see what had happened to the space she had decorated so lovingly. She knew that all the equipment had been sold. The cheque had just about cleared her overdraft. She wondered who had bought the kit she chose so carefully. It was all top-notch stuff. One day soon, when she pulled herself together enough to get a new job, perhaps she would find herself using some of the equipment she had bought for The Beauty Spot in a new place. It didn't bear thinking about.

In fact, the equipment Emily had chosen so carefully remained exactly where she had left it. Well, perhaps not exactly. The new leaseholder had chosen a slightly different layout for the new incarnation of The Beauty Spot. The walls between the treatment rooms had been torn down and repositioned a little closer together, to enable an extra treatment room to be squeezed into the same space. The pretty rag-rolled pink walls had been painted a luxurious shade of golden yellow. The gold was accented with lapis lazuli blue gloss on the coving and the skirting boards. The stencilled hearts around the tops of the walls were replaced by hieroglyphs, as befitted the new Egyptian theme.

Emily's country-dresser-style front desk was unceremoniously tossed onto a skip. In its place was a huge stone desk that rested on the heads of two slit-eyed cat statues of the kind that might have guarded a tomb. To the side of the door stood a full-size statue of Osiris, the dog-headed god of the underworld. In his left hand he held a flail. His right arm was outstretched. On his upturned palm was a small bowl containing complimentary breath mints.

It took just three weeks to transform The Beauty Spot into 'Luxoreus', Blountford's new Egyptian-style day spa, complete with Egyptian-style treatments. A notice in the window announced a variety of body scrubs incorporating genuine Nile mud and granulated papyrus. You could have a four-handed 'Egyptian' massage with precious Egyptian oil. Egyptian bikini waxing with special Egyptian strip wax. There was even a 'yummy mummy embalmification (sic) body wrap'. And for your refreshment while you were waiting, each client could choose between Egyptian coffee or a complimentary glass of Egyptian mint tea.

Luxoreus was quite the most exotic thing to spring up in Blountford since the very short-lived Japanese restaurant by the train station. Fortunately for the proprietor of Luxoreus, the good people of Blountford were more adventurous with beauty treatments than they were when it came to lunch. They awaited the opening of the new salon with great excitement.

One thing Emily did not get excited about any more was the arrival of the postman. Since the health and safety debacle, the post she received had become increasingly depressing as the interest built up on her overdraft and legal action was threatened regarding unpaid bills. So, when she found the stiff, creamy-coloured card in among the brown envelopes with cellophane windows, she was instantly intrigued.

The envelope was stamped on the back with a raised gold scarab. On the front, Emily's name had been written in careful calligraphy that was as close as one could get to Egyptian-style writing without using hieroglyphics. She opened the envelope eagerly.

'You are invited to the opening of Luxoreus.'

Seeing the address of her own salon printed neatly beneath the time and date, Emily felt a wave of nausea. But that was nothing compared to how sick she would feel when she found out the name of the glamorous owner of the new 'day spa'.

Carina Lees talked about her new business venture in her column in *Get This!* magazine.

'I've always wanted to be an entrepreneur,' said Carina. 'And ever since I was a little girl, I've been interested in the beauty business. Taking into account my recent appointment as spokesmodel for the Cellusmite fat control range of products, it seemed obvious to me that I should combine my two interests and open a salon. I found some great premises – a salon that had closed down because it was so badly run – and decided to go for it. My Luxoreus day spa will be opening next week.

'The Egyptian theme came to me in a flash of inspiration. Those of you who have been reading my column since the beginning will know that when Liyo Aslan regressed me to my past life on *Wakey-Wakey*, I discovered that I had been an Egyptian slave-girl who died when she was cast out of the palace for catching the eye of a pharaoh. So, I wanted to reflect my Egyptian roots in the decor of Luxoreus. And, because I was a slave-girl in a past life, I have decided to dedicate myself to helping women who find themselves in unfortunate circumstances in this life. Lots of the girls who are going to be working for me have said that, without me and Luxoreus, they really didn't think they had a future at all.'

The photographs that accompanied the article showed Carina 'working hard' to set up her salon. In the first picture she was wearing a hard hat and poring over some architectural drawings (in fact, they were plans for the photo-shoot stylist's new extension). In the second shot she was wielding a paintbrush in the direction of a wall that had in reality been finished for days. In the third shot she was seen chatting amiably with one of the girls she had rescued from having 'no future at all'. The girl smiled back at Carina adoringly, just as Emily had once done.

Emily read the article with a rising sense of disbelief and anger. When she had read the article three times, she took the magazine outside, along with the invitation to Carina's party, and set fire to them both on the patio. The flames leapt up immediately, as though Emily had turned on a living flame gas fire, but they didn't burn evenly. A half-burned fragment of paper floated up into the air and landed in Emily's eye.

41

On the day Luxoreus opened, Emily couldn't have walked past her old salon if she'd wanted to. The street was closed to all traffic, both automobile and pedestrian, from eight o'clock in the morning. Enormous bouncers dressed from head to toe in black Armani muttered into their headsets as they guarded the entrance to the Longbury Road as though guarding the entrance to a South Kensington club where Prince Harry was disporting himself.

The only people allowed to pass the velvet rope (they had actually strung one between a couple of lampposts) were the party planners. Towards the middle of the afternoon, when the interior of the salon was ready for the festivities ahead, a red carpet was rolled out for fifty feet in each direction from Luxoreus's door.

Blountford had never seen anything like it. The local people gathered on the wrong side of the rope and waited for the guests to arrive, like worshipful subjects awaiting their queen. In fact, a recent visit by the real queen to open a new wing at the hospital hadn't caused half such excitement.

At half past four the first limousine arrived.

'It's Posh and Becks!' someone shouted, causing a small stampede.

It wasn't Posh and Becks. But it was an up-and-coming Premiership footballer and his candy-floss-haired girlfriend. The paparazzi fired off a round of shots. The party had begun.

* * *

By seven o'clock, the party at Luxoreus was in full swing. Carina was delighted. The party planners (as recommended by Elton John. Though not personally) had done a fantastic job. Her dress was a triumph. Her hair had come out perfectly. The photographers kept her posing by the door for half an hour.

Everyone who was anyone was there. Carina felt an enormous rush of pride when she found herself sandwiched between two footballers' wives who swore that they would be getting their nails done at Luxoreus from now on. The Longbury Road would be the new Bond Street, one of them claimed. After that, Carina was covered in air-kisses by all three members of new girl band, 'Girlz Whirld'. Their songs may have been rubbish but they were the hottest thing in town since Erica, their leader, was rumoured to have dated both Orlando Bloom *and* Bruce Willis.

Girlz Whirld were followed by the winner of *Celebrity Jailbreak*, a chap called Pikey, who actually became a celebrity when he appeared on a documentary show about real-life prisoners during his stretch in Wandsworth Prison for aggravated burglary.

'Oh, he's lovely,' breathed Kenny, one of Mickey's assistants, as he watched Pikey showing two members of Girlz Whirld his tattoos. 'Hard to believe he broke a pensioner's legs for a fiver.'

Danny Rhodes put in an appearance. He spoke at length with one of the 3AM Girls about the continued respect he had for Carina despite their split. And of course he was more than happy to pose for a photograph.

And then Monkey turned up. At least, Carina thought it was Monkey . . . It was hard to know for sure.

Monkey was wearing a balaclava helmet pulled up so that only his eyes were visible. Or rather, they would have been visible were he not also wearing a pair of big black sunglasses.

He didn't say anything. Nor did he move. He was strapped to the gurney for his own safety, the nurse explained. And she couldn't allow him to be seen without sunglasses in case the flashbulbs set off some kind of fit. But, like Danny Rhodes and all the other celebs, he seemed happy enough to pose for photographs. Luckily the position he was holding at that moment involved an outstretched arm that Carina could snuggle beneath. For the benefit of the cameras, it almost looked as though he was hugging her.

'We're taking him straight out of here when the pictures are done,' the head nurse warned. Meanwhile her colleagues each downed a glass or two of champagne.

Carina didn't mind too much. The pictures were what counted. No one could say that her relationship with Monkey was a sham now. He had made it to the most important event of her life so far and the pictures would prove how much she mattered to him.

'I love you, Monkey!' she shouted passionately as he was wheeled back out to the ambulance to a round of applause. Then, after a couple of moments looking suitably dejected that her lover was headed back to the hospital, Carina plastered on her happy face (which actually more accurately reflected how she really felt) and set to work being the party girl again.

At eight o'clock there was a pause for the all-important ceremonies. Liyo Aslan gave a distinctly irreligious blessing and passed on best wishes from Carina's angel guide in the spirit world. The guests bent their heads as he intoned 'Good luck' in a voice strangely reminiscent of the Wizard of Oz. He also added that the spirit of Princess Diana would be among them later on. She never could resist a party, particularly when fashion or beauty were involved. After that little piece of excitement (which would make its way onto the gossip pages of the *Daily Express* as 'Queen of Hearts crashes beauty launch') there was a celebratory cake in the shape of a mummy and three cheers for the nation's favourite reality TV star.

Then the guests hit the dance floor, getting down to tunes spun by a former soap star who fancied himself as the next Pete Tong. Carina whipped off the detachable train of her fabulous dress – in the style of Bucks Fizz in their 1981 Eurovision Contest winning performance – and danced the night away. On the play-list were all her favourite songs, including the Pussycat Dolls' 'Don't Cha', which prompted a rush for the dance floor and had every woman in the place bump'n'grinding like professionals (which shouldn't have been surprising since so many of them were actual graduates of the Spearmint Rhino pole-dancing clubs).

At half past ten, Mickey beckoned to his favourite client. 'Time to go home,' he said.

'But I'm just enjoying myself.'

'So I see,' Mickey said paternally. 'But I think it's time we got you home before you get yourself snapped tripping over your shoes on the way to the limo.'

Carina did as she was told.

As the limo pulled away from the kerb outside the salon, Carina waved to the people who had been waiting all evening to catch a glimpse of her. As she waved, Carina thought she saw a familiar face in the crowd. She turned away. Luckily, her mobile phone was ringing to divert her attention. That person in the crowd wasn't someone she was prepared to deal with yet.

'Thanks, Mickey,' she said as she rested her head against his shoulder. 'This has been the best night of my life.'

42

The following day, the front desk at Luxoreus was mobbed as the good people of Blountford and beyond tried to get appointments for the Egyptian-themed treatments that Carina had talked about so glowingly just that morning on *Wakey-Wakey*.

'You don't look like you were up all night partying at the opening of your salon,' Patrick had said admiringly.

'That's because I treated myself to a fabulous Egyptian-style lymphatic massage facial,' Carina explained. 'It's one of the services we'll be offering at my new day spa . . .'

Within minutes of her utterance, the switchboard at Luxoreus was jammed.

Later that week, the Luxoreus manageress, Anita, oversaw the location of the first Cellusmite machine outside Germany in a treatment room at the very back of the salon. The staff at Luxoreus had been warned that the machine made a fair amount of noise when it was fully operational. It was not the kind of equipment that you wanted to have to listen to while you were having a nice relaxing facial.

The Cellusmite representative – Anneka Bloom from Cellusmite Headquarters in Cologne – visited Luxoreus three days later. Her smart white uniform, with a nurse's watch dangling from the breast pocket, underlined the medical overtones of the procedure. She gathered the Luxoreus girls together for a brief lecture on anatomy that would have gone over their heads even if it hadn't been delivered in an impenetrable Bavarian accent.

Carina didn't attend the lecture on how to use the machine. She arrived just as Ms Bloom was asking if anyone had any questions and receiving the most blank-faced response she had ever seen. Carina was there for the photos and a TV shoot. Naturally, *Get This!* magazine were thrilled to be able to run an exclusive on this 'revolutionary' new process. Cures for cellulite shifted almost as many copies as celebrity marriage breakdowns (though not quite as many copies as a celebrity marriage breakdown caused by cellulite). Especially cures that had been shown to have ninety-three per cent effectiveness in point two per cent of people in clinical trials.

Alongside the article, *Get This!* magazine was going to run a competition. The prize was twelve sessions in the machine, with a market value of more than six hundred pounds. They anticipated a huge take-up rate.

The team from *Wakey-Wakey* were also keen to get in on the act. Their competition surprise was a whole year's worth of free Cellusmite sessions. And, of course, unlike *Get This!*, they would be able to run actual footage of the fabulous new machine in action.

Carina posed for photographs next to the latest addition to her salon's impressive list of equipment, wearing what could only be described as a 'glamour' version of Anneka Bloom's clinical-looking outfit: a tight white shirt-dress with 'Luxoreus' embroidered on the breast pocket. It showed off her cellulite-free thighs to perfection.

Because they obviously couldn't do a 'before and after' comparison using Carina's own thighs, *Wakey-Wakey* had provided a willing guinea pig. A *Wakey-Wakey* viewer had travelled all the way up from Cornwall for the day and gamely stripped to a very ill-advised pair of thong panties for the cameras. Carina was filmed measuring the poor woman's thighs to ascertain the 'before' data.

Chris Manby

'Twenty-four inches,' Carina announced to the nation. 'For one thigh. That's bigger than my waist.'

The volunteer, one Jane Brady of St Austell, went crimson.

'Never mind,' said Carina. 'Ninety-three per cent of people who use Cellusmite lose two per cent of their body fat.'

The PR from Cellusmite wagged her finger at the *Wakey-Wakey* producer urgently. That claim would have to be cut.

'Let's start making you beautiful,' Carina told Jane warmly. She opened the door of the Cellusmite machine so that Jane could step inside. The machine itself resembled nothing so much as a gigantic white caterpillar's egg. Inside was a hard plastic seat, which vibrated when the door was closed and the machine was turned on. At the same time, steam – 'infused with herbal essences' – would be pumped into the Cellusmite's patented vacuum chamber, raising the temperature and causing the person inside to sweat out toxins and . . .

'Liquidated fat,' Carina told Jane knowledgeably.

'Actually,' said Erica Lay, the Cellusmite PR. 'You'll have to tell her she can't say that either. We make no claims about liquidating anything at Cellusmite. Especially not fat.'

Jane looked more than a little nervous as Carina closed the Cellusmite's heavy, curved white door so that only Jane's head could be seen, poking out of the top.

'Feeling comfortable in there?' Carina asked.

Jane nodded, though she didn't look comfortable in the least.

'You're in safe hands,' said Carina. 'I've been trained.'

'Has she?' Erica Lay asked Fräulein Bloom urgently.

Fräulein Bloom shook her head. 'She has not.' But it was too late now. Carina showed the camera the Cellusmite's remote-control handset. 'This is the control pad and here is where I make a decision about the level and time my client should be cooked for.'

'Uh-oh. No cooking jokes,' said Erica. 'The contract is quite specific about that.'

'I think we'll go for full power for twenty-five minutes,' Carina continued regardless. 'That should be long enough to get Jane's thighs to roughly the same size as a normal person's . . .'

'But not in one session,' Erica pointed out.

For the benefit of the camera, Carina turned the dial right up and pressed the big green button.

In the background the Cellusmite machine roared into life, sounding like a cross between a boiling kettle and a vacuum cleaner. The noise was so loud and so unexpected that Carina, who had her back to the action, jumped out of her skin.

'Oh my god,' said Jenny the producer from *Wakey-Wakey*. 'Is it meant to sound like that?'

'No. Absolutely not,' said Anneka Bloom.

'Help!' came a faint cry from Jane.

'You are only supposed to turn the power up very, very gradually,' said Fräulein Bloom, snatching the remote control from Carina's hands. 'Like this.'

She turned the dial right down.

The vibration had made it impossible to focus on Jane's face as she was jiggled violently from side to side. Now that she was only gently undulating, it was possible to see she was terrified. Her cheeks were already bright red. Puffs of steam emanated from the gaps around her neck. She looked like a missionary in a cannibal's pot.

'Do I really have to stay in here?' she asked in a tiny meek voice.

Jenny from *Wakey-Wakey* managed to persuade Jane that she should stay put for at least fifteen minutes with the promise of any other treatment she fancied for free afterwards. But after twelve minutes, at which point Jane's eyelids started to flicker as though she was about to pass out, Anneka Bloom intervened and poor Jane was released from the pod.

She got to her feet unsteadily and leaned heavily on Jenny the producer while she got her breath back. Fortunately, they weren't quite ready for the next bout of filming anyway. Carina was on the other side of the salon having her make-up retouched.

Eventually, having taken a couple of calls on her mobile phone, Carina was ready again. Jane climbed back up onto the podium in her thong and Carina wielded the tape measure.

'Exactly the same,' she announced with a hint of disgust.

'Just pull the tape a bit tighter,' Jenny suggested.

Carina did exactly that and managed to find a loss of half an inch on each of Jane's thighs. She measured Jane's waist too, pulling the tape as tightly as she could while Jane sucked her stomach in as far as she was able.

'That's fabulous,' said Carina.

Luckily the camera was focused on Carina when Jane finally stopped smiling and keeled over.

Despite her ordeal, Jane Brady went back to Cornwall a very happy woman. *Wakey-Wakey*'s Jenny handed over three hundred pounds' worth of vouchers for other treatments at Luxoreus and a fifty-pound voucher for Jigsaw that had in fact been a birthday present to the producer from her older sister. Never mind. She would be reimbursed by her accounts department. It was worth it to ensure Jane's agreement that the session had gone well and there was absolutely no way whatsoever that she would be contacting any magazine, news-paper or radio talk show to say otherwise.

By the time the Cellusmite segment had been edited and had gone out on *Wakey-Wakey* there was no hint that Jane might have had cause for complaint. The scenes were neatly cut together to show Jane arriving, being measured and leaving the salon with a huge smile on her face, stopping only to proclaim that her jeans felt much, much looser and she couldn't wait to get home and shag her husband silly, inspired by her new-found body-confidence (of course she didn't actually say she would *shag* her husband silly. This was morning TV).

Anyway, the idea of Cellusmite quickly caught the nation's attention. As soon as the show finished airing, the telephones at Luxoreus were once again red-hot with calls from women keen to try the treatment for themselves. Another machine was ordered to take up the slack. And Carina (or rather Mickey) quickly entered into negotiations with Cellusmite's parent company for the licence to import many more of the machines into the UK. Perhaps even to open an entire chain of salons specializing in anti-cellulite treatments based around Cellusmite's near-magical properties.

Everything in Carina's life was going according to plan. Her bank balance grew ever more swollen as her Cellusmite machines slimmed the thighs of a nation (or, at least, those who were able to get an appointment). Mickey had promised that he would try to work out a way to break things off between her and Monkey without making her look like a baddy. And it had been suggested that Carina might get to present an entire week's worth of *Wakey-Wakey* all by herself when Patrick and Trudy took some private time and went to the Dominican Republic to renew their vows over Christmas (the renewing of which would be aired live on the show, of course).

There was just one little fly in the ointment.

Carina's mobile phone buzzed into life. A number she didn't recognize appeared on the screen. Slipping into a corner of the party she was attending for a little privacy, she tentatively accepted the call.

'It's been four months,' said the familiar voice. 'You still haven't done what you promised.'

Carina snapped the phone shut as though Freddy Krueger's tongue had just slipped out of the receiver and into her ear. She had barred the caller once before. Now she did it again. And first thing the following morning she would have to go out and get a new telephone. Eventually all stalkers gave up if you stopped responding to them. Didn't they?

43

After discovering that it was Carina who had taken over The Beauty Spot, Emily went into a decline. Her parents began to worry about her. They hadn't seen their daughter leave the house without putting on her make-up since she turned twelve. The pride Emily took in her appearance had always been a great source of amusement to them. That she had lost that pride was not.

'Aren't you going to brush your hair, love?' Emily's mother asked as Emily headed out to buy a pint of milk one afternoon.

Emily scratched at her head. She hadn't washed her hair in a week.

'Why bother?' she said.

Emily looked far worse than Natalie had done on her first day at The Beauty Spot all those months ago.

Natalie had disappeared of course. For a few weeks after the salon closed, Natalie had called her former boss every day, eager to hear what progress had been made with regard to reopening The Beauty Spot and getting back to work. Emily had suggested to Natalie very early on that she might want to look for another job, but Natalie had continued to call. Right up until the day when Emily told her that she'd broken the rental agreement on the premises and The Beauty Spot had a new tenant. Natalie had sounded genuinely anguished as Emily confirmed that this really was the end. P45s all round. She'd promised to stay in touch, because they were friends as well as co-workers, weren't they? But that lasted for about a week. Emily no longer had any idea what was going on in Natalie's life.

She hoped that Natalie had been able to find a good position somewhere nice. Emily had written her a wonderful reference and, before discovering that Carina had slipped so neatly into her shoes at the salon, Emily had also suggested that Natalie might even call Carina for a reference too.

'Imagine how that will look in your CV,' she said. 'You're a celebrity beautician.'

She wondered if Carina had given Natalie a reference. Or perhaps even a job . . .

'You need to start looking for a job yourself,' said Eric Brown to his daughter over breakfast about four months after The Beauty Spot closed. He hoped that having to get out of her pyjamas every day might be the first step in Emily's recovery. 'Your mother and I love having you here,' he said. 'But I'm sure you'd like your own space again someday.'

It was the hint she needed. Emily went out that day and bought copies of all the trade magazines. She swallowed her pride and applied for the type of jobs that she had so recently been interviewing other women for. She didn't get any of them. When she called, one of the salon owners explained, 'Well, you're a bit too fancy for us, love. You've had a salon of your own. You'd be bored here. You might start a revolution!'

That knowledge didn't much help Emily. What could she do? Leave her two years as a salon owner off her CV?

One afternoon, as she was walking to the post office to send off another armful of applications, she bumped into Malcolm of Herr Kutz. Malcolm threw his arms around her in a bear hug.

'My poor love,' he said. 'You look done in.'

'Thanks.'

'Did you find yourself a new job?' he asked.

Emily shook her head.

'Thank goodness for that,' he said. 'Come in here.'

He pulled Emily into his salon and invited her into the private back room. He made them both a cup of tea and began to outline his own plans for world domination.

'You can't just be a hairdresser these days,' he said. 'You've got to offer added value. I've been thinking about it for quite some time. I've got room at the back of my place for a treatment room. Are you interested in coming in on it?'

Emily said that she might be. Malcolm clapped his hands with delight.

It didn't take long for the old storeroom to be converted into a little treatment room with dimmable lights and a surround-sound system for the whale music. Malcolm paid for an advertisement announcing the expansion in the services Herr Kutz had to offer. When she didn't have clients, Emily manned the phones for the entire salon. It was a comedown from being her own boss, but it wasn't too bad. Malcolm soon became a firm friend.

Emily's parents were delighted that she'd found herself something to do all day other than watch *Wakey-Wakey* and hiss at the screen whenever Carina Lees's face appeared. The day before she started working for Malcolm, Emily gave herself a mani/pedi and threaded her own eyebrows back into perfect shape.

'It won't be long before she's back to being the Emily Brown we all know and love again,' said Malcolm to Emily's dad.

'It's every girl's prerogative to look her best,' Emily said with a smile.

44

Six months later

Carina had spent the entire morning at Luxoreus being preened and pampered and plastered with acrylic bits. It was especially important that Carina look her best that day. It was her birthday. She'd been planning her party ever since the salon's opening night. It had to be good. The salon opening party was going to be a difficult one to beat. So many celebs had turned out for that evening. The press coverage had been amazing. Carina had been showered with gifts by people she hardly knew. She'd received thank-you notes from people she hadn't knowingly invited.

Since that first party had been such a triumph and people seemed to enjoy the novelty of the venue, Carina considered holding her birthday bash at Luxoreus too. It was on Mickey's advice that she plumped for a nightclub (coincidentally part-owned by one of Mickey's old friends). The Lotus Rooms had just opened in Enfield. It was loosely based on the Los Angeles club of the same name. (Very loosely, in that it neither looked like the LA Lotus Rooms nor would it attract the same clientele.) Back in October, when Luxoreus opened to great acclaim, the owner of the Lotus Rooms said that he would be delighted to host Carina's birthday in return for nothing more than a namecheck by her influential self on her TV show or in her magazine column.

Six months later, he wanted a namecheck in both, *and* ten thousand pounds.

'Ten thousand pounds!' Carina yelled at Lucy. 'But we're doing him a favour. Remind him about the publicity.'

'Apparently, if you're not prepared to cough up, Kelly from Girlz Whirld has said she wants the room for her cousin's baby shower.'

Carina coughed up. She had to. The invitations, on lotus-embossed cards, had already been sent out. The caterers had made thousands of lotus-shaped vol-au-vents. She'd already bought her outfit. Carina was stuffed.

The unexpected invoice incident left a very bad taste in Carina's mouth. And so the party started badly. The room was as lovely as Carina remembered from her visit to the club, and it had been decked out fabulously – Egyptian theme as usual – but though Carina waited a full hour after the time stated on the invitations to make her entrance, she still found she was the first person to arrive. Not even the paparazzi were ready for her. Only Mickey's assistant Lucy was already there, standing by the door with her clipboard, chewing nervously on the end of a pencil.

'Where's Mickey?' Carina snapped.

'Meeting,' said Lucy. 'He says he'll be here later on.'

'You're telling me he arranged a *meeting* for the night of my birthday party?'

'Emergency,' said Lucy. 'Danny Rhodes was arrested for indecent exposure on Clapham Common last night.'

'He did that deliberately!' Carina wailed. 'He's always trying to steal the limelight.'

'I really don't think he intended to get arrested,' said Lucy.

'You have no idea how manipulative that man is,' Carina assured her.

Thankfully the guests started arriving not too long after that. If you could call them guests, thought Carina nastily. The first ten were all staff from Mickey's agency and a couple

Chris Manby

of girls from the tabloid gossip pages. Junior girls at that. Still, they got stuck into the champagne and made the place look a little busier.

It was another half an hour before Carina was gratified to see the familiar firework glitter of flashbulbs as a new batch of guests walked in. But if the paparazzi recognized them, she didn't . . .

Twenty people in a row arrived without triggering any kind of recognition in Carina at all. Was she going mad? Where were Elton and David? Liz and Arun? Peter Andre and Katie? Even Michelle Heaton – and that husband of hers whose name Carina could never remember – would have done.

The twenty-first person was a girl who looked a bit like Jordan. At least her extensions and implants probably came from the same salon and doctor. Accompanying the pneumatic brunette was a scruffy-looking man who was wearing a porkpie hat and chewing gum manically and open-mouthed.

'Who are they?' Carina asked.

They seemed to know her.

The newcomers made a beeline for Carina and air-kissed her extravagantly while the party photographer snapped. Then they posed for more pictures. The girl, who was wearing a *very* mini-skirt, even wrapped her leg around Carina as though the birthday girl were a pole in a lap-dance club. Carina was horrified (as a nation would see in the photos that graced the *Sun*'s Bizarre page two days later).

But that wasn't the worst of it. When the pole dancer unwrapped herself from Carina, the girl's behatted date stepped forward and suddenly honked Carina's implants as though they were antique car horns.

'Honk, honk,' he said as he did it. 'Honk honk!' Then he walked off in the direction of the bar without so much as an 'excuse me'.

'What the . . . ?' Carina was stunned. She cupped her breasts protectively.

'Don't worry about it. That's his *thing*,' said the girl with the implants, patting Carina on the arm. 'Now, where's the champagne?' She flicked back her hair and followed her boyfriend towards the drinks.

Carina grabbed Lucy by the elbow and marched her into a corner.

'Did you see that? You've got to do something. Random members of the public are getting in,' she complained. 'And I've just been assaulted. I want that man in the stupid hat thrown out of here at once. He grabbed my boobs and honked them.'

'Oh, that's his *thing*,' said Lucy. She didn't seem shocked. She just shook her head.

'What the hell does that mean? His *thing*? Who is he?'

'He's going to be one of the contestants on this year's *Living Hell*.'

'You mean he hasn't even been on TV yet?'

'No. But by the end of the summer he'll be a household name, just like you are. Honker's what he likes to be called. He honks anything he can get his hands on. It's his USP. His unique selling point.'

'I know what a USP is,' said Carina. 'But I still don't want him in here. Or anyone else I don't know. Or haven't heard of. I mean, what's her bloody USP?' Carina stabbed a finger in the direction of Honker's girlfriend.

'Now she is just hilarious,' said Mickey's assistant. 'Her name is Mystique. As in *feminine mystique*. At her audition for *Living Hell* she turned her eyelids inside out and then farted the National Anthem. The idea is that when Honker and Mystique come out of the house, they'll make a novelty single of Slade's "So Here It Is, Merry Christmas", comprised entirely of farts and honks.'

'Give me that.'

Carina grabbed Lucy's clipboard and looked down the guest list. The names of all the people who had RSVPd in the positive to her 'save the date' email (sent out six months earlier) had been neatly typed out but there were no ticks confirming arrival next to any of them. At the bottom of the list, however, about forty names Carina had not seen before had been added in Lucy's biro scrawl.

Carina thrust the clipboard back at her.

'I haven't heard of any of them. These people are all nobodies!' Carina complained.

'But without them there would be literally *nobody* here.'

Lucy had a point. Elton and David Furnish were no shows. Likewise Liz Hurley and Arun. Liyo Aslan texted Carina to say that he would have loved to be there but he was psychically exhausted. Of course he would be there in spirit, he signed off.

'Funny he didn't see that earlier on,' Lucy quipped.

Then Mickey texted Lucy to say that his meeting, which involved mysterious transatlantic conference calls, was likely to go on all night.

Not even Carina's nan made it to her party. She texted, 'I'd love to come dancing but my sciatica is playing up.'

At half past nine, when the pyramid-shaped birthday cake was brought out, a room full of people Carina had never met before sang 'Happy Birthday' in the most ear-splitting fashion possible. It seemed that every single stranger present hoped one day to have a record deal. Thus every single one of them added his or her own peculiar vocal quirk to the melody. A little bit of unnecessary vibrato here, a Fugees style 'yeah, yeah, uh, uh' there. Carina even heard someone rap, 'It's a Happy Birthday, y'all, check *this* out.' Of course, Honker and Mystique did their own honking, farting reprise. And then Mystique blew out Carina's candles. No prizes for guessing how.

Then, singing over, the unwanted guests vanished as quickly as they had appeared. (The reason for this mass exodus was that, in fact, they had all arrived together on a coach hired by Shore Thing PR and it would be dropping them all off again at Victoria.) Most of Mickey's staff left at the same time. The tabloid gossip girls were long gone. Only Carina and Mickey's assistant Lucy remained. At which point they were interrupted by one of the club's bouncers.

'The boss says we have to open the VIP room up to the general public now,' he told them apologetically. 'You're not spending enough money at the bar.'

It wasn't quite ten o'clock.

'Happy birthday,' said Lucy, handing Carina an envelope.

'Oh, thanks,' said Carina. At least Lucy had remembered to buy her a card. Perhaps she wasn't all bad.

But it wasn't a card. It was an invoice.

'Mickey wants to change your arrangement from a commission to a retainer,' Lucy explained. 'I'm sure it works out better for you.'

Carina had her driver take her straight home. What a miserable birthday she'd had. And it wasn't about to get any better. The postman had been since Carina left the house early that morning to prepare for what should have been a big night. There was a little pile of envelopes on the welcome mat. Three cards. One from her mum and stepdad. One from her nan. And one addressed in handwriting that she didn't recognize.

Carina opened that card first, not moving from the doormat to do so. Who could it be from? The writing looked shaky. Perhaps it was from Monkey. She pulled out the card.

'With Sympathy,' said the legend above a wan-looking bunch of roses.

Seeing the condolence card where a birthday card should have been, Carina started with fright. She dropped the card

243

onto the hallway floor and instinctively picked up the base-ball bat that she kept beside the door in case of burglars. Then, and only then, did she feel safe enough to pick the card back up and read what had been written inside. Perhaps this card wasn't meant for her. Perhaps whoever sent it had been writing a condolence card at the same time as Carina's birthday card and got the two mixed up. It was probably from her ancient auntie Joan. She was going round the bend.

But the words inside the card offered Carina no comfort.

'Happy Birthday. Perhaps it'll be your last. No birthday presents for people who don't keep their promises.'

She knew at once who had sent the horrible thing. But how did she know where Carina lived? Carina had never told her the address of the executive home with Mediterranean-style conservatory and American kitchen. Mickey wouldn't have given it out. Would Lucy? Carina dialled Lucy at once and prepared to tear a strip off her.

'Of course I wouldn't do that,' said Lucy, sounding strangely sympathetic. As if she almost cared. 'Client addresses are absolutely private except on a need-to-know basis. You know that. Are you OK? You want me to call the police?'

'No,' said Carina, deciding quite suddenly that it was best not to involve the law. 'I'm fine. I'll be fine.'

She slept with the baseball bat beside her that night.

45

The day after her disastrous birthday party, Carina took herself off to a spa on the Surrey/Hampshire borders where she lounged around looking significantly incognito. When she got back to Luxoreus, her salon manager Anita handed her the post, which contained the usual A4-sized Manila envelope full of press cuttings from Shore Thing. That day, Carina seized the envelope from Anita with particular eagerness. She needed the boost of a nice photo of herself. She had twirled on the red carpet outside The Lotus Rooms for the benefit of the snappers for what seemed like an hour. She'd been wearing a fabulous cobweb dress by a hot new designer. There was bound to be at least one picture of that.

There were several. But the captions weren't exactly what Carina had hoped for.

'Would you let your daughter go out looking like this?' asked the front page of the *Daily Mail*. 'Would she want to?' asked one of the newspaper's bitchier columnists inside.

'Has Halloween come early?' asked *Heat*.

Even *Get This!* – the weekly that had practically been a Carina Lees fanzine for the past year – had stuck her and her cobweb dress in their 'when bad clothes happen to good people' section. 'Sorry, Carina,' the caption said. 'Ordinarily our star columnist never puts a foot wrong when it comes to red carpet glamour. But look at this mess of a dress. What happened???'

Without saying a word to Anita, Carina left the salon and jumped back into her Range Rover. Forty-five minutes (and two speed-camera flashes) later, Carina was standing in the lobby of Shore Thing PR. Mickey was out, the girl on reception told her. Carina had to wait half an hour for Lucy to see her instead.

Carina brandished the cuttings under Lucy's nose like a dog owner drawing a puppy's attention to a widdle.

'What the hell is this?' she asked.

'It was just a bad choice of dress,' said Lucy simply. 'Everyone gets it wrong sometimes.'

'I don't. I don't get it wrong. Get Mickey on the phone now. Tell him that I'm never wearing that designer again. I don't care whose nephew he is. Tell him I want Dior for everything from now on. If I ever appear in the worst-dressed columns again, heads will roll!'

To underline that she meant business, Carina picked up Lucy's phone and handed it to her.

'Carina,' said Lucy, replacing the receiver in its cradle without dialling anybody. 'Mickey is in a very important meeting.'

'This is important to me!'

'I'll let him know you're upset, but really, there isn't anything else I can do right now. It doesn't matter. Today's news, tomorrow's chip paper.'

Carina didn't see it like that. She saw nominations for 'worst-dressed celeb of the year' on the horizon. She told Lucy as much.

'There's no point getting into a sweat about it,' Lucy tried again. 'You'll just have to make sure you're wearing something really amazing next time you go out. Then the status quo will be restored. No one will remember you a year from now.'

'What?'

'I mean,' said Lucy hurriedly, 'no one will remember you wore one bad dress a year from now.'

Lucy's telephone buzzed. She picked up.

'He's here? Oh, great. Send him through.'

She put down the phone and looked up at Carina, who was still standing in front of her desk, with an apologetic smile.

'I'm sorry, Carina. I'm going to have to finish this conversation. Mickey's next client is here.'

'Who is it?' Carina asked. She wanted to know who could be more important to Mickey than the business of reassuring her about those horrible pictures. She soon found out.

Honker crept up behind Carina, put his arms around her and 'honked' energetically on her breasts.

Carina whirled around and slapped him about the head with her limited-edition Chloé clutch bag.

Lucy shook her head at him, but she was secretly glad that Honker had managed to achieve what her gentle entreaties hadn't. Carina stormed out of the building.

Back at home, Carina shut herself in the bathroom. She sat on the closed toilet seat and examined the pictures again. It was just the dress, wasn't it, which had drawn such bitchiness from her usual allies in the press?

But then she read through the 'anonymous' snippets of gossip in Bizarre.

'Which reality "celebrity" ate too many pies before attending her own birthday party in a dress straight out of *The Munsters* that did nothing for her cellulite?'

Judging by the Halloween comments in *Heat*, they had to mean her. But cellulite? That was just spiteful, wasn't it? Carina didn't have cellulite. How could the owner of a salon that boasted Britain's first and only Cellusmite machine possibly have anything but perfect thighs?

Carina pulled down her jeans and balanced on the toilet seat so that she could see her bum and thighs in the mirror above the Tuscan marble double basin. She grabbed at the spare flesh at the top of each leg and squeezed it until she found a dimple.

'I've got cellulite!!!' she squealed in disgust.

Emerging from the bathroom, she got straight back into the Range Rover and drove to Luxoreus. It was almost closing time. Once everyone had gone, she would lock herself in there and Cellusmite her thighs into oblivion. No one would ever, ever take a bad photo of her again.

46

'I've got something that'll make your morning,' said Malcolm as he walked into Herr Kutz on the Tuesday after Carina's birthday. 'Have you seen this week's edition of *Heat*?' He waved the magazine in front of her nose.

Emily caught sight of the headline – Carina As You've Never Seen Her – and made a grab for it. Malcolm quickly moved the magazine out of her reach.

'Uh-uh-uh,' Malcolm wagged his finger teasingly. 'It's not polite to snatch. What do you say?'

'Please may I have a look at that magazine?' asked Emily in a singsong voice. 'Pretty please.'

'Not yet,' said Malcolm, hiding it behind his back. 'We'll look at it together. Put the kettle on first.'

While Emily filled the kettle, Malcolm lay the magazine in the middle of the kitchen table, smoothing it out lovingly. Emily made the tea. Malcolm heated up the chocolate croissants he had also bought on his way in that morning. Only when their breakfast was properly prepared and set out did Emily and Malcolm get round to opening the magazine. Emily couldn't wait to see what was inside. The picture on the front cover alone would have been enough to keep Emily smiling for a week.

It was a snap of Carina getting out of her Range Rover in front of Luxoreus. She looked a far cry from the glamorous girl that graced the sofa at *Wakey-Wakey*. An unfortunate gust of wind lifted her hair so that you could see the knotty join between platinum-blonde extension and mousy locks beneath. She wore no make-up. Her face was pale. Her mouth, turned down at the corners, only added to the impression that she had aged ten years in as many days. As she climbed out of her car, her tracksuit bottoms got caught up on her seat-belt clip and were tugged down to reveal the waistband of a pair of large greying knickers.

'Ewww. My mother always told me you should never leave the house without clean underwear,' Malcolm commented.

'Make that *good* clean underwear,' Emily elaborated. 'I'd be embarrassed to use a pair of pants like that for dusting.'

'Find the other pictures,' said Malcolm gleefully as Emily turned to the contents.

The other shots of Carina were on pages 4, 5 and 6.

There she was, preening for the cameras in that cobweb dress again, blissfully unaware that she was showing cellulite. For the benefit of its readers, the magazine had kindly circled the offending dimpled fat in red. The next shot showed her arriving at a film premiere, lifting her arm to wave at the crowd. Another red circle helpfully drew attention to an underarm sweat patch on her pink silk dress. There was a picture of her bending over in a shoe shop (Gina on Sloane Street), revealing a 'whale tail' of thong. And a 'muffin top' roll of fat. Finally, most horrific of all, they had printed a picture sent in by a reader, of Carina sitting in her car at traffic lights, obviously (hopefully) unaware she was being observed as she excavated the contents of one of her nostrils with a long acrylic fingernail.

'My god,' said Malcolm. 'She's putting me off my chocolate croissant.'

'They must have been saving up all these bad pictures for months,' said Emily. 'I wonder why they're printing them now?'

'I guess her fifteen minutes must be nearly over,' said Malcolm.

* * *

Indeed, that very same day, Mickey took a call from the editor of *Get This!* magazine. He had placed a call to her the previous afternoon, reminding her that it was almost time to discuss terms for the renewal of Carina's contract. When Kathleen the editor didn't return his call right away, Mickey had an inkling that something was afoot. He braced himself for an uncomfortable discussion about the kind of fee Carina could expect. His most pessimistic estimate was that they might try to offer him half the previous rate. He had not expected Kathleen to say, 'We're thinking about a complete change of style for that page . . . Basically, a change of celebrity.'

'You're saying Carina's pissed you off,' said Mickey perceptively.

'She keeps calling Alice at three in the morning,' Kathleen confirmed. 'I don't know, Mickey. Maybe you should have a word. Alice says that sometimes it's like Carina's got no one else to talk to.'

It wasn't a total disaster for Mickey Shore. The replacement celebrity Kathleen suggested was actually another of his clients and thus Mickey would retain his obscenely high commission. But breaking the news to Carina would still be difficult. He decided that he would have a nice long lunch first. Steel himself up.

However, it was while Mickey was having a nice long lunch and half a bottle of Pouilly Fumé that things took a turn for the worst. Having been expressly told not to interrupt his moment of reverie before that afternoon's horrible business, Lucy called Mickey just as his coffee and mints arrived.

'I told you not to bother me,' he said. 'What part of that simple instruction didn't you understand?'

'Actually,' Lucy pointed out to him, 'what you said was that I shouldn't contact you except in case of dire emergency.'

'And . . .' said Mickey grumpily.

'We are having a dire emergency. Right now.'

Mickey folded his napkin and asked for the bill, cursing that he would be wracked by indigestion all afternoon.

When he got back to the office, Lucy was clutching her forehead, squeezing her brow muscles together in an attempt to stave off a tension headache.

'The *Sun* have already been on the phone,' she told him.

'How did they know about this before we did?' Mickey wanted to know.

Jane Brady, the girl from Cornwall who became the first-ever British woman to use a Cellusmite machine for the benefit of *Wakey-Wakey*'s viewers, was suing Carina Lees. Her claim was that the reality star had ruined her life. She had, said her deposition, been subjected to a humiliating and painful ordeal at Carina's hands. Since her twenty minutes in the Cellusmite machine she had suffered debilitating flashbacks, insomnia, claustrophobia, even piles . . . You name it; Jane Brady was suffering from it, and all because of Carina Lees and the Cellusmite machine.

Before Mickey could phone Cellusmite, their managing director was on the phone to him. But, rather than promising to work with Mickey to clear Carina's name by presenting evidence that Jane Brady's malaise could not possibly have been caused by their fabulous machine, the Cellusmite boss said that he too was planning to sue Mickey's client.

'Our Cellusmite machines are perfectly safe,' he asserted. 'In the hands of *trained* therapists. As far as we at Cellusmite are concerned, we cannot and will not be held responsible for any unforeseen consequences arising from the operation of our machines by untrained individuals. It said as much in our contract. Our public relations officer Erica Lay and head of training, Anneka Bloom, will both attest to the fact that Miss Lees chose to operate the machine without training and against our advice. She refused the opportunity to be properly trained in our safety procedures. Our responsibility is completely absolved.'

Mickey sought legal advice at once, of course. And so did Cellusmite. Their lawyer called to say that the machines at Luxoreus should be rendered inoperational at once.

Mickey phoned the salon.

'I've got clients all afternoon,' said Anita.

'You'll have to send them home,' said Mickey.

Finally, he got round to calling Carina. She was at a hair-dressing salon in Mayfair, having extra extensions woven into her already prodigious fake locks. When she saw her agent's number on her mobile, Carina launched straight into a rant.

'Have you see the *Sun* this morning?' she asked. 'There must be something you can do to stop them printing that picture of me in that stupid cobweb dress. Tell them that if they say I've got cellulite one more time, we'll sue them for libel. Princess Diana did it, didn't she? When they said she had cellulite on her bum. It was just the imprint of her car seat. That's what you can see on my legs too. We need to sort this out, Mickey. This could affect my new deal with Cellusmite. How the hell can I have cellulite when I'm the face of the most effective fat-reducing regime in the world?'

'Not any more,' said Mickey. 'Carina, I need you to come into the office at once.'

Carina was so shocked by news of the lawsuit that Mickey decided it might be best if she didn't go back home.

'There might be paparazzi,' he reasoned.

Instead, he had Lucy book Carina a room at a Central London hotel. It wasn't a swanky one, but it was one where he could trust the staff not to reveal their guest's identity when the Cellusmite lawsuit hit the papers the following day.

Now it was Jane Brady's turn to have her fifteen minutes. The *Sun* had paid for her to travel up to London again and pictured her looking sad beneath the inevitable headline: 'Carina Lees turned my life into a Living Hell.' Jane talked about the downward spiral her life had taken since she volunteered to try out Cellusmite for *Wakey-Wakey*.

'Before Carina measured my thighs,' said Jane. 'I hadn't really thought about how big they were. I mean to say, I wasn't entirely happy with my figure – what woman is? – but I had never considered myself to be *disgusting*. That was how Carina described me. They cut that from the bits they aired on the *Wakey-Wakey* show, but I heard it and it stayed with me when I went back to Cornwall. All the way home her comments were ringing in my ears. She called me "fatty" too. When she thought I wasn't listening. My husband noticed that I was different at once. We'd always had a very healthy sex life but, after Carina's nasty comments, I didn't want to get undressed in front of him at all.'

The timing could not have been worse. For the past month the *Wakey-Wakey* show had been running a campaign called, 'Just say no to size zero'. It was Trudy's idea. In the wake of a couple of widely reported anorexia-related deaths in the modelling community, she said that she wanted to celebrate female beauty in all its forms. She insisted that the sofa be filled with 'plus-sized' guests for the next four weeks, 'to help re-educate the viewers in their ideas about what's really attractive'.

Wakey-Wakey had scored an enormous coup in the form of a guest appearance by a young Oscar-nominated British actress who spoke movingly about her battle with eating disorders, made worse by the tyranny of the Hollywood mania for skinny. So when it was revealed that Carina Lees had made 'fattist' comments, what could the show do but disown her? The day after the *Sun* ran Jane Brady's Cellusmite sob story, Trudy of *Wakey-Wakey* was delighted to make an announcement.

'I do believe that Carina is a good person at heart,' said Trudy almost sincerely. 'And so it is with great regret that we have to say farewell to her. However, both Patrick and I believe that we have a duty to educate as well as entertain. And the young women who watch this show every day need to know that it is OK to be whoever you really are. Thin or fat. We can only apologize if Carina's Makeover Magic segment on this show gave any other message to you, our beloved viewers.'

In the production office, Christian made gagging motions. Maddy slapped him.

At home on her sofa in Essex, Carina blinked back tears.

'This is a bloody disaster,' said Mickey, fresh from a call to the publishing company, which had decided not to release the paperback version of Carina's makeover book after all.

'Shall I get Carina on the phone?' asked Lucy.

'Nah,' said Mickey. 'No point. But see if you can get that Jane Brady's number, will you?'

By the end of that afternoon, Jane Brady, Cornish Cellusmite Victim, would be a client of Shore Thing PR.

47

Carina Lees was desperate. She couldn't understand how, seemingly overnight, she had gone from being the nation's darling to public enemy number one. There were vast groups on Facebook dedicated solely to Carina's vilification.

How was it possible that one moment everyone had loved her makeover segment on *Wakey-Wakey* and now even the team at *Wakey-Wakey* themselves were declaiming makeover shows as the very worst example of exploitation television? Trudy Blezard had taken to appearing on the show without make-up. She was allowing her grey roots to grow out and proclaimed proudly that she had given up calorie counting and Pilates.

'It's important to be authentic,' she said. 'This is the way I really am. I'm not going to hide my blemishes behind make-up and Botox any more.'

(Meanwhile, Patrick embarked on an affair with Maddy, the *Wakey-Wakey* production assistant, who never left the house without her YSL *Touche Eclat*.)

Anyway, suddenly it was open season on Carina Lees. The photo spread in *Heat* was the very least of it. Carina had no idea how often she picked her nose until the tabloids printed the evidence. At first she tried to tough it out. She would get up, put on her make-up and make the journey into Central London to Mickey's office for more crisis talks (or at least to hang around at Shore Thing in the hope that somebody would have a crisis talk with her). But, no matter how good she thought she was looking when she left the house, the papers would somehow produce a picture of her looking terrible. Like those pictures of Robbie Williams, fresh out of rehab, looking heavy-lidded in a stoned sort of way when, in reality, he'd probably just blinked at the wrong moment.

Now Carina dared not open her mouth for fear that a paparazzo would catch her mid-sentence and the paper would present her as a snarling beast hurling obscenities at anyone bigger than a size eight. And so going out became an increasingly difficult prospect. Carina's nan moved into the executive home to keep her company and she stayed indoors instead, watching endless reruns of 1970s sitcoms, not daring even to turn on the BBC news in case some Tory backbencher was attempting to gain brownie points with the general public by denouncing Carina's lookist stance. A double whammy. At the same time proving that he was 'down with the kids' by even knowing who Carina was.

'You need to do something, Mickey,' Carina begged him. 'You need to rehabilitate me.'

Mickey made soothing noises. 'I'm doing my best, my dear,' he promised. 'I'll come up with a way to get you back where you belong.'

In a funny way, Mickey was doing exactly what he said. He was coming up with a way to put Carina back exactly where he thought she belonged.

The truth was, Mickey Shore actively despised most of his clients. When he started out in the management business, the people who put themselves forward for representation usually had a recognizable talent. They could sing, they could dance, or they could act. Now all it took was the slightest brush with some other 'celebrity' to send the kind of people who should have contented themselves with staying at home, watching *Who Wants to Be a Millionaire?*, rushing to Mickey Shore's door.

From time to time, the scumbags who solicited his services had a story that would genuinely interest the tabloids
for a couple of weeks. Maybe even a whole month. But that
– fifteen minutes of fame and a down-payment on a top-of-
the-range BMW – was no longer enough for most of them.
After that they wanted the recording contract, the modelling
assignments, the leading role in the next Tom Cruise film . . .
They thought their brief moment in the spotlight was the
start of an actual career, for heaven's sake! Sooner or later
they all started to get cocky. Phoning Mickey on a Sunday
morning, like he was some kind of employee. One builder
from Newcastle, who shagged the ex-wife of a Premier League
footballer, had actually asked Mickey to have Select Model
Management send him their book so he could pick out a
girlfriend, as though the agency was a private dating service.
Talk about delusions of grandeur. These people had no idea
of their limitations.

And Carina Lees had reached hers. She couldn't sing, she
couldn't dance, she couldn't act. Even if she agreed to get her
kit off – which she would; they all did in the end – she had
a maximum of two years left in her as a glamour model.
Mickey might have rehabilitated her, found some way to
convince the public of her contrition, but why bother? A fresh
bunch of reality TV graduates had recently hit the market
and the public eye was turning on them. She was old news.

So Mickey Shore was cashing in on Carina Lees. She was
on the downslide; it was time to bring the skeletons out. While
the papers were still vaguely interested.

He didn't feel too bad about it. He might even take Carina
out for lunch one day this week and explain to her that, in
a way, this continued bad press was doing her a favour. It was
keeping her in the public eye and reigniting interest in her. In
a best-case scenario, Carina's fans would rally round and he
could engineer her 'comeback' in that year's *I'm a Celebrity*.

In a worst-case scenario, they could make a few quid from rebuttals before Carina's flame of fame was extinguished once and for all. He'd point her in the direction of a good financial advisor. He wasn't that cold-hearted.

Mickey clicked on an email from Jane Brady, the Cellusmite 'victim'. The title was 'Three in a Bed'. For a second, Mickey was very excited. Then he read: 'I've written this screenplay called *Three in a Bed*. Can you get it in front of Quentin Tarantino?'

'No,' said Mickey, pressing delete.

If there was just one silver lining to the clouds that had gathered over Carina's life, it was that her stalker seemed to have given up on her. She hadn't had a letter from her deranged nemesis in weeks. She'd had plenty of other hate mail, but nothing in the familiar handwriting that made her heart sink to her boots and left her regretting that she had ever been born. Perhaps even her stalker felt sorry for her.

48

Matt Charlton was at home nursing a cold. He and Cesar sat side by side on the sofa. Matt had a Lemsip. Cesar was contemplatively gnawing on a dog-chew. Matt would not ordinarily have been watching *Wakey-Wakey*.

The 'Fatty-Gate' affair had largely passed Matt by. His information about current affairs generally came from *Newsnight*, and Jeremy Paxman had yet to chair a debate about the rights and wrongs of the nation's obsession with dimply thighs. But when he heard Trudy's heartfelt speech about the dismissal of Carina Lees from the *Wakey-Wakey* team, it captured Matt's attention in a big way.

Over the previous couple of weeks, memories of that night at the house Natalie Hill shared with the interior designer from Dyfed had been coming back to Matt like shards of glass hidden in a shag-pile carpet. Each time he found one, it was an acutely uncomfortable sensation. But Matt was gradually piecing those memories together and the picture they created was unexpected. Seeing Carina Lees's face on television prompted the final piece to fall into place.

He'd been through what he remembered so many times. The walk home from Emily's house had always been pretty clear. Natalie had been drunk. She had leaned on Matt heavily as they crossed the quiet streets. She was weaving so much it took longer than Matt had expected to get her safely home. By the time they reached her door, it was almost one in the morning. Matt had a meeting first thing. All he wanted to do was see Natalie safely inside and walk the remaining three streets to his own house. Cesar was equally keen to be curled up inside his own bed with its tartan blankets.

'I'll make you a cup of coffee,' said Natalie.

'That's OK,' said Matt. 'I really should be getting home.'

'I can't let you go without making you a drink,' said Natalie. 'That wouldn't be very nice.'

'No need at all, I promise. I won't be offended.'

'I would be.'

Natalie had already grabbed his collar and was pulling him inside the door.

Cesar hesitated outside until Natalie grabbed his collar and hauled him over the step as well. The dog sat down on the doormat, looking disgruntled. Nobody, but nobody, pulled Cesar by the collar. Natalie was lucky that he was trained not to bite despite terrible provocation.

Once she had them inside, Natalie ushered Cesar and Matt into the sitting room and practically pushed Matt down onto the sofa.

'Take your coat off,' she told him.

'No need,' he said, 'I'll only have to put it back on again in a minute.'

'Take your coat off,' Natalie insisted. 'You won't feel the benefit if you don't.'

By this time, Matt didn't really have a choice. Natalie was already wrestling the coat off his right arm. It seemed easier to acquiesce than risk a dislocated shoulder.

'What do you want to drink?' asked Natalie. 'I've got Baileys.'

'Tea,' said Matt.

'That's not a real nightcap.'

'I've got a meeting first thing in the morning.'

'Fine,' said Natalie. 'I could put some Baileys in your tea, if you like?'

'That sounds disgusting,' Matt told her.

'Stay there,' said Natalie. 'Don't move.'

She wobbled off into the kitchen.

Matt didn't move a muscle. Instead he listened carefully to the sound of Natalie moving about the house. She had moved from the kitchen. He heard her walking up the stairs. Thundering, was actually more accurate. He heard the sound of her tripping over the final stair and cursing loudly. He heard her heavy footsteps in the room above his head. He heard a wardrobe being opened.

When Natalie came back downstairs she had changed. She was no longer wearing the demure skirt and top. She was wearing something that was probably a nightdress. She sat down on the sofa beside him and, before he knew what was going on, she had tucked her hand inside his shirt and was twisting his chest hair.

'Er, Natalie,' he said. 'I've got to go.'

'No!' Natalie's face crumpled. She pouted. He guessed that she thought it was an alluring pout, but it reminded him of his two-year-old nephew preparing for a tantrum. 'I just want to talk to you,' she said. 'I've been really upset about the way things are going at The Beauty Spot,' she continued. 'I'm so worried.'

'OK,' said Matt, softening. He couldn't leave her in distress. 'But can we have that cup of tea first?'

'Alright.' Natalie bounced to her feet again.

As soon as she was out of sight, Matt went in search of the bathroom. Cesar followed.

'We'll get out of here just as soon as we can,' Matt promised him, grabbing his coat from the banister as he passed. 'Half a cup of tea and we're going.'

Cesar's shiny brown eyes seemed to convey his agreement. Matt found the bathroom and his little dog squeezed in there after him.

Matt undid his trousers and started to pee. As he stood at the toilet, his gaze wandered around the walls of the tiny little room. Natalie had told him all about her flatmate, Morgan, whom she had met at sixth-form college. He had gone on to study at art school and now he was training to be an interior designer. Certainly the whole flat bore the hallmarks of someone who was interested in the way things looked. It was just an ordinary rental flat: magnolia walls, IKEA furniture, but someone had added a certain flourish. The sitting room was covered in cushions and wall-hangings reminiscent of a Moroccan souk. A garland of fairy lights festooned the banisters. There were candles everywhere. Unusual artworks lined the walls. Even in the littlest room.

Morgan obviously had a wicked sense of humour. He had decorated the bathroom walls with prostitutes' calling cards. The kind of brightly coloured postcards you find blu-tacked to the walls of call boxes all over London, promising 'hot young models' 'new to town'.

There was quite a collection. Must have taken some time to put together, Matt thought. He couldn't help but be fascinated. He wasn't the gay man everyone seemed to think he was, after all. He read a few and chuckled at the spelling mistakes. But there was one card that truly shocked and surprised him.

The card was illustrated with a busty redhead, who pouted at the camera with the kind of pneumatic lips that suggest a plastic surgeon who ought to be struck off. She was (barely) covering her nipples with her long acrylic fingernails. And beneath her was a phone number that Matt recognized at once. Unbelievable. He checked it against the number in his phone.

He plucked the card down and tucked it into his coat pocket.

Now, as Matt watched Carina Lees crying her way through

another apology on television, he finally remembered what Natalie had told him just before he passed out.

'Come on, Cesar,' he said. 'We've got someone to see.'

And as if Matt needed further confirmation that he'd solved the mystery of that night at last, when he pulled on the jacket he hadn't worn in almost a year, he found that card again.

49

Seven months had passed since Malcolm asked Emily if she would like to set up a treatment room at the back of Herr Kutz and she'd grudgingly accepted. She hadn't been ecstatic about the prospect – anything was bound to be a comedown from running her very own salon – but the surprising and wonderful fact was that it was working out just perfectly. Emily enjoyed Malcolm's company. He didn't treat her like an employee. He was fast becoming a friend. It was hard to believe that she had ever suspected him of having her salon robbed so that he could gain a professional advantage.

Malcolm understood Emily very well. He too had worked hard to set up his own business, and the thought of losing it gave him sleepless nights. Lately he had begun to talk about the possibility of opening another place, with Emily at the helm.

'Renting space from you?' she asked him.

'No. As a partner, of course.'

Emily was thrilled and agreed to the idea at once.

'We could call it Herr and Beauty,' Malcolm suggested.

'Perhaps,' said Emily.

It was something to work towards. A short while later, Malcolm and Emily sat down and did some financial projections together. Emily couldn't help thinking of Matt as she and Malcolm discussed their plans. She could almost see Matt's approving nod as she actually suggested that Malcolm rein in some of his more extravagant impulses.

Emily had been thinking about Matt quite a bit lately. She

wondered how he was getting on. She thought she'd seen him walk past Herr Kutz one afternoon and was tempted to go after him. Just to say 'hello'. Give Cesar a pat on the head. But it had seemed wrong. Disloyal to Natalie. Though Natalie had been increasingly blasé about her 'trouble' with Matt towards the end of their time together at The Beauty Spot, and lately she had disappeared from Emily's life altogether, still Emily felt she had to stick by her promise to keep away from Matt Charlton. She couldn't ignore the possibility that Matt wasn't the nice guy she had once believed him to be. And so her thoughts about him were always tinged with guilt.

Emily's thoughts about Carina were altogether less complicated. Planning her new venture with Malcolm not only made her think of Matt, it made Emily remember how far she had got in achieving her ambition before Carina snatched her salon out from under her nose. Carina's fall from grace had gone some way to cheering Emily up, but it wasn't enough. Carina had stolen Emily's life. She'd had to change so many things as a result.

Malcolm caught Emily with a frown on her face.

'What are you doing?' he said, sticking his thumb firmly on the furrow between her brows in an attempt to make her forehead relax. 'Do you want to have to start using Botox?'

'Sorry,' said Emily.

'Want to come for a drink after work tonight?'

'Not tonight,' said Emily, narrowing her eyes as an idea crossed her mind. 'There's something I've got to do.'

50

Carina promised Anita that she would close up the salon herself that night.

'But you don't know what to do,' said Anita reasonably.

'I think I can work it out,' said Carina. 'I did have a proper job before I became a celebrity, you know.'

'Well, don't blame me if we get robbed because you did the alarm wrong,' said Anita as she shrugged on her coat. She was bothered, but not that bothered. She had a feeling that Luxoreus wouldn't be around for that much longer anyway. She'd already started looking for another job. 'Night.'

Carina waved Anita off distractedly.

'Yeah. Night.'

Though the Cellusmite machines were officially out of action, waiting for the manufacturers to send a van to take them back to Germany, Carina had been using the machines in secret every night. She wasn't convinced that she could see all that much difference to the size and texture of her thighs, but she had grown somewhat addicted to the sensation that being inside the machine afforded her. Twenty minutes in there with the dial set to low was almost like being in a floatation tank. It was the nearest she got to feeling relaxed. And protected.

Certain that she wouldn't be disturbed, Carina started to undress. She was just taking off her new shoes when she heard the tinkle of the bell above the salon's front door. She hadn't locked the door after Anita. She quickly buckled her shoes back on. The last thing she wanted was to be caught using the Cellusmite.

'Hello?' she called. 'Hello, Anita? Is that you?'

No answer.

'Anita?'

Still nothing.

But there was definitely someone in the lobby. Carina could hear them moving around. Her heart began to beat faster. Was someone going to rob the salon? And if they were, what was Carina's best course of action? Should she confront the intruder? Or hide?

She hesitated behind the door to the treatment room, opening it just a crack to try to get a view of the lobby. It wasn't much of a view. She couldn't see past the industrial-sized stack of paper towels in the corridor.

Carina suddenly thought to call someone on her mobile phone. But, even as she was feeling pleased with herself for coming up with such a clever and obvious solution, she remembered that her phone was still in the pocket of her jacket. The jacket that was hanging from a cat-shaped statue by the front desk . . . She wasn't going to be calling anyone.

She heard the sound of footsteps on the marble floor of the lobby. Then the sound of someone opening the stiff drawers in the front desk. The intruder coughed. Whoever it was, he or she didn't seem that bothered about anyone knowing they were there. They seemed to be taking their time. Looking round. Perhaps it was just one of the girls, Carina told herself hopefully. Forgotten something.

'Hello,' she called again, affecting a cheery, confident tone. 'I'm back here in the treatment rooms. Make sure you don't lock me in on your way out, won't you?'

Spa Wars

The door to the treatment room in which Carina was cowering suddenly swung wide open. And standing in the doorway was an unwanted visitor whom Carina knew only too well.

51

'Get out!' said Carina, summoning all her power to push the intruder back into the lobby. She tried to sound authoritative but there was an edge of panic to her voice. 'Get away from me. Go to the papers if you want to,' said Carina. 'Do whatever you want. I don't care any more. I just want you out of here.'

But the intruder was going nowhere. In fact, slowly and surely Carina was losing ground again, being backed further into her own salon. Carina continued to shout and shove but her opponent just shoved back. And back and back and back until Carina realized to her horror that she had been backed into the corridor that led to the treatment rooms and could no longer see the front window of the salon, which meant, of course, that no one passing by the salon would be able to look in through the window and see her.

'Get out of here. Let me go!' Carina shouted. 'You'll be sorry!'

'You're just the same as her,' the stalker was saying quite calmly. 'You think I'm some kind of joke, don't you? You feel sorry for me. You think you're better than me, just because you've got the right clothes and the hair extensions. I bet you had a real laugh about me behind my back, didn't you?'

By this time, Carina had been backed right up against a door. She stared with horror into the face that loomed over hers. There was a manic glint in those eyes that she hadn't seen before.

'It's alright for you. You've always had it good. You've

always been pretty and popular. You've always had everything you wanted. You don't know what it's like to be picked on because your hair's too frizzy or your nose is too big. I bet you were a bully. I bet you've been making fun of people like me your entire life . . .'

'No, no,' said Carina. 'I haven't. I swear. You've got it all wrong!'

Carina's protestations fell on deaf ears.

'Well, now you're going to find out what it's like when the boot is on the other foot!'

Carina's escape plan came to her in a flash. She could climb out through a treatment-room window! She leaned heavily on the door and scrabbled behind her to find the door handle.

'Please, God, don't let this door be locked,' Carina offered up a little silent prayer. Her prayer was answered. The handle turned easily and the door opened behind her. Carina slipped through it, quick as a fish darting under a rock, leaving her pursuer gawping. Carina slammed the door behind her and leaned against it, breathing hard. Safe for the moment.

'Come out of there.'

The door handle rattled.

'No way,' Carina shouted back, bracing herself against any attempts to smash the door down.

With her back against the door, she had a moment to consider her options. All she needed to do was wedge the door shut while she climbed out of the window . . .

But there was nothing in the room to use as a wedge. And there was no window.

'What?' Carina exclaimed.

She had been tricked into the one treatment room that had no window of its own. This was the extra, tiny room she had squeezed onto the end of the row after ripping out the original room divisions that Emily had installed. Never before had making space for extra treatments seemed like such a bad idea. A room with no windows. Carina remembered with shame how she had told the Luxoreus beauticians that having no natural light was no real hardship.

'I'm coming in to get you!' The stalker's voice sounded a little further away. As though someone was taking a run-up.

'Oooof!'

Eleven stone two hit the other side of the door. The impact was too much for Carina on her kitten heels. The door burst open and sent Carina skidding across the tiny room and onto her knees, ricocheting off the treatment couch and banging her head against the hard exterior of a Cellusmite machine as she fell.

'It's payback time,' was the last thing Carina heard before she passed out.

'Where am I?'

When she came to, Carina was seeing stars. She put a hand to her head. A tender lump the size of a duck's egg had already formed where she had crashed her skull against the Cellusmite. She began to be aware of her surroundings. She recognized the Egyptian-themed design stencilled at the top of the wall around the coving. She could see one of her little white shoes on the other side of the room. She picked it up and went to put it back on but discovered to her disappointment that the heel had snapped. What had happened? Carina considered the possibility that the broken heel was a clue to her predicament. She'd sue that Jimmy Choo . . .

'Anita!' Carina shouted. She needed some help to get up. But Anita didn't answer. 'Anita!'

She got to her feet alone, quite unsteadily, hanging on the treatment bench for support. Her head felt terrible. She examined herself in the mirror that hung over the basin. There were no obvious signs of damage, apart from the fact that one of her false eyelashes had come loose and was resting on her cheek like a big black spider. Carina was starting to put the lash back where it was supposed to be when she noticed that the shadowy figure of someone else had appeared in the reflection beside her.

'Anita?'

'Anita isn't here. No one's here except you and me.'

Suddenly it all came back. Carina's amnesia was cured.

Natalie Hill.

'I'll call the police,' Carina protested.

'How exactly do you plan to do that?' Natalie asked.

Carina patted her pockets for her phone. Of course it was still in the jacket draped over the stone cat.

'Besides,' Natalie continued, 'if you could call them, what would you say?'

'I'll tell them you've been stalking me!'

'Just chasing an unpaid debt. It's not going to look good, Carina,' said Natalie. 'And neither are you.'

Natalie glanced to the corner of the room, drawing Carina's attention to the wax kettle that she had recently plugged in. The heated wax made a gurgling sound. Natalie stepped towards it.

'What are you going to do with that?' Carina asked.

It was a stupid question.

Natalie grinned.

52

Emily hadn't walked down Longbury Road since the night the officer from the Department of Health closed The New Beauty Spot down. It was time to change that. Apart from anything else, the Longbury Road was the fastest route between Herr Kutz and the town centre. It was a complete pain to have to take a ten-minute detour in each direction when you only had forty minutes for lunch. And so Emily decided it was time she got over it. She would walk past Luxoreus and with her head held high. At the top of the road she paused and took a deep breath. And then she set off, heart pounding.

At the other end of the Longbury Road, Matt Charlton was also preparing to confront his fears. He had also been avoiding walking past Emily's old salon, for fear that Natalie would rush out and have him arrested for stalking her. Now that he knew she had no grounds, however, it was a different matter. Matt was on his way to clear his name. He walked with his head held high too.

The former friends met right outside the front door of Luxoreus.

Cesar, remembering Emily's generosity with the dog-chews, wagged his tail and was immediately at her pockets.

'Matt, I . . .'

'Emily, you . . .'

The two humans danced around on the pavement, unsure whether to shake hands or embrace or keep on walking in opposite directions.

In the end Matt simply shoved the prostitute's calling card into Emily's hand.

'Look at this,' he said.

Emily shrieked.

'Ohmigod, what is this?' Emily let the card drop to the floor and tried to rush past him. 'Natalie was right about you. You're a pervert. Just leave me alone.'

'Wait! You've got to read it. Read the number!'

Before Matt could begin to explain, from inside the salon came a bloodcurdling scream that stopped Emily in her tracks.

53

Laughing maniacally, Natalie dipped a spatula into the wax pot, whipped it out and thrust it at Carina. Carina ducked out of the way. Natalie wielded the spatula like a light sabre, sweeping it from side to side right in front of Carina's face. Carina tried desperately to defend herself, but to no avail. Natalie loomed over her with the wax, flicking the horrible yellow stuff all over her with glee. Carina's Dolce & Gabbana shirt, her Versace trousers and her Jimmy Choos were all covered in the stuff. No dry-cleaner in the world would be able to rescue them. And soon Carina had been backed up against the Cellusmite machine once more.

The machine was open. Natalie darted the spatula at Carina's face. Carina jerked out of the way and suddenly found herself sitting on the hard plastic seat inside the Cellusmite. As Carina struggled to get back up, Natalie advanced. And stuck the spatula-full of hot wax right in Carina's hair!

Instinctively, Carina's hands flew to her head; it was while she was busy trying to get the sticky spatula out that Natalie slammed the Cellusmite's heavy door shut and locked it with the bar. The bar you were only ever meant to employ while moving the Cellusmite machine from one premises to another. Never were you supposed to use it while someone was actually inside!

'What are you doing?' Carina shouted. 'Let me out.'

'Not yet,' said Natalie. 'I haven't finished your treatment.'

'Oh god!'

Carina had always assumed that the Cellusmite had some

kind of safety facility that meant it would shut off automatically if the bar was employed while someone was inside it. That was what the therapists always told their clients. There's no need to worry if the treatment gets too intense, they'd say. The Cellusmite machine is perfectly safe. No need to worry at all. There's no way you can get trapped inside while the machine is working! You can get out of there at any time! Any time you like!

Well, they were wrong. If the 'safety' bar was down, you were stuffed. Carina quickly lost all her acrylic fingernails finding that out.

'Natalie! Let me out of here.'

Meanwhile, Natalie picked up the remote control for the unit – the remote control that you were meant to hand to the client so they could regulate the settings themselves – and set the Cellusmite to 'fast' and 'hot'.

'What are you doing!?'

As the machine whirred into life, Carina began to jiggle as though stuck with electric cattle prods.

'Turn it off!!!!'

'Come on,' said Natalie. 'You can't expect me to do that yet. This is more fun to watch than *Living Hell*. Or the humiliation of Makeover Magic.'

Carina tried desperately to reach the lock on the safety bar but her arms simply were not long enough. Her face grew redder and redder through exertion and the rapidly rising temperature inside the machine. Her eye make-up began to run down her face in long black streaks until she looked like a cheap plastic Pierrot doll melting in front of an electric fire.

'Let me out! Please! Please! I'll do anything! Do you want money? I can give you as much money as you want!'

Carina's voice grew ever more shrill as her panic rose, but Natalie was immune to Carina's entreaties. Instead, she stood calmly by the wax pot, watching the orange-yellow gloop inside it bubble. Then she took another spatula, loaded it up and promptly stuck it to Carina's fringe.

'Aaaaaagh!' Carina yelped.

Carina grabbed for the spatula but that only made things worse. Now the wooden stick was stuck to her hair *and* her hands. And Natalie was still coming at her with yet more wax. Natalie laughed gleefully as she glued yet another spatula to Carina's ridiculously expensive real false hair.

'Stop it! Stop it!' Carina screamed. 'Stop it!'

'Hold still,' said Natalie. 'And I'll get the removal strips.'

'No!' Carina wailed.

'This is going to hurt you much more than it hurts me,' said Natalie. 'Here.' She stuck a muslin strip to a patch of the wax and ripped it off, taking an inch-square clump of hair with it. 'Oh, hang on,' she said. 'You've got more unsightly hair here too!'

'Aaaaaagh!' Carina yelled as Natalie ripped the other four wooden spatulas from her head. But there was nothing she could do. She was absolutely trapped inside the Cellusmite machine which was still running at full power, making unsettling 'kettling' sounds like a household boiler about to burst.

'Please let me out of here,' Carina begged one more time. 'I will give you anything. You can have all my money. You can have Luxoreus. You can sell your bloody story to the *News of the World*.'

It made no difference. It was as though the spirit of a medieval torturer had possessed Natalie and she was completely unable to resist his commands. Carina didn't know how things could possibly get any worse.

Then Natalie slapped the spatula against one of Carina's eyebrows.

'Whoops,' she said.

'No! No! Noooo!'

54

'That wasn't a scream,' said Emily, shaking her head.

Standing on the pavement outside Luxoreus, Emily and Matt were trying to convince themselves that nothing was awry. It was Cesar who wouldn't let the matter drop. Hearing Carina's continuing whimpers (which were too quiet for the humans to hear) and recognizing them as the sound of distress, Cesar – good rescue dog that he was – was trying to draw Matt's attention by taking a mouthful of Matt's trousers and tugging him towards the door.

'Are you going to have a fit?' Emily asked nervously.

'No,' said Matt. 'This is different. Something's going on in there.'

Cesar now stood with his nose right against the door, listening intently.

'Perhaps she's being burgled,' said Emily, folding her arms. 'That would serve her right.'

'Ssssh!' Matt put his finger to his lips. 'If it was just a burglary, why would we have heard a scream?'

'It wasn't a scream,' Emily insisted, looking worried all the same.

'Aaaaaaiiiiieeee!'

Emily and Matt might not have had Cesar's near-supernatural powers of hearing, but this time they didn't need them.

'Someone's definitely in trouble,' said Matt. He tried to push open the door to the salon but it was locked shut.

'Let's just go,' said Emily, pulling Matt's arm. 'It's probably nothing.'

'Help!' screamed the voice inside.

'That doesn't sound like nothing.'

Matt leaned hard against the door. It wouldn't give.

'I had much better locks fitted to that door after The Beauty Spot was burgled,' said Emily. 'We're never going to get in.'

'But we've got to. It sounds like someone's being murdered.'

'Or waxed,' Emily joked, having no idea how close to the truth she really was.

The shouting continued. Cesar was getting more excited. He scrabbled at the bottom of the door as though trying to dig a rabbit out of its hole. When that brought him no closer to getting inside the salon, he started to bark.

'There must be another way in,' said Matt. 'How about the back door?'

'There is a back door,' said Emily. 'Of course. But we'd have to get in via the back yard.'

'We've got to try.'

'This is ridiculous,' said Emily. 'It's none of our business.'

'Cesar doesn't think so. We've got to do something.'

Feeling very unsure that she wanted to be there, Emily led Matt and Cesar down the alley between the Carphone Warehouse and the organic butcher's shop that led to the back of the parade. She didn't have to wonder for a second which of the doors in the wall led to the back of her old salon. She went straight to it. And of course, it was locked.

Matt looked at the wall. 'We can get over that. Easy.'

He dragged a wheelie bin across the yard and used it in place of a ladder.

'I can't get up there,' Emily warned him. 'I've got mules on.'

'You don't have to,' Matt reassured her. He sprang down into the courtyard and seconds later he had opened the door to the yard from inside.

The shouting was much louder at the back. No longer could Emily kid herself that it was the sound of a leg-wax virgin. Now she agreed with Matt that they had to get in there. While he tried to get into the back door of the salon itself, Emily dialled the police.

'Locked again,' Matt told Emily.

They would have to wait until the police arrived with a battering ram, unless . . .

Emily glanced at the little stone planter beneath the kitchen windowsill. When The New Beauty Spot first opened, Emily had tried to make this tiny back yard a tranquil haven for her staff. There had been a wrought-iron picnic table with an umbrella, a couple of chairs, and that planter had been full of pretty flowers. Now the table and chairs were gone. The flowers were dead. The only thing planted there now were cigarette ends but . . .

Emily started to scrabble in the dirt.

'I buried a key to the back door in here. In case of emergencies.'

And there it still was.

'Perhaps they haven't changed the locks at the back here.'

Matt fitted the key into the lock and turned it triumphantly. They were inside.

55

'Do something!' Emily yelled to Matt who, having been so determined to help, was now standing at the door of the treatment room where Natalie held Carina captive, frozen to the spot with horror. Girls fighting was a sight to make most men quail, and Matt was no exception. Cesar, however, was braver. He was barking frantically, straining at his lead.

Thinking quickly, Matt unleashed his little dog.

Cesar set off across the room like a cat with a rocket tied to its tail. He made straight for Natalie, leaping into the air most balletically to attach his teeth to her bottom.

'Oooooowwwww!'

Natalie immediately dropped the spatula she had been wielding and reeled back from the Cellusmite machine, arms flailing as she tried to detach Cesar from her bum. But Cesar was as persistent as that hot wax. He hung on as tightly as he could, sinking his teeth deeper and deeper into Natalie's flesh, giving Matt and Emily time to make their move.

'How on earth do you turn this off?' Emily rushed to the Cellusmite.

'The handset! The handset!' Carina cried out weakly. But the handset was beneath the treatment bench. Emily couldn't find it. Eventually she worked out which of the plugs in the wall belonged to the infernal machine and yanked that out instead. The Cellusmite machine shuddered to a halt.

Meanwhile Matt turned his attention to Natalie. He had to get his dog off her bottom while avoiding being waxed himself. Natalie was deranged. She was bellowing with pain but Cesar would not let go. The brave little mutt seemed oblivious to the fact that he had a waxy spatula sticking to his own furry bottom.

'Stop struggling and he'll let you go,' Matt shouted to Natalie. She didn't seem to hear him and the fight between woman and beast continued.

'What can I do?' Matt asked Emily as he ducked another spatula.

'Use this.'

Emily threw Matt what appeared to be a surgical bandage. Actually, it was a surgical bandage (trade price: seventy-nine pence), used for the famous Luxoreus 'mummy' wrap (cost to the client: seventy-nine pounds fifty).

While Natalie's efforts were focused on detaching Cesar from her buttocks, Matt fashioned a sort of lasso out of the bandage. He flipped it over Natalie's head and allowed it to fall about her shoulders before he pulled tight on the free end, pinning Natalie's arms to her sides.

'Hey!' Natalie exclaimed in surprise as Matt ran around her a couple of times to make sure she was properly tethered.

Sensing that his work was done, Cesar dropped from Natalie's bottom to the floor. Matt backed Natalie up to the treatment bench so that she had no choice but to sit down. Once she was there, he lashed her tightly to it.

'Don't try anything else,' he warned her. 'The police are on their way.'

Emily was still struggling with the safety catch on the Cellusmite machine. It was so 'safe' that in the end it took both Matt and Emily to release it. Carina stood up, eager to escape, and promptly fell back down again in a heat- and stress-induced faint. Matt caught her beneath the armpits and helped her out into the cool air of the corridor, where she sank to the floor once more.

Emily pulled a papyrus fan out of one of the enormous Egyptian-themed floral displays and used it to waft a breeze over Carina's face until she started to come round.

'Did she get my eyebrows?' was the first thing Carina asked her rescuers.

Matt nodded solemnly.

'Oh nooooo.'

Natalie had 'got' every single hair on Carina's head.

Carina Lees was as bald as a boiled egg.

And, at last, Emily Brown could recognize her.

56

The real reason Carina Lees didn't want anyone to know about her early life was because she had spent the past decade running away from it as hard as she could. Carina Lees wasn't even her real name. That was Karen Lavers.

Life as Karen Lavers was far from the party-filled lifestyle of a reality TV star. The bullying started early. If she was honest about it, little Karen's mother had noticed it even when her only daughter started nursery school. Something about her marked her out as a victim. Like the smallest pig in the litter, the tiniest kitten, the ugliest duckling. Except that Karen wasn't small. Not even when she was three years old. She hadn't been an enormous baby, but by the time she started nursery school, the health visitor would give Karen's mother a lecture about Karen's weight every time they visited the clinic to get Karen's asthma medication.

By the time she was seven, Karen wore clothes made for ten-year-olds. By the time she was ten, she was wearing a size fourteen adult's dress. Add that to the asthma, and the short-sightedness that required a pair of lenses so thick that when she put her glasses on Karen looked as though she was wearing a pair of those comedy specs with the eyeballs on springs.

She tried hard to blend into the background. That seemed to work at junior school. But in a secondary school full of girls, the way you looked was suddenly the only thing that mattered. Whenever Karen walked into the classroom, she felt a dozen sets of eyes swivel in her direction for all the wrong reasons. Each time she left, a wave of girlish giggles followed in her wake. School was purgatory for Karen Lavers.

Emily Brown's experience of school had been entirely different. She was firmly ensconced in the popular crowd from day one. She was pretty and petite. She always wore the right clothes. She was the girl you looked to if you wanted to know exactly how to dress or wear your hair. And, as she grew interested in becoming a beauty therapist, Emily established herself as the class beauty guru too.

Though wearing make-up was strictly forbidden at the Blountford High School for Girls, each lunchtime Emily would set up shop on a bench beneath a tree in the school playing field. She'd translate the beauty trends in *Just Seventeen* using her big vanity case full of Max Factor and Rimmel. It was rumoured she even had a couple of lipsticks by Chanel.

How Karen Lavers longed to be part of Emily Brown's carefully chosen circle. Like most girls in her class, Karen had her own subscription to *Just Seventeen* and read it avidly, but she didn't know where to start when it came to transforming her own looks. Each lunchtime, she felt a pang of envy as she watched the popular girls troop out onto the playing field to talk about boys and learn about the mascara that could stop a fifteen-year-old lad in his tracks.

So Karen was thrilled when Emily invited her to join them one afternoon.

'Me?' She was so surprised that she looked behind her to see if Emily was in fact addressing someone else.

'Yes. You. We've all been thinking how pretty you could look if you just made a bit more effort.'

It wasn't exactly the most charming of invitations, but Karen accepted at once.

'Tomorrow lunchtime. Under the oak tree in the corner of the field,' Emily told her.

As if anyone in the entire school needed to be told where the unofficial 'Beauty Club' met.

That night, Karen had felt as though her life was just beginning. She was too excited to sleep. Instead, she sat up in bed, reading *Just Seventeen* and trying to make a Curly Wurly last for more than thirty seconds. Actually, she found to her delighted surprise that she did make her Curly Wurly last for more than thirty seconds that night. Her stomach was churning so hard with anticipation she didn't feel like eating much at all.

She carefully cut out three beauty looks that she was particularly interested in. She knew that was what the Beauty Club did. Each girl picked out a picture and Emily did her best to recreate it. Karen chose a 'natural' look (that nonetheless required three different shades of eye shadow). Then she chose a look with green eye shadow, which would apparently bring out the green flecks in her hazel eyes. Finally she chose a look with smoky eyes and bright red lipstick. It was the most glamorous make-up she could imagine. It probably wouldn't suit her but what the hell . . . If anyone could work a miracle it was Emily Brown.

Next morning, Emily actually said 'hi' to Karen as she walked into the classroom.

'You're still coming out onto the field with us at lunchtime?' Emily asked.

'Oh yes,' Karen squeaked.

All morning her stomach continued to churn. She couldn't concentrate in double maths. Mrs Greenaway ticked her off in front of the whole class for daydreaming.

When Karen sheepishly glanced across at Emily, Emily rolled her eyes in sympathy. Karen gave Mrs Greenaway the finger from behind the cover of her textbook. Emily gave Karen the thumbs-up and laughed.

After double maths came double PE. Ordinarily, this was Karen's least favourite lesson. It might as well have been called 'double humiliation'. First there was the embarrassment of having to change out of her long skirt and baggy jumper into her stupid little Aertex top and gym shorts, without revealing her enormous bra. Once someone had caught sight of the 38DD label sticking out of the back of it. Later the same day, an anonymous wag drew a picture of Karen in her bra on the blackboard and annotated it with the shameful size.

That day, however, Karen changed into her gym kit without attracting any attention at all.

Ordinarily, the next stage would have been the humiliation of picking teams. Karen was always one of the final two to be chosen. Her partner in shame was Effie Barker, who had such a severe astigmatism that she was allowed an extra half-hour in any exam to give her time to read the question paper. Nobody wanted Effie on their team. She never saw the ball unless it hit her squarely between the eyes.

'We want Karen.'

Emily chose Karen for her rounders team right after the school team players had been divided up. And no one laughed when Karen didn't hit the ball.

Karen had no idea why Emily Brown suddenly wanted to be her friend, but she was delighted.

At last lunchtime arrived. Karen raced straight for the playing field and the bench beneath the oak tree. The other girls were already there.

Emily's make-up box had pride of place in the middle of the bench. It looked like a tool box but, instead of nails and screwdrivers, it was full of lipsticks and eye-shadow palettes. Emily patted the bench beside the box and instructed Karen to sit down. As she did so, Karen glanced inside and was sure that she saw the mythical Chanel logo on the end of one of the lipstick tubes.

Emily perched on the other side of her make-up box. The rest of the Beauty Club sat around her in a semi-circle on the grass.

'So, Karen. How do you think you want to look?' Emily asked.

Karen shyly handed over the three pages she had torn from *Just Seventeen*.

'Hmmm,' said Emily, looking from each picture to Karen's face. From time to time she held her fingers up like a little frame as though she were a photographer. The beauty gang looked on in silence as Emily made her decisions.

'Well,' she said at last, 'I think we can do something with this.'

She held up the photograph of the model wearing smoky eyes and red lipstick. Karen was shocked.

'I think this look on you could be stunning.'

'Really?' asked Karen. 'I just brought that one along on the off-chance really. I mean, that model has got dark hair and I've got mousy brown. I didn't think it would suit me.'

'Red lipstick suits everyone,' Emily announced. 'It's just a matter of finding the exact right shade, isn't it, ladies? Smile.'

Karen smiled.

'With your teeth,' Emily said patiently. 'I've got to see how yellow your teeth are.'

Karen attempted a toothy grin that came out as more of a grimace.

Emily's mouth twitched up at one corner as though in disappointment. It was the look a plumber gets the minute before he tells you that your 'simple' job ain't going to be so simple after all.

'Your teeth are pretty yellow,' Emily announced. 'But we can offset that with a blue-based red like this one.'

Karen tried to hide her excitement as Emily brought a lipstick out of her box.

'This is Chanel,' said Emily. 'It cost me fifteen pounds.'

'And you're going to use it on me?'

'Yes. Because you're worth it,' said Emily, mimicking the L'Oréal ad. She winked at her circle of admirers. Then she asked Karen to hold her hair out of her face while she painted in a cupid's bow.

'Press your lips together,' she instructed. Karen did as she was told.

'Can I see it yet?' Karen asked her.

'No. I'm going to do your eye make-up.'

Karen dutifully closed her eyes and tried not to twitch while Emily applied three colours of eye shadow with ticklish little brush strokes. Then she opened her eyes and tried not to blink while Emily curled her lashes and applied not one but four coats of glossy black mascara. She had a sense that an amazing transformation was taking place when she sneaked a glance at the girls in the semi-circle. They were rapt, watching Emily's every move like pupils of some guru in an ashram.

'You've got very nice skin,' said Emily as she applied a little cream blusher. 'You don't need any foundation at all. I'm jealous.'

Karen felt a bubble of pride rise in her churning stomach. Emily Brown was jealous of her.

'I guess I'm lucky,' she said in response.

'Yes, you are. I would kill for skin like that.'

At last Emily's work was finished. She sat back as if to better appraise what she had done. The girls in the semi-circle looked on reverently.

'You can have the mirror now,' she told her model. Karen took the black-rimmed hand-mirror from her, suddenly understanding why those women on makeover shows often seemed on the verge of weeping before the drapes were whipped away from the glass. Had a miracle taken place?

'Oh my god,' said Karen. Her mouth dropped open. 'Oh my god. You've made me look . . .'

'Beautiful,' Emily prompted her. 'You see? I knew there was something worth looking at hiding underneath your horrible greasy fringe.'

Karen didn't even mind the greasy comment. Because Emily Brown had seen something in her and managed to bring it out with a few small pots of face paint. The smoky eye shadow made her bog-standard blue eyes look dark and mysterious. The red lipstick made her lips look so smooth and her teeth look so white.

'Thank you, thank you, thank you.'

Karen leapt up from the bench and risked all by giving Emily a hug. Emily received it with a bemused look on her face.

Karen was delighted. She didn't even care when she was given a detention for wearing mascara in class. She kept the make-up on for as long as she possibly could. That night she sat in front of her dressing-table mirror for three hours, just staring at the face that Emily Brown had found beneath her puppy fat. She wondered how she could ever repay her. A gift was in order. Some chocolates? No, Emily didn't eat chocolates. Some flowers? Too cheesy. Maybe a funky make-up bag? She spent ten quid on one the following day. It was the money she had been saving for her summer holidays, but what price popularity?

Karen had been over the moon when, about a week later, Emily had informed her during morning break that she would like to experiment with some new techniques on Karen's 'perfect' face.

'With your great skin you're the ideal blank canvas,' she said. 'But you know,' she added as they sat under the tree at lunchtime, 'you'd look even better if we did something about your eyebrows.'

Karen raised her eyebrows as if to ask, 'What do you have in mind?'

'They're a little bit bushy. They overwhelm your face. Have you ever had them plucked?'

Karen shook her head.

'I didn't think so. But a more delicate arch would draw attention to your pretty eyes and might even make you look slimmer.'

'Really?'

If it would make her look slimmer, Karen would have agreed to have her eyebrows waxed right off.

Which is exactly what happened . . .

'It was a terrible mistake!' Emily insisted, but the laughter of her friends suggested otherwise.

Karen never went back to school. The following morning, she feigned illness. Her mother didn't need to ask what was really wrong. That was as clear as the nose that looked even bigger in the middle of Karen's face without the balancing effect of her bushy eyebrows. Mrs Lavers didn't try to force Karen back to school. Instead, she had a quiet word with Karen's form teacher who agreed that the best thing would be for Karen to stay home and swot for her GCSEs there. Karen's teacher thought she would be confident enough to come back when her eyebrows had regrown. But she wasn't. She flatly refused to go back into the classroom, threatening suicide if forced. She missed her exams and officially left education completely unqualified.

Eventually, Karen gave up leaving the house altogether. She rarely left her room except to go to the fridge. After a year, her mum and stepdad decided that drastic measures were needed. A psychiatrist diagnosed depression and advised that a stint as an inpatient at a newly opened mental health facility called The Bakery might help.

By the time Karen left The Bakery three months later, a transformation had begun.

Losing five stone was just the start. She got a job working as a secretary in a solicitor's office. Since she didn't have any friends to speak of and wasn't often invited to go out, it was easy for her to save the money for a nose job. Her mother and stepfather gave her the cash to have a boob operation for her twenty-first birthday – dieting had left her looking more flat-chested than she liked. The 38DDs that had been the bane of her life at school would have looked wonderful above her new tiny waist.

The surgery was a big success. When she looked at her face through blackened eyes the day after she had her nose job, she knew she had shed more than the bump on the bridge of her schnoz. She had shed Karen Lavers.

Her mousey hair was highlighted blonde. She bought a whole new wardrobe. She left her job at the solicitor's office and took a job as a receptionist at a health club instead. People started to notice her. Other girls asked her where she bought her clothes. Guys suddenly began to ask her out. The final part of her transformation came when she started to call herself Carina (she'd change her name by deed poll shortly after). She accepted a date with a courier who delivered packages to the office where she worked.

Carina Lees had her first kiss aged twenty-one . . .

It was the type of Cinderella story that Mickey Shore would have loved to sell to the networks as a drama-documentary, but the truth was that Carina had never been certain of her happy ending. The memory of that horrible afternoon out on the playing field was as fresh as it had been the day after she lost her eyebrows. It could still reduce her to tears. Likewise, though those three months in The Bakery had kick-started her transformation, Carina would never forget how difficult her time there had been.

She had never expected to see Emily Brown again. When Carina walked into that silly little salon and saw her nemesis still alive and well and as obsessed with the way people looked as ever, she almost turned around and walked back out. She seriously considered the possibility that she should go to the awards ceremony with a broken fingernail rather than have Emily recognize her and smirk that stupid smirk as they both remembered their last meeting.

But Emily didn't recognize her.

Carina was astonished. She had a new nose and new boobs but her eyes were the same, her voice was the same. These were the things she was sure would give her away. But there was no flicker of recognition in Emily's face at all, beyond the usual open-mouthed surprise she saw whenever members of the public found themselves face to face with someone they knew off the telly.

And so Carina stayed and allowed Emily to fix her nail. It had come to Carina as she sat at the manicure table. She was being given her chance for revenge. Just as her grandmother had always promised her.

'It may take a long time,' Nan Lavers had warned. 'It could take years! But that doesn't matter. Revenge is a dish that's best served cold.'

57

Getting Natalie to help exact that revenge had been easy . . .

Natalie had believed that Emily Brown was a good friend
to her. That was why she had been prepared to work so hard
to help Emily expand her business and move from the little
salon on School Street to the huge premises on Longbury Road.

The truth came as a shock. It was Carina who told her,
that day when Emily didn't have time to give the reality star
a facial herself. Emily was right to have fretted about what
might be being said inside that treatment room. Starting with
the whole story behind that 'random' makeover.

Carina spared no detail. 'She told me you were letting the
entire salon down . . .'

Then she told Natalie that Emily felt nauseous every time
she thought about the horrible feet and manky toenails that
might be hiding inside Natalie's thick-soled boots. She told
Natalie that Emily felt sick when she saw her scratching her
head with a pencil. She even told her that Emily actually
gagged when she caught sight of a big yellow zit on the back
of Natalie's neck.

'She said that when you shook your head over the kitchen
table one lunchtime, she saw something jump out and run
across your sandwiches.'

'She never mentioned this to me.'

'What on earth would she have said? Natalie, you're
infested? She said that from time to time when you walked
past, she got a whiff of something that reminded her of graves.
Is your house damp? I told her that might be it.'

The catalogue of cattiness continued. Still, at the end of it, Natalie tried hard to see the good side.

'She wanted to help me, I suppose.'

'It's patronizing,' said Carina. 'She sees you as her project. A poor silly girl from Wales who doesn't have a clue. She thinks the best thing that could happen in your life is to be made into a clone of her. I would think better of her if she had taken you aside and broken the news to you gently, like a grown-up, but she didn't, did she? She wanted to get a laugh out of you. She jumped at the chance to humiliate you on live TV. Chloe was in on it, too.'

Natalie's stomach started to churn.

'I don't know what to do,' she said. 'I can't stay here knowing that they said those awful things about me. I'll have to give up my job. I'll have to go back to Wales.'

Carina took the cucumber slices off her eyes and sat up.

'But what would that prove? That you're a quitter?'

'I *want* to quit.'

'Natalie, if you hand in your notice right now, what will you have achieved? Emily and Chloe will be mildly inconvenienced, but in a week or so they'll have a new therapist working in this room and, by this time next year, they'll be struggling to remember your name. Meanwhile, they'll carry on being the bitches they've always been. They'll be making fun of some other poor girl. They'll have had no comeuppance.'

'No. I'll tell them why I'm going. They'll be ashamed.'

'What makes you think that? It takes a bit of niceness to be ashamed. Remember what Emily said about that zit on the back of your neck?'

Natalie swallowed hard.

'I've got a far better way for you to get over the nasty things you've heard today. You're going to hit Emily Brown where it really hurts.'

And that was when the plan was hatched. Carina merely

hinted at sabotage. It was Natalie who ran with the idea, fired up by the thought that Emily and Chloe had been laughing about her behind her back for weeks.

'You know,' said Carina then. 'If The Beauty Spot were to fold, I can think of someone who might be interested in taking over the lease.'

She outlined her own plan for Emily Brown. Or rather, for her business.

'What's in it for me?' Natalie asked.

'One of the production girls at *Wakey-Wakey* told me that you really wanted a chance to sing.'

Natalie nodded.

'If you can close this salon down, I'll introduce you to Mickey Shore. My agent. One day you too could be a star.'

Natalie got to work right away. She came up with the idea for the Man-tenance package while sitting on the loo, looking at Morgan's collection of phonebox cards. Morgan was only too pleased to make Natalie some cards of her own using his computer.

'This week's special,' the text announced. 'Man-tenance package at The Beauty Spot. Come in for a nice thorough once-over.' And following it, The Beauty Spot's number. They looked very authentic.

That was just the start. Disabling the answer-machine was an easy way to stop clients from getting appointments, as was turning the ringer on the phone right down so that nobody ever heard a call. The burglary was a coincidence, but Natalie turned it further to her advantage by slipping the appointments book into her bag while pretending to inspect the damage as Emily sat in shock on the pavement. It was easy to frame Chloe for that.

Matt was different.

* * *

Natalie had hoped Matt might even become an ally. But then, on the night of Emily's dinner party, he found the Man-tenance card.

'What is this?' he asked. 'Are you trying to stitch Emily up?'

'Oh, come on, Matt. Don't look at me like that. Do you think she doesn't deserve it? Smug cow.'

'What are you trying to do? Ruin her business?'

Natalie didn't deny it.

'Look, I know you like her, Matt. It's obvious from the way you were mooning over her tonight. But the feeling isn't reciprocated. She used to feel sorry for you, but just the other day she said that you've really been getting on her tits. She does a really wicked impression of you.'

'She does?'

'Oh yes.'

Natalie got up and walked across the room, lampooning Matt's walk exactly. Matt was horrified. He'd always been slightly self-conscious about the way his feet turned out, but his mother had promised him that no one else really noticed.

'But—'

'Oh sure. I know what you're going to say,' Natalie adopted a whining voice. 'She was always so *nice* to me. She invited me to her house for dinner. That means she must like me.'

Matt couldn't help nodding.

'You're in a dream world, Matt. Emily would not be interested in you in a million years. She invited you and me to dinner because she feels sorry for us both. We're her charity project. It makes her feel really great to know that she's helping the little folk. The helpless types like you and me.'

Matt shook his head.

'Well, I don't know about you,' said Natalie. 'But I'm sick of being patronized. Do you still feel quite so loyal now?'

When he frowned, Natalie thought she had him.

'But what do you have to gain if the salon fails?' he asked. 'I mean, you may feel like you've got your own back on Emily for patronizing you, but you'll be out of a job too.'

Natalie smiled broadly. 'Do you really think I want to be a beautician for the rest of my life? I've got bigger fish to fry. Getting my own back on Emily is just a happy side-effect of my grand plan. You know Carina Lees? The reality star who comes into the salon sometimes? Me and her, we've become quite friendly over the last few months and . . .'

It was at that point that Cesar began to scratch frantically at the leg of the chair Matt was sitting on. Matt was so absorbed by Natalie's revelation that he didn't take notice of Cesar at once. And then it was almost too late. Matt just about got himself into the recovery position before the fit started.

'What the hell?' Natalie shouted.

Matt had no idea how long he had been on the floor but, when he came round, Natalie was standing above him. She looked dishevelled. Her flimsy dress was falling off her shoulders to reveal a good part of her bra.

'You bastard!' she spat at him, yanking him onto his feet. 'Get out of my house. Get out before I call the police! I can't believe you did that! You pervert! You beast!'

Matt left Natalie's house in a daze.

Natalie genuinely believed that Carina would hold up her end of the bargain. It was the only thing that kept her going through the darker moments of the next few months. Whenever she felt a twinge of guilt as she thought about the damage she was causing, or the lies she'd told Emily about Matt, she told herself that it was worth it. When she became a big star she would make amends. That's what she told herself when she made those anonymous calls to the Department of Health. And when she watched Emily write a cheque to the 'financial advisor' who would hasten her ruin . . .

Even after The Beauty Spot closed and Luxoreus opened in its place, Natalie kept her word, keeping their association a secret until the 'right moment'. Carina did not keep hers.

58

What Carina didn't know was that the day after the eyebrow incident, the laughter on the playing field had already become a distant memory. The mood was far more sombre. The headmistress of the Blountford High School for Girls gave a short but passionate speech about bullying at morning assembly. She didn't mention any specific incident, but Emily knew that the eyes of the entire school were upon her. There wasn't a girl in the place who didn't know what had happened. For days afterwards, weeks even, Emily's progress around the school corridors was accompanied by a soundtrack of whispers.

Emily and her friends from the Beauty Club were called in to see the headmistress, of course. They were put on detention for a whole month. Emily accepted her punishment almost gratefully. She hoped it would make her feel better.

During that month in detention, Emily went over the incident in her head a hundred-thousand times. She tried to convince herself that she hadn't really intended to do it. She told anyone who would listen that she had wanted to help Karen Lavers make the most of herself. She just wanted to make her look tidy. Better. She'd never used the wax strips before. Should have read the instructions more carefully.

'It was an accident!' she said again and again and again. But gradually Emily came to admit that she had been a bully.

Karen Lavers may have left the school altogether, but Emily

equally felt that her life had been ruined. The lunchtime makeover club was disbanded. Several of her former friends no longer spoke to her. Instead, Emily spent her lunch breaks in the library revising for the GCSEs she needed to train as a beauty therapist. She still clung on to that ambition, though she didn't like to say it out loud any more.

It took a long time before Emily believed that she was a good person again. Years. She compensated for her feelings of guilt by offering free beauty treatments to pensioners and the unemployed while she was training. She tried hard not to be judgmental when she met someone who really needed sprucing up.

She often wondered what had become of Karen Lavers. She hoped that Karen was happy wherever she had ended up. Once or twice Emily had even thought about writing her a letter. Saying that she was sorry in print. But she didn't know where to find her.

Would it have made a difference, Emily wondered as she and Carina/Karen sat side by side on a bench at the police station while Constable Garfield questioned Natalie in an interview room? Would she still have sought revenge?

'It was clear that you hadn't changed at all,' said Carina, remembering their early meetings. 'You had every opportunity to say how sorry you were when I told you I was making a show called *Confessions*. But you just carried on like butter wouldn't melt, telling me that you'd never done anything to hurt anyone and then complaining about how bad Natalie looked. You hadn't changed at all.'

Emily closed her eyes in shame.

'I had to get my own back on you. You had it all,' Carina concluded. 'Now your salon is finished. I'm going to be bankrupt in a couple of weeks. Neither of us has anything any more.'

Without saying a word, Emily reached for Carina's hand.

* * *

Carina decided not to press charges against Natalie Hill.
How could she? When it was her turn to be interviewed,
Carina had to admit that Natalie's 'fanciful' story about the
plot to sabotage The Beauty Spot was in fact true, and so
Carina had to accept some of the blame for the hot-wax
incident. When she was questioned, Emily told Constable
Garfield that she felt no need to pursue the allegation that
Natalie had deliberately sunk her business either. And so
both Carina and Natalie were released without charge,
though Constable Garfield muttered darkly about wasting
police time. At home later that night, Constable Garfield
weighed up his career in the police force against the money
he could make if he sold the story of that night's work to
the tabloids.

His wife advised him against it.

Outside the police station, Carina, Emily and Natalie found
themselves together once more in the car park.

Sensing a big story in the making, Mickey Shore had, for
the first time in a long time, thrown himself into action upon
receiving Carina's call. He abandoned the contracts he had
been working on to support her. (The contracts were for
Monkey Gordon, with Whittaker's crisps. At last Monkey
had been discharged from The Bakery.) Mickey arrived at the
police station in a stretch limo, ready to whisk Carina off for
an exclusive photo-shoot before she got her hair fixed – the
obligatory 'misery' shot. He was surprised to see her standing
outside the police station with the girl who had, it seemed,
wanted to kill her.

'What's going on?' he asked, as the limo glided to a stop
by the girls and he rolled down the window. 'Why isn't she
in custody? Get in the car.'

Carina hesitated.

'The photographer is waiting,' said Mickey.

'I don't want to do any photos,' she said. 'But you could give all of us girls a lift to my house.'

'Even me?' Natalie asked.

'Especially you,' said Carina. 'I think we all need to talk.'

59

Matt had not been at the police station. Constable Garfield took his statement on the spot, then agreed that it was more important for Matt to take Cesar straight to the vet than hang around.

Cesar comported himself heroically as the vet removed the sticky wax from his hindquarters. It took a long time. But the news was good. Cesar had come out of his brush with the hot wax with nothing worse than a bald patch.

'It will *probably* grow back,' said the vet.

As he walked back from the vet's, Matt accepted Natalie's apology by telephone. He knew that he would have been justified in feeling much angrier, but when it came down to it, all thoughts he'd had of revenge and retribution were overcome by relief. Relief that he definitely hadn't acted like a monster and relief that Emily knew the truth at last.

The following day, Matt knocked on the door of Emily's flat for the first time since the night of the ill-fated dinner party. He was as nervous as he had been when they'd bumped into each other on the pavement but, this time, rather than a prostitute's calling card, he thrust a bunch of roses into her hands.

Emily blushed. 'They're beautiful,' she said. 'Do you want to come in?'

Cesar was already on his way down the hall to the kitchen.

The old friends talked at length about the previous day's revelations. Matt told her how much he'd missed hanging out at The Beauty Spot. Emily admitted the truth about her history with Carina Lees.

'I've always been too quick to jump to conclusions,' she said. 'To make judgments about people based solely on the way they look.'

Matt nodded. 'Like you did with me.' Natalie had told him that Emily assumed he was gay.

'I'm sorry,' she said. 'But you've got to admit you're very well groomed for a straight man.'

'I'm working on it,' he said, loosening his tie.

'I can think of one other way you can prove that you're into girls,' Emily added with a smile.

Matt didn't need to be asked twice. His heart beating so hard he thought it might explode from his chest, he finally enfolded Emily into his arms and kissed her.

60

A few days later, Carina and Emily met up again in Carina's executive home. Carina didn't look too bad, considering what she'd been through. She'd been fitted for a wig: a short, chic crop à la Kylie Minogue. Emily had shown her how to draw in a pair of particularly natural-looking eyebrows.

The girls spent the afternoon together, talking about their lives since the original eyebrow-waxing incident. They also talked about life before that awful day. Emily recalled a time she had been envious of Carina for winning the school cookery prize. Carina could recall far too many moments when she had been envious of Emily.

'But you got the last laugh,' said Emily. 'You became a celebrity.'

'And threw it all away. Thank god.'

They were interrupted by the arrival of Natalie. She brought with her a child's inflatable swimming ring to sit down on. Cesar had bitten her bottom very hard.

It was as Natalie was leaving that she told Carina about the phone call.

'I got a message from that agent of yours. Mickey Shore. He said something about being able to sell my side of the story. Seems a bit disloyal to me. I reckon you ought to sack him.'

'Already have,' said Carina. 'I'm through with being a celeb.' But then she had a light-bulb moment. 'Did he really say your story was worth selling?'

'Definitely.'
'How much?'
'He said I could get . . .'
Natalie whispered a very large number.
'Call him back and say you will!'
'But . . .'
'Natalie,' said Emily. 'We need that money.'

EPILOGUE

Emily handed in her notice at Herr Kutz. Much as she loved working with Malcolm, she knew that he didn't quite share her vision for the future. She didn't leave him in the lurch, however. She was able to recommend the perfect partner for his new venture, 'Herr and Beauty'. Chloe had just returned from a season working in a salon attached to a holiday resort in Puerto Pollensa. She was only too glad to hear from Emily, to truly accept her apology for the events at The Beauty Spot and to step into her shoes as Malcolm's partner.

Luxoreus, Blountford's 'premier day spa' was never to reopen. Local residents began to wonder whether the former hairdressing salon on the Longbury Road was in fact cursed. When a notice in the window announced the imminent opening of the third new beauty salon on the premises in eighteen months, the man in the betting shop across the street said he would open a book on how long this new place managed to stay open.

Beauty Secrets was the new salon's name. The gaudy faux Egyptian fixtures and fittings that had been the trademark of Luxoreus were put up for auction on eBay. Osiris and the two slit-eyed stone cats were sold to an amateur theatre director who was staging a production of *Antony and Cleopatra*. The Cellusmite machines were returned to the factory in Germany. The life-size portrait of Carina Lees dressed as Nefertiti that had once graced the waiting area was sold to a crazed fan who hung it on the ceiling above his bed.

The decor of Beauty Secrets was a welcome departure from the camp high glamour of Luxoreus and the sweet kitsch of The Beauty Spot. Instead it echoed the Zen trend started by some of New York and London's top interior designers. The walls were stripped of the gold paint and painted pale cream. The stone desk was replaced by a bench of beautiful untreated wood. On the walls hung calm oriental-style brush drawings. Above the bench was a piece of Chinese calligraphy. Translated, the precise brush strokes read, 'Dreams come true.'

The proprietors? Three girls who had made a lot of money with three consecutive features on bullying and its ugly consequences in *Get This!* magazine . . . Carina, Natalie and Emily Brown.